Blueberry Hill

by

Jean Varner

AmErica House
Baltimore

First printing

ISBN: 1-58851-914-7
PUBLISHED BY AMERICA HOUSE BOOK PUBLISHERS
www.publishamerica.com
Baltimore

Printed in the United States of America

To my friends

Ruth Riach and Wanda Wright

and to my daughter
Pat Shelton

1 Thessalonians 5:11

CHAPTER I

Somewhere in the Pacific
July 1945

Darkness closed in on Joe as he crept through the jungle. He couldn't see his men, but he knew they were there. The overgrowth was so thick that had to cut their way through. Suddenly lights flashed as machine guns rained bullets into them. Ambush! His men fell all around him. Screams of agony tore from the throats of the wounded and dying. Hordes of Japanese soldiers surrounded them. By the flashing lights he saw a raised hand with a grenade. He opened his mouth and shouted, "No-o-o-o!" At the same time, he raised his gun and fired. The Japanese soldier fell and the grenade exploded in his hand. The blast threw Joe backwards onto the hard ground. Shrapnel pierced his body. Searing pain filled his chest and he blacked out.

Silence greeted the six marines as they came upon the scene of the ambush. With wide-open sightless eyes, the bloody bodies of fellow marines lay scattered about.

"They're all dead!" whispered a private.

A low moan broke the stillness.

"This one's alive!" shouted a corporal. He turned to the medical corpsmen. "Over here! Get him to the camp pronto! Maybe he can be saved."

At the base hospital, the doctor shook his head and said, "I don't know if we can help him but let's try. Ready him for surgery stat! Start plasma and type and cross match him for four units of blood. What's his name? Does anyone know him?"

"Yes. He's Sergeant Joe Sullivan," the captain answered. "A brave marine! He was in charge of this search platoon. We thought the area was clear of enemy soldiers, but evidently we were mistaken."

"I was in his platoon once," a corpsman said. "He was a great guy. Everyone liked and trusted him."

The corpsmen readied Joe for the operation. As one of them removed his watch and an ID bracelet, he noticed the name "Maggie" engraved on the inside of the bracelet.

"I wonder who Maggie is?" said the corpsman who knew Joe. "He never mentioned her."

While Joe was in surgery, the corpsman picked up the bloody, torn uniform shirt. "Might as well throw this away," he said, and then added, "There's something in the pocket."

He reached in and pulled out a New Testament. The metal cover was dented. When he opened it, a picture fell out. He picked it up and looked at it. Long lashes framed beautiful eyes under the arched brows of the pretty girl who gazed back at him. Her straight nose tipped up slightly at the end and her lips curved sweetly in a smile. A mass of dark curly hair surrounded her oval face and a black drape covered her, leaving her shoulders bare.

"Look here," he said, handing the picture to his buddy. "Joe never showed us this picture. What a beauty she is! If I had a girl who looked like that, I'd be bragging and showing her picture around."

"It looks like a graduation picture," his friend said. Turning it over, he read, "Mary Margaret Mitchell, Sr. 1944. Maggie is a nickname for Margaret. She's probably the girl who gave Joe the bracelet."

The first corpsman took the picture back and gazed at it for a long time. "She looks like a nice girl. Do you suppose she's waiting for him?" he mused. "If she is, she might be waiting in vain. Doc thinks Joe hasn't a chance of pulling through the surgery."

His friend looked over his shoulder at the picture and said, "She's gorgeous! I wonder what kind of a girl she is? I'd sure like to meet her."

CHAPTER II

Oak Grove, Oklahoma
June 1940

Dark clouds gathered overhead as Meg and her three friends came out of the theater. Thunder rumbled across the sky and flashes of lightning illuminated the surrounding hills of the small town of Oak Grove in southeastern Oklahoma. All day the sky had been overcast and now a storm threatened to break.

Other movie patrons hurried to their parked cars or nearby homes, but the four teenage girls huddled together, talking excitedly about the movie.

An ancient Ford convertible pulled up to the curb, and the young man in it honked loudly.

"There's my brother. I'll see you all tomorrow," Meg called as she sprinted to the car. She climbed nimbly over the side and dropped into the seat beside him.

The other girls called their good-byes as they scattered to their own homes.

"When are you going to enter the car like a lady?" Bob teased as he turned the car around and headed home.

"When you get out and open the door like a gentleman."

"Ha! That'll be the day! Me open the door for my freckle-faced, dishwater blonde, tomboy sister!"

"Sticks and stones!" Meg said. "Can't you say anything good about me?"

"Yes, Mary Margaret Mitchell. You have beautiful dark-blue eyes that are exactly like our mother's."

"Why, thanks, Bob." Her voice softened. "That's the nicest thing you've ever said to me. Are you gonna see The Sea Hawk?"

"Sure, Joe and I are gonna see it tomorrow night. Stay for the midnight horror show, too."

"Will Dad let you? You have to be up early for church."

"Listen, baby sister, I'm eighteen, a high school graduate, and holding down a job. I can very well do as I please."

Meg gazed admiringly at her brother. How handsome he was. Wide-set gray eyes, a straight nose, and a firm chin gave him a clean-cut appearance. The damp wind ruffled his blond hair, causing it to curl. His medium height and compact, muscular build made him a good athlete. And he was smart, too. Not only had he lettered in three high school sports, he had also been the valedictorian of his graduating class. She was proud of him, but she'd die before she'd let him know it.

"In a few days I'll be fourteen," she sighed. "It will be four long years until I can do as I please!"

At that moment, the wind gusted and brought a shower of rain upon them. "Put the top up!" Meg cried.

"It won't go up," Bob said. "I tried to get it up before I left home. You'll just have to get wet."

Bob and Meg lived with their parents and younger brother Johnny in an old farmhouse two miles from town. Their father, Sam Mitchell, owned the hardware store in downtown Oak Grove, but he and his wife Sarah preferred to live in the country. They had a few acres of land on which they planted vegetables and raised chickens and hogs. These enterprises along with their milk cow provided most of their food. Their children helped with the chores.

"I wonder what's going on at Joe's house," Meg said as they approached the O'Brien home. "All the lights are on."

Joe Sullivan lived with his Aunt Peg and Uncle Dan O'Brien. Orphaned at an early age, he had not had an easy life. His aunt drank too much, and his uncle was a bully who frequently mistreated them. Officially Dan owned the saloon in Oak Grove, but unofficially he was the local bootlegger. Hard liquor was illegal in Oklahoma. Dan had his own still and he also shipped bottles in from Texas. All the chores on the acreage were left for Joe. He had the total care of the garden, chickens, hogs, and cow. Often Bob helped him so that he would have time for fishing, hunting, and high school sports.

A shrill scream splintered the air. Through the lighted kitchen window, Bob and Meg saw the figures of two men fighting.

Bob abruptly turned into the drive of the ramshackle house.

"Stay here!" he ordered as he hopped out of the car and ran toward the side kitchen door.

Without a moment of hesitation, Meg jumped out of the car and followed him into the kitchen. A single bare light bulb, dangling from a frayed cord, swayed crazily and cast grotesque shadows on the walls as the two men fought. Although Joe was three inches taller than his uncle's five-foot-nine, he was no match in weight. Dan weighed more than two hundred pounds, and even though he was in his fifties most of that was muscle. At eighteen Joe had not attained his full growth, and Dan was getting the best of him. Joe's bloody nose and bruised face horrified Meg.

"Stop it, you beast!" she yelled at Dan.

Dan's large right fist smashed into Joe's abdomen, knocking him to the floor. He leaned over with doubled fists to hit him again, but Bob jumped on him, knocking him away from Joe. The force of Bob's hurtling body carried them both to the floor. Then Dan rolled over and Bob was trapped under him.

Joe staggered to his feet and reached for a shotgun leaning against the wall. He grasped it and looked down the barrel at the back of his uncle's head. His jaws were clenched and his eyes had turned gray like twin points of steel.

Panic-stricken, Meg's heart nearly stopped beating. She had only enough breath to whisper, "No, Joe! Don't do it!"

Aunt Peg slumped in a corner of the kitchen. Tears streamed down her bruised face. She sobbed, "Please, Joe. No!"

Joe hesitated for a second, gun in hand. Turning the gun around, he gripped the barrel. Then whack! He hit his uncle over the back of the head. Dan went limp, and Bob crawled out from under him.

Joe grabbed his jacket off a kitchen hook, picked up a small bundle from the floor, and started toward the door. "Don't leave, Joe," begged Aunt Peg.

"I gotta. For the past ten years Dan has made my life miserable! I'm not putting up with it any longer."

Bob grabbed his arm. "What about college? We're going to OU together this fall."

"I don't have any money and I won't stay in this house another minute!" Joe jerked his arm out of Bob's grasp.

"You can stay at our house, Joe. You know you can," Meg said tearfully.

"I hafta get away!" Joe paused briefly at the door. "Aunt Peg, I'll write. Let you know how I am," he said, and disappeared into the night.

Meg ran after him. The rain poured down and lightning flashes crisscrossed the sky, accompanied by a boom of thunder.

"Joe! Joe! Come back!" she called. But her voice was lost in the storm. She stood there, her wet hair plastered to her head and soaked clothes clinging to her slender figure.

As Meg and Bob entered their home, they heard the whistle of the ten o'clock train. It slowed as it picked up the mail on the way through town.

"Joe's on that train," Bob said thoughtfully, as he gazed back out of the door into the darkness.

"How do you know?" she asked.

He shut the door and said, "Whenever things went bad for him at home, he'd say he wished he could hop on that train and never come back."

Bob and Meg relayed the details of the fight between Joe and his uncle to their parents and about Joe leaving. Their mother asked about Aunt Peg.

"I'll make some chicken soup for her tomorrow," she said.

Meg smiled to herself. Chicken soup had been her mom's cure-all for any illness or problem for as long as she could remember.

After a long relaxing bath, Meg shampooed her hair. She sat in front of the mirror at her vanity table and flipped a comb through her curly hair while it dried. Tonight she didn't see her reflection. She saw Joe. He had been like a member of the family. When things got too rough for him at home, he came to their house. Some nights he stayed over and slept on the other bunk in Bob's room. He often ate meals with them.

After breakfast the next day, Meg took the path through the fields to the O'Brien's house carrying the pot of chicken soup her mother made. She went around to the kitchen door and knocked.

"Come in, honey." Aunt Peg sat in a worn rocking chair by the unlit kitchen stove. The house wasn't as old as the Mitchells', but it was dirty and rundown. Limp curtains hung at the windows, unwashed dishes covered the wooden counter, and a table and four straight-back chairs stood in the middle of a cracked and peeling linoleum rug.

Meg found some matches, lit one of the gas burners of the stove, and placed the pot of soup on it. While it warmed, she took a clean bowl and spoon out of the cupboard and set them on the oilskin tablecloth. When she judged the soup to be hot enough, she poured some into the bowl.

"That soup sure smells good," Aunt Peg said as Meg helped her out of the rocker and into one of the chairs at the table.

In the light from the window Meg thought Aunt Peg looked ill. Her dry skin had a yellow tinge, and bruises circled her watery blue eyes. Matted lackluster gray hair straggled around her ravished face. Meg had seen a picture of her as a young girl and she had been pretty. Everyone knew she drank a lot, even though she tried to hide it. With a husband like Dan, it was easy to understand why she had begun to drink.

Aunt Peg hungrily ate the soup, but often a hacking cough choked her and caused her to clutch her chest in pain.

"Thank your mother for this soup, Meg. It's delicious."

"She's coming over later," Meg said as she cleaned out the sink and filled it with hot water. She made suds from a bar of P&G soap and tackled the stack of dirty dishes on the counter top.

"Leave the dishes. I can do them later," Aunt Peg said in a weak voice.

"I want to help you," Meg said. "It's obvious that you aren't feeling well."

When Aunt Peg finished the soup, Meg washed her bowl and spoon and scrubbed the table and the counter tops.

"Do you want to brush your teeth and wash your face now?" Meg asked. "Can you make it upstairs?"

"It's hard for me lately, so I've been sleeping in the downstairs bedroom and using this bathroom off the kitchen."

While Aunt Peg washed her face and brushed her teeth, Meg found her comb and brush. She helped her back into the rocking chair and began brushing her hair.

"That feels good," Aunt Peg sighed. "I'm going to miss Joe," she added abruptly.

"Why isn't he going to Oklahoma University with Bob this fall?" Meg asked.

"Because Dan made me give him Joe's money," she said.

"Joe's money? Had he saved enough for college?"

"No, his father left him the money. You knew his father was my brother Mike, and he was killed in a car wreck?"

"Yes, along with Joe's mother and little sister. Joe told us. He loved his little sister, Callie. She had been his only playmate most of his life."

"Mike's farm in western Oklahoma didn't prosper, so he sold it and packed up his family and possessions in his old truck to move to California. Before they got out of the state, they were hit by a car that ran a stop sign. His Indian wife Little Doe and daughter Callie were killed instantly. Joe had been riding atop the mattress and other possessions in the truck bed and was thrown clear. He only suffered a few cuts and bruises." Aunt Peg paused and reflected on the tragedy and then continued, "Mike lived long enough for us to get to his bedside. He woke up while Dan was out of the room and told me to take his billfold and save the money in it for Joe. There was nearly five hundred dollars. I hid the money and kept it a secret from Dan."

Tears came to her eyes and she said, "After Joe graduated from high school, I told him about it. I knew how much he wanted to go to OU with your brother. When he wrote for a catalogue from OU Dan became suspicious.

"Last night Dan came home drunk and shouted at me, 'Where did Joe get enough money for college?' I said, 'I don't know. Ask him!' and then he began slapping me around. He grabbed my arm and said he would break it if I didn't tell him!"

Tears ran down her cheeks. She began coughing and clutched her chest. Meg handed her the cough medicine sitting on the table and she took a large swallow.

"You better rest now," Meg said. It pained her to see Aunt Peg so upset.

Aunt Peg rocked a few minutes and then cried, "He was hurting my arm so badly that I had to tell him about the money! After he got it, he slapped me for keeping it from him all of those years. Joe came in from work and hollered at him to leave me alone. 'He's got your money, Joe!' I shouted. 'I'm keeping the money to pay for your room and board for all the years you lived here,' Dan snarled. Without a word Joe went upstairs, tied a few clothes in a bundle, and said he was leaving. 'Joe has more than paid for his room and board by all the work he's done around here,' I told Dan. It made Dan so mad that he knocked me into the corner, and that's how the fight started!"

"My family's going to miss Joe," Meg said sadly.

"So am I, honey," Aunt Peg said. "So am I."

The night that Joe left was the last time Meg saw him until after December 7, 1941. "A Day That Will Live in Infamy," as President Roosevelt called it.

CHAPTER III

December 7, 1941
Oak Grove, Oklahoma

On a cold crisp Sunday afternoon Meg walked briskly down the country road toward town. The brilliant colors of autumn were gone and dark bare branches of trees now stood out against the blue-gray sky. Fallen leaves and dead grass formed a drab protective covering over the earth.

Meg passed the O'Briens' house and remembered that Aunt Peg had died the past winter, but they had been unable to reach Joe in time for him to attend the funeral. A cold wind blew across the fields. Meg shivered and pulled her coat tight. Wisps of brown hair escaped her bright red knitted cap and danced around her face. Matching red mittens and scarf added a touch of color to the somber scene.

By the time Meg reached Main Street, her cheeks were reddened with the cold, and her eyes were filled with moisture. She hurried to Glass Drug Store where most of the teenagers gathered on Sunday afternoons. The drug store and the Main Street Café were the only businesses open on Sundays, so few people were downtown.

When she opened the door, a gust of wind tore through the store, and Meg laughed with exuberance as she struggled to close it. The musty and pungent medicinal odors mixed with cologne, newsprint, and new magazines combined to assail her nostrils with a pleasant and familiar scent.

"Hi, gang!" She returned the greetings of the teenagers sitting at the marble-topped tables as she crossed over to the soda fountain.

"Hi, Meg. What'll you have?" Red-haired Jimmy Lester gave her a toothy grin from behind the counter. A high school senior, he worked at the soda fountain after school and on weekends. She knew he liked her by the way he looked at her. It pleased her even though she didn't feel attracted to him. During the past year she had grown out of her tomboyish ways and had discovered boys. In the fall she had crushes on the football players, and now it was the basketball team that held her interest.

With the braces gone, her teeth gleamed white and even. Her streaked blonde hair had darkened to a nut-brown shade that enhanced the deep blue of her eyes. When she looked in the mirror, it pleased her to see how much she resembled her mother. She thought her mother was beautiful.

Pulling off her cap, she gave her short hair a flip. "I'll have a strawberry soda," she told him.

Jimmy mixed a soda with extra ice cream and set it on the counter with a flourish.

Meg thanked him, put her money on the counter, and joined her friends Amy, Sue, and Sylvia at one of the tables.

Amy said, "We've been talking about the Christmas program at your church, Meg. You'll be a perfect Mary."

Meg replied, "Thanks. I wonder who'll be Joseph?"

Sue looked at her in surprise. "Jimmy Lester, of course."

Sylvia added, "It'll be a musical, and you and Jimmy are always singing together. Besides," she said with a sly look, "you make such a nice looking couple. I've heard other people say so."

Meg felt her face burn. "Be quiet, Sylvia. He'll hear you," she whispered.

"Hey! Kids!" Mr. Glass, the pharmacist, came out of his office and waved his hands excitedly. His face displayed shock and his pale blue eyes looked startled behind the steel-rimmed glasses. "Pearl Harbor has been attacked by the Japanese! I just heard it on the radio."

The young people looked blankly at him.

Meg asked, "Where is Pearl Harbor?"

Sue looked puzzled, "Yeah, and what has that to do with us?"

Mr. Glass was exasperated. "Don't they teach you kids anything in school? Pearl Harbor is in Hawaii and it's part of the United States. We have a large naval base there, and they're bombing our ships!"

"Now I remember," Don Anderson said. "We did study that in history. Guess it didn't make much of an impression on me."

"You'll remember Pearl Harbor the rest of your lives," Mr. Glass said sadly. "This means war!"

"War!" several of the teenagers exclaimed in unison. A general hubbub arose. Everyone tried to talk at once. One little seventh grade girl began to cry.

"I always thought that if we entered the war, it would be in Europe," Meg told her friends. "It never occurred to me that we would fight the Japanese!"

All the way home Meg thought about this new development. This would change all of their lives. Already some of the senior boys talked excitedly about volunteering for the service right away. She knew her brother Bob would go, but she hoped her father was too old. This certainly would change things.

War did sound exciting, though. "I wish I could go," she thought. "Girls miss out on everything!"

When Meg got home the family discussed the latest news. Her parents opened the atlas and showed her and her brother Johnny where Pearl Harbor was located.

"Hawaii isn't a state, but it is a territory of the United States," Dad explained.

The telephone rang and Dad answered it. It was Bob.

"Dad," he said, "I'm quitting college and joining the marines."

"No, Bob. I know how you feel, but don't rush into anything now. Wait until the Christmas break, and we can discuss what would be best for you to do."

"But, Dad, we're at war, and every able-bodied man is needed to defend our country. You enlisted in the last war."

"Bob, listen to me. You have more options than I had. Wait until you get home. The service needs educated men, and the war won't be over for a long time. You'll still have plenty of time to serve."

"Okay, Dad, I'll wait until after Christmas to enlist, but nothing you can say will change my mind."

When Meg came home from school a few days later a surprise awaited her. A tall dark young man rose from a chair and said, "Hello, Maggie."

"Joe!" she exclaimed. She ran swiftly across the room and threw herself into his arms. "I'm so glad you've come home at last! We've missed you."

He held her close and then released her. "I've missed you too, Maggie. I came home to see you all before I joined the marines."

"I'm not surprised that you're joining the service," Meg said.

"That's all the boys at school talk about. Some are dropping out of school now and others are waiting for graduation. All of us girls feel left out. We would join if we could."

"Ha! That'll be the day!" Johnny exclaimed.

"You will stay until after the holidays, won't you, Joe?" Mom asked. "Bob'll be home soon and will want to see you. That other bed in his room is still available."

"We're having one of your favorite meals tonight," Meg said. "Pork chops with mashed potatoes, gravy, black-eyed peas, greens, and hot biscuits."

"How did you know that I'd be here today?" Joe asked with a laugh.

"Here comes Dad," Johnny said. "He'll be glad to see you."

Dad came in pulling off his coat. "It's getting colder all the time," he said as he hung it on the coat tree in the hall. Turning around he saw Joe grinning at him. "The prodigal has returned," he said, slapping Joe on the back. "Welcome home!"

"Thank you, sir. Good to be back." Joe took his hand and shook it vigorously.

"Sorry about your Aunt Peg, son," Dad said. "Everything possible was done for her."

"I know. The news didn't reach me until it was too late, or I would have come home. Poor Aunt Peg. She had a hard life. The doctor wrote that it was pneumonia complicated by too much alcohol in her system."

"Dan O'Brien has a lot to answer for," Dad said.

"Someday I'll see that he does," Joe said with a grim look.

All through the meal Meg covertly glanced at Joe from across the table. He had always seemed like a brother to her, but now he was different. Time had changed him. Although he was the same age as Bob, nearly twenty, he seemed older, larger, and more mature. Almost a stranger. "Maggie" had been his pet name for her. She had insisted that everyone call her "Meg" after she had read Little Women, but he wouldn't comply with her request. "I like 'Maggie' best, and it fits you," he had said.

"Where have you been and what have you been doing since you left here, Joe?" Dad asked.

"I've had a lot of different jobs around the country," he answered.

"Lately I've been working in the Texas oil fields."

That evening as they sat around the fireplace, Joe told them of his travels. He had picked fruit in California and cotton in Georgia, worked on a fishing boat out of Galveston, and had gone to New York City "to have a look."

When Meg awoke the next morning, the first thought she had was that Joe was back at last. It gave her a happy, expectant feeling. Too bad she had to go to school today! She hurriedly dressed and went downstairs. Joe was seated at the breakfast table drinking coffee.

"Breakfast is nearly ready," Mom said. "Get the butter and maple syrup out. We are having Joe's favorite, pancakes and sausages."

"I thought you would sleep late, Joe," Meg said. "I heard you and Dad talking long after bedtime."

"I'm an early riser," he said. "Thought I'd go to town and look around today."

"Since tomorrow is Saturday and I won't be in school, we could take the dogs out tramping in the woods. The old tree house is still intact," Meg said.

Joe glanced at her affectionately. "I remember how you tagged after Bob and me. Bob was sure mad when you discovered our secret retreat."

Meg blushed. "You didn't mind, though, did you?"

Saturday morning the weather was sharp and clear. The sun was trying to shine and dispel the wintry gloom. After breakfast Meg made ham sandwiches, put them in an empty bread wrapper, and filled a canteen with water. She dressed warmly in coveralls, an old jacket of Bob's, and her red knitted cap, scarf, and mittens. Joe wore khaki trousers, an old red hunting coat and cap, and a pair of work gloves. The hound dogs, Buck and Duke, were excitedly running to and fro.

"They miss hunting with Bob," Meg said. "Hope they don't mind it when we don't shoot whatever they scare up."

The terrain around Oak Grove was rugged and hilly. It was in the foothills of the Ouachita Mountains and was filled with oak, elm, ash, pine, dogwood and redbud trees. Thick underbrush made it difficult to get around. Bob and Joe had made paths through it. Meg knew these trails because she had followed them often, much to

Bob's chagrin. The boys had become experienced woodsmen and hunters in this wilderness. Soon they came to the Poteau River where they had spent many summer hours fishing and swimming.

"Look!" said Joe. "There's the old rope that we used to swing out on and drop in the deep water. We felt like Tarzan."

"Johnny and his friends come out here now," Meg said. "They had to replace that old rope with a new one."

Joe skimmed a rock out over the water where it eventually sank, leaving ever increasing circles.

"Bob saved my life here," he said quietly.

"Saved your life? What happened?"

"When I first came here to live, I was only eight and was so shy that it was hard for me to make friends. One day I stumbled on Bob and a bunch of guys swimming here. They hollered at me to come on in, but I was afraid. I didn't know how to swim and was ashamed to admit it. As I turned to leave a couple of them grabbed me and threw me in, clothes and all."

"How awful!" Meg exclaimed.

"It was the deepest place and I panicked. I thrashed around and began sinking."

"Boys can be horrid!"

"No, just mischievous. They were all laughing, and Bob was the first one to notice that I was really in trouble. He dived in and pulled me out. Nothing was hurt except my dignity."

"Why did I never hear of this?"

"We kept it quiet so that no one would be punished. From then on the guys accepted me, and Bob and I became best friends. I think he felt responsible for me. It didn't take me long to learn to swim after that experience!"

Meg and Joe followed the river south for a mile and then turned west on an almost invisible trail into the thickest part of the woods. The dogs ran ahead, joyfully sniffing along the path, stirring up an occasional rabbit. Squirrels scolded as they scrambled among the tree branches. In an open space Joe stopped and took hold of Meg's arm and pointed. A pair of deer were grazing on the edge of the clearing. The dogs stood quietly in point position until the deer lifted their graceful heads and disappeared into the foliage behind them.

"I think the dogs are disappointed in us," Meg said.

A little farther on, Joe stopped again.

"Here it is," he said, looking up at the weathered boards of the tree house.

Meg noticed that his face had clouded over, and she remembered that many times he had come here after a beating from his uncle. The tree house held sad as well as pleasant memories for him.

"Let's climb up to it," she said.

"I'll go first and see if it's safe," he said as he started climbing the tree. "Seems solid enough, but it's full of bugs and dead leaves." He took off his hat and brushed the trash out. "Give me your hand, and I'll help you up."

Meg scrambled up the tree. "I can still make it on my own," she said with a laugh.

Sitting on the planks of the tree house floor, they ate the sandwiches and shared the canteen of water.

"Did you see anyone in town from your high school class yesterday?" Meg asked.

"Yes, several. Barry at the gas station, Leon at the garage, and Bud at the Dixie Clothing Emporium. They plan to go into the service after the holidays. We ate lunch together at the Main Street Café. Sally Ray is a waitress there. Most of my old classmates are in college, working in Oklahoma City, or in military service."

"You'll see them next week when they come home for Christmas."

"It'll probably be the last Christmas everyone will be home until after the war is over," Joe said sadly.

Meg sat quietly as she thought about his words. The war could change everything. Some men would never come home. Suddenly she was afraid! Bob and Joe and the rest of the men and boys of Oak Grove were putting their lives on the line for their country. Would theirs be the ultimate sacrifice? She shook off the feeling of gloom. God wouldn't let them die. Of course Bob and Joe would come home.

"I hope everyone has the best Christmas ever!" Meg exclaimed. "I know we will because you'll be here with us."

Joe was silent, and Meg noticed that he had become moody.

"What's wrong, Joe?" she asked quietly

"I discovered what my uncle did with my money," he said

bitterly. "He bought a roadhouse out on the highway west of town."

Meg glanced quickly at him. His eyes were narrow slits. Hate twisted his face. She placed a hand on his arm and said earnestly, "Don't think about it. You can't do anything about it, and hate will only hurt you."

Joe laughed cynically, "Such wisdom! You've grown up, Maggie."

"I'm glad you noticed."

"I've noticed something else. It's getting colder. We'd better start for home." He brushed the crumbs out for the birds, put the canteen strap around his neck, and swung down to the ground. Then he turned to help her, and lifting her from the last branch, he kept his hands around her waist a fraction longer than was necessary. Looking into her eyes he said, "You have grown up."

In the evening the Mitchell family gathered around the fireplace. The dogs stretched out on the hearth rug before the crackling fire. Dancing flames cast lights and shadows over the room.

"Bet I can still beat you at a game of checkers, Joe," Dad said.

"You're on!" Joe replied.

Mom pulled out her knitting, and Johnny flopped down on the hearth rug with the dogs and began reading his latest comic book.

"I'm going to finish reading Macbeth," Meg announced. "We may have a test over it Monday."

She curled up in a chair beside the fireplace with the book in her lap and covertly watched Joe. How strong and handsome he looked. Straight black hair, thick black eyebrows that nearly met over a high-bridged nose, high cheekbones, and a firm chin attested to his Indian blood. In the firelight his eyes alternated from gray to green, and they stood out in contrast to his swarthy skin. The softness of boyhood was gone, and his face appeared grim. Suddenly he glanced up and saw her watching him. He grinned at her, his eyes lit up, and his face appeared boyish again.

Meg smiled back and then looked down at her book, embarrassed to be caught staring. For some unaccountable reason her heart had fluttered when their eyes met.

CHAPTER IV

Sunday morning turned colder. The sky was overcast, and a hint of moisture hung in the air. Joe accompanied the family to church and sat with Mrs. Mitchell while Meg and her father sang in the choir. Johnny forsook his buddies to sit with Joe. They sang the old familiar Christmas carols and listened to a sermon about preparing to receive the Christ Child.

After the Sunday dinner, Joe offered to help Meg with the dishes. Usually washing dishes was drudgery for Meg, but with Joe drying the time went by fast. She had a lighthearted sense of humor and discovered that Joe shared it. They took turns recounting the amusing and absurd things that had happened in their lives during the past year and a half. When they finished the dishes, they went outside for a breath of fresh air.

"Let's walk off that dinner," Joe said. "It was delicious, but I ate too much."

They walked up the road until they came to the O'Briens' house. Joe's expression changed to brooding hatred. Meg guessed that he was remembering the hard times he and his aunt had suffered at the hands of his uncle. All her attempts at conversation failed, so she suggested they go back.

At home Joe and Dad resumed their game of checkers until Meg reminded her father of choir practice.

"We don't usually have choir practice on Sunday afternoons," Dad apologized, "but we haven't much more time to practice on the Christmas cantata."

Johnny had come in from playing outside and said, "Meg is going to sing with Jimmy Lester. They're sweethearts!"

Meg was furious with her nine-year-old brother. "We are not! How dare you say such a thing!"

She glanced at Joe and he grinned at her.

"Are you coming to church tonight, Joe?" Mom asked. "It starts at seven."

"No, I'll stay here and read the Sunday paper," he said.

"I'll stay home and keep him company," Johnny offered.

"Okay, you can stay home this time, Johnny, but don't think you can make a habit of it," Dad said.

The rest of the week flew by for Meg. During the day she went to school, but the evenings were spent in Joe's company. Joe came to town every afternoon to visit friends or play pool. Since Dan had sold the saloon and pool hall, he didn't mind going there. Meg would meet Joe after school at the Glass Drug Store for a soda or hot chocolate. They would talk to the other young people and then walk home together.

In the evenings they played dominoes with Dad and Johnny, or, when Meg had homework, Joe and Dad played checkers. On Wednesday evening the Mitchells attended prayer meeting followed by choir practice, and Joe went bowling in the nearby town of Wolfeton with Barry, Leon, and Bud.

Friday was the last day of school before the holidays, and Bob came home from college. Meg had mixed feelings. She was glad to see her brother, but she knew she would no longer see as much of Joe. Every day she had looked forward to spending time with him. They shared similar thoughts. Many times their eyes would meet in agreement or amusement at some incident.

Bob had good news for his family.

"I've decided to finish the next semester of college. It will give me two years and then I'll enlist in the air force for pilot training. Several of my friends are planning to do that also."

"Sounds like a good idea," Dad said.

The family didn't see much of Bob and Joe Friday night or Saturday. Choir practice took place both nights, so Meg didn't have much time to miss them. Sunday morning the boys attended church with the family but had plans for the afternoon.

Mom asked them the question that was uppermost in Meg's mind. "Are you coming to the cantata tonight?"

"Wouldn't miss it!" Bob replied. "Heard that Meg and her boyfriend will sing a duet."

"He's not my boyfriend!" shouted Meg. "I'm tired of everyone teasing me about him!" She stormed up to her room and slammed the door. Throwing herself on the bed, she sobbed in frustration. "What's the matter with me?" she thought. "I'm so hateful and crying about nothing."

By evening Meg's spirits had risen with the excitement of the forthcoming performance. She dressed in her costume that included a white gown and a blue veil. Examining herself critically in the mirror, she was pleased with the effect. Her cheeks were flushed, and her eyes sparkled under the dark, naturally-arched eyebrows. Carefully she reddened her lips with a touch of lipstick and stood back to admire her handiwork.

As she descended the stairs her father looked up at her. "Our little girl is growing up," he said fondly.

"You look nice," Mom added.

"Wow!" Johnny exclaimed. "Wait 'til Jimmy sees you!"

Ignoring Johnny, Meg asked, "Isn't Bob home yet? I-I wonder if he'll make it to church tonight."

"Sure!" Dad exclaimed heartily. "He wouldn't miss his little sister's big moment."

The pews of the small Baptist church overflowed as the choir filed into the choir loft. At first Meg was nervous, but as soon as the music began, her confidence returned. She had a good soprano voice and sang often in both school and church events.

When it was time for the manger scene, she and Jimmy took their places on the platform with the baby Jesus doll in the crib. Jimmy gave her a wink and a toothy grin from under his headdress. His tenor voice blended pleasantly with Meg's.

After the program, they enjoyed a reception for the choir in the church basement. Coffee, hot chocolate, cookies and dainty little sandwiches were served. Meg looked around eagerly, but did not see Bob or Joe. People came by and complimented her on her singing. She tried to keep her mind on their comments in order to make proper responses but found it difficult.

Dad came up behind her and said, "Bob and Joe were here for the cantata, but didn't stay for the reception."

Meg continued to receive congratulations with a smile fixed on her face to hide her disappointment.

"Would you like for me to get you a plate of food and some hot chocolate, Meg?" She turned around in astonishment. It was Don Anderson, a senior and the star center on the basketball team. Every girl in school had a crush on him, including Meg. At least she thought she had.

"Thanks," she replied. "You can't carry it all. I'll get the chocolate while you get the food." He came back with a plate piled high with sandwiches and cookies, and they joined the other young people in a corner of the room. Jimmy sat on the other side of her.

"Do you think you'll get a basketball scholarship?" Jimmy asked Don.

"Maybe. I won't take it anyway, because I plan to join the navy after I graduate this spring. Have some more food," he offered Meg.

Meg was so excited that she could only nibble at a sandwich and sip her chocolate. "I'm too full. You go ahead and eat all you want," she said.

"You sure?" he asked, and when she nodded, he wolfed down the rest of the cookies and sandwiches.

CHAPTER V

The next morning Bob, Joe, and Johnny left early for the nearby woods to get a pine tree for Christmas. Meg and her mother spent the morning cleaning house. When they finished, Meg went to the attic to get the Christmas decorations. The boys had not returned by noon, so the two of them ate a light lunch.

"They're probably goofing off, tramping around in the woods," Meg said. "May I go to town for some last-minute shopping?"

"Yes," Mom said. "It gets dark early, so ride home with your dad."

Main Street was festively dressed up with wreaths of pine branches, big red bows, and silver bells. Loudspeakers played Christmas carols for the shoppers.

The first person Meg met in town was her friend Sue Gregory. At Sue's suggestion they went to the drug store to have a Coke.

"Guess who walked me home from church last night!" Sue said breathlessly.

"I can't imagine. Dracula?"

"Be serious! It was Brock Vandenberg!"

"The Third?"

Sue responded with levity, "You don't think I'd be thrilled with the First or Second, do you? Even though they are rich bankers."

"The first is widowed and available. You could be a rich man's darlin'."

"Not only is Brock rich, he also happens to be the handsomest boy in school."

"Did he try to kiss you?"

"Naturally. I would have been disappointed if he hadn't. I didn't let him, though."

"Enough of these true confessions. I've got some shopping to do. Want to come with me, or have you finished?"

"I'm through, but I'll come along to keep you company."

They walked up to the end of the block to the jewelry store where Meg picked up the I.D. bracelets that she had engraved for Bob and Joe.

For the rest of the afternoon Meg and Sue laughed and enjoyed themselves as they explored all the merchandise in the stores. Meg had finished her shopping but couldn't resist buying a pretty handkerchief with the letter 'S' for her mother. Sue liked it so well that she bought one with her mother's initial on it also.

"I better get more wrapping paper and ribbon," Meg said as they came to a gift wrapping display.

She paid for the items and then glanced at her watch. "It's time for Dad to close the store! I'll have to hurry. He doesn't know that I'm in town. See you later, Sue."

It had darkened considerably outside and the Christmas lights seemed brighter as they twinkled cheerfully over the town. Her father's hardware store was at the far end of Main Street, and Meg had to pass by the dimly lit saloon and pool hall to get to it. Only men ever went there, for it was strictly their domain. She had always been curious about this mysterious place, but avoided it as did all the other women in town.

As she hurried by, the door opened, and a huge man lurched out in front of her.

Meg tried to go around him, but he grabbed her arm and pulled her to his side.

"Where are you goin', my pretty?" His voice was slurred, and he leered at her with bloodshot eyes. The strong smell of alcohol and body odor nauseated her as he wrapped both arms around her.

"Let me go!" Meg shouted as she tried to escape from his grasp.

He tightened his hold on her and said, "How 'bout a kish for ole Unca Dan?"

Meg reached up and slapped his flushed face with a sharp stinging blow.

"My, aren't we feisty," he said with a laugh.

"Leave me alone!" she shouted again. A note of terror had crept into her voice.

"I like a gal with spunk!" he said. "If you can run around with that half-breed nephew of mine, you can spare me a little time."

Meg gasped for breath. The tightness of his embrace and the strong odor of alcohol choked her as his wet lips sought hers. She jerked her head to one side, and the kiss landed on her cheek. Her mind was in a turmoil. This couldn't be happening to her!

Suddenly she was released and dropped to the ground, as Dan was jerked backwards. She heard a resounding crack of fist on jaw, and Dan sprawled on the ground near her.

Joe spoke in a furious voice, "Keep your filthy hands off her!" He stood over Dan with clenched fists. "If you weren't so old and drunk, I'd beat you to a pulp."

Tenderly he helped Meg to her feet. "Are you okay?" he asked.

Sobbing, she threw herself into his arms. "I'm glad you came, Joe. I was so afraid."

Dan sat up and rubbed his painful jaw. "I'll get you for this, Joe!" he hissed. Sluggishly he got to his feet and staggered down the street.

Meg shuddered and clung tightly to Joe. She looked up into his face with tear-filled eyes. "He-he's terrible!" she said.

Joe gently brushed her hair back from her forehead with his right hand while he held her around the waist with his left arm. "Maggie!" he whispered huskily, and his lips came down on hers. Without thinking, Meg responded ardently to his kiss. Warmth and excitement surged through her, and she felt safe and secure in his strong arms. He was her hero. He had rescued her from that awful man.

Just as suddenly as the kiss had begun, Joe put Meg away from himself. "I'm sorry, Maggie. I shouldn't have done that." Quickly he gathered her scattered packages.

Meg was bewildered by his change of attitude. Numbly she got in the car as he held the door open for her, and then she sat huddled against the side.

"When your father came home without you, your mother was worried. I volunteered to come for you," Joe said when he got into the car. They drove the rest of the way home in silence.

When they reached home, Meg hurried up to her room with her purchases. Composing herself, she combed her hair and washed her face and hands. Her mother would be in the kitchen waiting for her to help with dinner.

Over dinner Joe carried on with her in the same half-teasing way he always had. If she didn't know better, she would think she had just imagined his kiss.

After supper the young people began decorating the tree. Mom popped some corn, and Dad read the Daily Oklahoman.

"Is this the best tree you could find?" Meg asked. "It looks lopsided."

"Most of it is in good shape," Bob said with a laugh. "Put the bare spot facing the window."

"Great!" Meg responded. "Then everyone who passes will be able to see it."

"We could cut off some branches to even it up," Joe said. "But then there wouldn't be any place to hang the ornaments."

With much bantering the tree was finally trimmed with shiny ornaments and glittering tinsel. Joe placed the star on top as a crowning touch. When Johnny plugged in the lights, they all stood back to admire the lovely symbol of joy and celebration.

"It's beautiful!" Meg said.

Johnny went outside and came back to report that the bare spot wasn't noticeable.

Later in her room Meg sat at her dressing table mirror brushing her hair. "I'm a little bit angry with Joe," she thought. "He shouldn't have told my parents about Uncle Dan. Now they'll watch me like hawks and may not let me go to town alone. Believe me, I'll never get caught in that situation again!"

Turning off the light, she slipped into bed. Her mind went back to the terror she experienced and then the thankfulness she felt when Joe rescued her. In the darkness of her room, she let her mind dwell on Joe's kiss. Again she felt his lips on hers. How insistent they were, and she had responded so shamelessly! It made her blush to think about it. What must he think of her? She remembered the feel of his strong arms around her and the closeness of his body. "Joe," she thought, "I love you." Suddenly her eyes popped open and she sat up in bed. "I love Joe," she thought. "I love him, I love him, I love him!" Warmth and happiness flooded her as the awareness of her love for Joe possessed her. Then she slumped back in her bed. "But does he love me?" she wondered. "Why did he kiss me like that? Does he feel this way about me, or was he only relieved that I was okay?"

Sleep did not come easily and most of the night she spent tossing and turning.

CHAPTER VI

Christmas Eve fell on Wednesday and as was their habit, the Mitchell family prepared to go to prayer meeting.

"Bob, are you and Joe coming?" Dad asked.

"Sure, some friends from our high school class will be there," Bob replied.

"I'm glad you have such a good reason to go," Dad said with irony.

Upon arriving, Bob and Joe joined their friends outside the church, while the rest of the family went inside. On this night Meg and Johnny sat with their parents instead of their friends. Dad led them down the middle aisle and stood aside while Meg and her mother entered the pew. He came next, followed by Johnny.

When they stood to sing the first verse of "O Come All Ye Faithful," Bob and Joe had not yet come in. During the second stanza Meg felt someone enter from the side aisle and take hold of her book. She looked up into Joe's face. He grinned at her and began singing in a baritone voice. She thrilled at his closeness and the sound of his voice, but tried to remain outwardly calm. Glancing back she saw Bob standing beside Betty Connors. Meg had always thought Betty to be a pretty girl. She had graduated with Bob and was also home from college for the holidays.

The rest of the prayer meeting went by quickly for Meg. She found it hard to concentrate on the service with Joe so close. They sang several more traditional carols, and then different members of the congregation prayed. Brother Cunningham opened his Bible and read the Christmas story from the second chapter of the Gospel of Luke. The meeting ended as everyone joined hands in a circle and sang "Silent Night."

At home Mom played the piano while they sang several more carols. The warmth of the fire as well as the scent of the pine needles mixed with the aroma of spice cake and cookies filled the house.

"I wish this evening could last forever," Meg sighed.

"Time to open the presents," Dad said. "Who wants to be Santa and pass them out?"

"I do, I do!" shouted Johnny.

"Let the twerp do it," Bob said. "He's got to learn how since I probably won't be here next year." Turning around he saw the look of sadness flicker across his mother's face. "I'm sorry. I didn't mean to upset you, Mom."

"I'm fine," she said with a smile.

The first gift Johnny handed out was a gift to Meg from her mother. Eagerly she tore the red ribbon and colorful wrapping paper off the large box and opened it. From the tissue paper inside she pulled out a red corduroy dress. It was princess style with short sleeves and a scooped neckline.

"Oh, Mom," she cried, hugging her, "I love it! Thank you. When did you make it?"

Mother laughed and said, "I worked on it while you were at school and choir practice."

Johnny passed the rest of the presents out one by one as he came to them. He waited while each individual gift was opened for everyone to admire before proceeding to the next one.

Meg was delighted with all of her gifts, which included a music box that played "Always" from Dad, a red compact with her initial on it from Bob, and a box of talcum powder from Johnny. Last of all she opened her gift from Joe. In the small velvet lined box she found a solid gold locket on a gold chain.

"Joe, it's beautiful," she breathed. She nearly flung her arms around him as she would have done in the old days, but since their kiss, she was too shy.

Dad gave the two older boys cameras, and Mom gave them small New Testaments with metal covers.

"Place them in your shirt pockets over your hearts for protection from bullets," she said, "and don't forget to read them."

"Okay, Mom," Bob said. "Tomorrow we'll take pictures of everyone so we won't forget what you look like. Ha ha!"

"I got the best presents of all," Johnny said. "Can I sleep in my new pup tent tonight?"

"Only if you pitch it in your room," Mom said.

Bob had given him a canteen and a set of camping utensils to go with his tent and Meg had given him a flashlight, which he kept shining in everyone's eyes until Mom made him put it away.

"At least I can read the Zane Grey books that Joe gave me," he said.

"You'll have to wait until tomorrow," Mom said. "It's past your bedtime."

"Gee whiz!" Johnny said as he gathered his gifts in both arms and headed up stairs.

"Watch your language, son," Dad said. "That's slang for Jesus, and Christians must not say it."

"Sorry, Dad. I didn't know that. I won't say it again."

"I think I'll turn in," Mom said. "Tomorrow is going to be a busy day. Thanks again for the dresser set, kids. Joe, I'm going to wear this cameo pin that you gave me tomorrow and Sunday. It's exquisite."

"I won't wear this tie clip until Sunday, Joe," Dad said with a grin, "These nice warm house shoes will come in handy tonight, though. Thanks all of you for the presents, and good night."

Before Meg got in bed, she sat at her dressing table and brushed her hair. Her mind focused on Joe and her emerging feelings for him. Although she knew she loved him, she couldn't tell if he returned her deep affections. She put the brush down and picked up the locket. It was beautiful and real gold, too. He must like her a lot to give her such an expensive gift.

Closely examining her face in the mirror, she wondered if he thought her pretty. Just thinking about him made her dark blue eyes sparkle with happiness.

She sank to her knees beside her bed and prayed for protection for Joe and Bob and for all of the men who would be fighting in the war. Then she kissed the locket, put it back in its box, and placed it under her pillow.

"Maybe it'll cause me to dream about Joe," she thought as she slipped under her covers.

CHAPTER VII

Christmas morning Meg arose early to help her mother with the cooking. She dressed warmly in a gray skirt and red sloppy-joe sweater and went downstairs. Mom was preparing the turkey for the oven.

"Want me to fix breakfast, Mom?" she asked.

"Yes, thanks."

While she was beating the batter for waffles, Meg said, "I'm glad that Grandma and Grandpa Mitchell are coming."

"Yes, and your Aunt Barbara and Uncle Harry and their boys."

"You mean their three little horrors!"

"Meg! They're just young boys. Of course they don't mind very well."

"They don't mind at all! The last time they were here they emptied my red fingernail polish all over my underwear drawer and my powder all over my dressing table and rug. On top of that, they pulled up your prize pepper plant. All Aunt Barbara said was, 'Tell them you're sorry.' Which they did very sweetly, but after they left we discovered hair cream all over the bathroom walls.

"We'll keep better watch over them this time," Mom said.

"Who in the 'Lonely Hearts Club' is coming?" Meg asked.

"Meg! I'm ashamed of your callousness. These people are old and all alone in the world. I can't bear to think of them spending Christmas by themselves."

Meg hugged her and said, "I'm sorry, Mom. I shouldn't tease about something like that. Really, I'm glad to have them here, and I'm lucky to have a mother who cares for others."

Her mother was touched. "Thank you, dear. I've invited Miss Patty, Doc Sheffield, and Jack Higgins and his seeing eye dog Scout."

"That means we'll have a jar of sweet pickles that Mrs. Sheffield put up before she died, a jar of blackberry jam from Miss Patty, and a bag of pecans from Jack Higgins," Meg said. "Also cakes, pies, candy, relishes, and various other food that Grandma and Aunt Barbara bring."

Dad came in from milking the cow and said, "Something smells good."

"Call the boys, Meg," Mom said.

Meg went to the foot of the stairs and called, "Breakfast!"

Bob and Joe ate in a hurry because they wanted to get the chores done and go hunting before dinner. They chopped wood for the fireplace, threw hay out for the cow, and slopped the pigs. Johnny fed the chickens and gathered eggs.

"Let's go," Bob said.

"I'm ready," Joe said.

"So am I," Johnny said.

"No," Bob replied. "The little cousins will be here soon, and you need to stay here to keep them out of everyone's hair."

"I'm on the way to get the special guests," Dad said as he took his coat off the kitchen hook by the door.

Meg helped Mom prepare the vegetables and salads. The pies, cakes, and cookies baked the day before lined the cabinets. She enjoyed helping her mom in the kitchen, especially on Thanksgiving and Christmas. The pleasant aroma of the food permeated the warm atmosphere of the kitchen as they worked and sang carols together.

Soon Dad returned with the elderly people. Miss Patty came in the back door first with a small covered basket on her arm. "Here's some blackberry jam," she said. "What can I do to help?" She was a little bird-like woman of uncertain age. Small black eyes in a heavily powdered and rouged face darted around the room, missing nothing. Rubies shone in her petite pierced ears, and chains of gold and strands of beads hung around her wrinkled neck. Rings sparkled on several of her fingers. No one knew if her jewelry was real or fake, but her abundant black hair was obviously a wig.

Behind her came Doc Sheffield, a short rotund man with a balding head and large blue eyes under shaggy gray brows.

"I brought a jar of sweet pickles that my dear wife Mary put up before she passed away," he said.

Jack Higgins, a large burly old man with a thatch of white hair and dark glasses, came in led by his German Shepherd seeing-eye dog Scout. He carried a bag of nuts.

"My old pecan tree produced a bumper crop this year," he said. "Scout kept the squirrels away so I could gather a few. Anything I can do to help?"

"You men can get the extra leaves for the dining room table from the hall closet under the stairs," Mom said. "It will take all of them to seat twelve. After you put them in, Meg and Miss Patty can set the table."

Just as they finished setting the table a large Buick sedan drove up.

"They're here! They're here!" shouted Johnny as he ran through the house to open the front door.

Three little tow-headed boys, ages seven, five, and three, tumbled out of the car and ran for the house. "Hi, Johnny!" they shouted in unison. "You should see what Santa Claus brought us," Charlie, the oldest added.

"Come see my presents!" Johnny invited, and they all dashed into the house, nearly colliding with the Mitchells and the three elderly people coming out.

The rest of the relatives climbed out of the car, and Uncle Harry opened the trunk and began passing out boxes to be carried in.

"Sam, you can carry this large box," he said.

"Here are a few things we didn't have room for in the trunk," Aunt Barbara said. "I hope the boys didn't squash anything. They've been in high spirits all the way here. Couldn't keep them still."

Grandpa stood behind her nodding his head and rolling his eyes upwards. Meg had to control herself to keep from laughing out loud.

"There's enough stuff for everyone to carry," Uncle Harry said. "You didn't forget the kitchen sink, did you, Babs?"

This time Meg did laugh. "Uncle Harry!" she said.

"Don't mind him," Aunt Barbara said. "Where did those kids get off to?"

"Johnny took them upstairs to see his presents," Mom said. "You remember Miss Patty? And our other guests, Doc Sheffield and Jack Higgins?"

"Oh, yes. They were here last year," Aunt Barbara said. "Glad to see you again. Harry, Maw, Paw, you remember them, don't you?"

"Sure," Uncle Harry said. He shook hands with them and then handed them each a package to carry in.

"Okay, everyone," Mom said, "take the food to the kitchen and put the gifts under the tree."

"Everything looks so nice, and the food smells delicious," Grandma said as they entered the house. "Where's Bob?"

"He and his friend Joe Sullivan went hunting," Mom said. "They'll be here in time for Christmas dinner, never fear."

"Is he that Indian kid that lived over yonder with Dan and Peg O'Brien?" Grandpa asked. "Thought he left town."

"He's back on a visit before he joins the marines," Mom answered. "Since he and Dan don't get along, he is staying with us. I had better see about dinner."

The men stayed in the living room discussing the war, while the women accompanied Mom into the kitchen. A few minutes later, Bob and Joe came in the back door.

"Hi, Grandma," Bob said and gave her a hug and a kiss on the cheek. "Good to see you, Aunt Barbara and Miss Patty. Have you met my friend Joe Sullivan?"

"Sure, I remember Joe," Grandma said. "Was sorry to hear about your aunt's passing."

"Yes, we miss Peg. She was always so kind," Miss Patty added.

"Thank you," Joe said. "It's nice to see all of you again."

"How is your uncle doing?" Aunt Barbara asked. "He must be lonely without Peg."

"Can't really say," Joe replied. "Only saw him briefly."

Meg quickly glanced at him, but his face was impassive.

"Is dinner ready?" Bob asked.

"It will be by the time you and Joe get cleaned up," Mom said.

"Hey, Meg!" Bob said. "We got two rabbits for your favorite food, rabbit hash." Ducking the pot holder she threw at him, he dashed down the hall and took the stairs two at a time.

Joe laughed and followed him.

"You like rabbit hash, Meg?" Miss Patty asked. "I like it also. Can't say it's my favorite food, though."

"Oh, Miss Patty," Meg said. "It's not really my favorite food. Bob likes to tease me because when I was little I wouldn't eat the 'cute little bunnies' that he and Dad shot. Mom made the best hash, and I would eat it with relish. I didn't catch on until I was older that it was those rabbits."

By the time Bob and Joe came back downstairs the table was heaped high with food. The younger boys were rounded up and seated at the breakfast table in the kitchen with filled plates.

"That turkey smells good," Grandpa said as he came into the dining room.

"Looks delicious, too," added Uncle Harry. "Browned just right."

"This is one time that too many cooks didn't spoil the soup," Dad added with a grin.

"Where do you want us to sit, Sarah?" asked Grandma.

"Sam will sit at the head of the table, and I will sit at the foot," Mom replied. "Babs and Harry can sit on Dad's right and you and Paw on his left. Jack will sit on my left, so I can help him a little. Miss Patty next, and then Doc. Joe, Meg, and Bob will be on my right."

When they were seated, they bowed their heads while Dad prayed. "Father, we thank Thee and praise Thy name. Especially we thank Thee for our Lord Jesus Christ, Your Son, whose birth we celebrate today. Bless this food and the hands that prepared it. Bless each one at this table who partakes of it. Thank You for friends and loved ones. In Jesus' name we pray. Amen."

Dad carved the turkey, placed a generous portion on each plate, and passed them down the table.

Mom placed the food on Jack's plate and told him where each helping was clockwise. Doc Sheffield was hard of hearing and smacked loudly as he ate. Miss Patty, eating fastidiously between the two men, gave Doc an occasional hard look. When Jack's hand got too close to her plate, she would move it back to his side without missing a dainty bite. Uncle Harry, Aunt Barbara, Dad, Grandma, and Grandpa quietly conversed at their end of the table as if nothing were amiss. Mom was concerned that the food was passed and that everyone had enough to eat.

Meg felt as if she were at the Mad Hatter's tea party. Once she turned her head and caught Joe's amused eyes on her. The urge to laugh overcame her, and she grabbed a napkin to cover her mouth and try to stifle the giggles but only succeeded in choking in it. This caused unwanted attention.

"Help her!" Aunt Barbara cried. "Meg is choking on a piece of turkey!"

"Oh, Meg!" Mom's face was white. "Spit it out!"

Dad got up quickly and rushed down to her and began pounding her on the back. "Cough it up, sweetheart," he said.

"Dad, stop! I'm OK. I only coughed."

"Sounded like you were choking," Grandma said.

The rest of the meal passed quietly. Meg kept her eyes on her plate, not daring to look at Joe.

After the meal the women cleared the table and did the dishes while the men gathered on the porch to talk. Johnny and the little cousins took his new tent out to the back yard, set it up, and pretended they were camping in the wilderness. They found sticks in the woods to use for their hunting guns.

Meg took the table scraps out to the dogs and found Scout finishing the rabbits. Gleefully she went to the front porch and announced, "Mr. Higgins, you'll be glad to know that Scout had a good Christmas dinner also. He ate a couple of rabbits." With a wicked grin at Bob and Joe, she disappeared into the house.

When the kitchen was clean they all went outside to pose for Bob and Joe, who wanted to try out their new cameras.

"Now it's time to go into the living room and open presents," Mom said.

The four younger boys received their presents first and quickly tore off the brightly colored wrapping papers to discover games, puzzles, books, marbles, and toy cars. They exclaimed happily over each gift and wanted to go immediately upstairs to play with them.

"You'll have to wait until the rest of us open our gifts," Aunt Barbara said.

Mom had wrapped a gift for each of the elderly people so they wouldn't be left out of the exchange.

When all the presents were opened and the wrapping papers were thrown away the little boys ran upstairs to play. The adults relaxed in the living room with cups of coffee.

"This has been a wonderful day," Miss Patty said with tears gathering in her eyes and threatening to run down her rouged cheeks. "I can't thank you enough for everything."

"Scout and I would have spent Christmas alone," Jack said.

"It has been so lonely without my Mary," Doc added.

"We've been more than glad to have you," Mom said.

"Yes, we have," Dad said. "Now I'd better get you home before dark."

"We have a few more things to send with you," Mom said and sent Bob, Johnny, and Joe to the cellar to get the three boxes that she had filled earlier with home-canned fruits and vegetables and a small ham.

With tears of thanks the three elderly people were loaded into the old Ford and driven home by Dad.

"I'm glad you all are going to spend the night with us, Grandma," Meg said. "We can put my new puzzle together."

"I bet Sam will want to play dominoes when he gets back," Grandpa said.

Meg got the dominoes, checkers, and puzzle from the hall closet, while Bob and Joe set up the folding table and chairs.

"We can work the puzzle on the library table in the corner," Meg said. "Who wants to help me?"

"I will," Joe volunteered.

"Who's ready to get beat at a game of dominoes?" Dad asked as he came in the front door and hung his coat on the hall tree.

"Harry and I will beat you and Barbara," Grandpa said.

"You're on!" Aunt Barbara said as they gathered around the folding table.

"Do you want to play checkers with me, Grandma?" Bob asked.

"Sure, unless your mother wants to play."

"You go ahead, Mother Mitchell," Mom replied. "I'll sit by the fire and knit."

Meg enjoyed the closeness of Joe as they worked the puzzle. They kept up a casual conversation, but when their hands occasionally touched as they reached for the same piece, Meg felt a tingle go through her. She would glance up quickly at Joe, but his face remained impassive.

As the afternoon drew to a close, Mom said, "It's getting late. I'll make coffee and turkey sandwiches. There's plenty of pie and cake left. Everyone can help themselves when it's ready."

"Need help, Mom?" Meg asked.

"No, I don't need any help." She paused, listening. "I wonder what the dogs are barking at."

There was a loud banging on the door, and Mom started to answer it, but Dad said, "Wait, Sarah, let me."

He opened it, and Dan O'Brien stood there in a disheveled state.

"Where's that good for nothing nephew of mine?" He was drunk. "Doesn't he have the courtesy to come shee his ole Unca Dan on Chrismush?"

Joe hastened to the door and asked angrily, "What are you doing at decent people's homes in that condition?"

"I-I," Dan started to say and then fell on his face with a thud that shook the house.

Joe bent over and touched him. "He's hot as a firecracker!" he exclaimed.

"Bring him in and put him on the couch," Mom said.

"I'll call Dr. Newberry," Dad said.

Joe and Bob carried Dan to the couch.

"Who is he and what's he doing here?" Grandma asked.

"It's Dan O'Brien," Grandpa told her. "You know him. He lives over in the next house."

"He's Joe's uncle," Aunt Barbara explained.

Dan's breathing was shallow and wheezing, and his face was flushed with a bluish tinge around his mouth and nose.

Hearing the commotion, the little boys had rushed downstairs to see what all the excitement was about. They stood staring in wide-eyed awe at Dan.

"Johnny, you and Charlie take Todd and Timmy back upstairs," Uncle Harry said.

"Aw-w-w, we want to stay here," whined Charlie.

"Yeah-h-h," Todd and Timmy agreed.

"Come on, guys, we better mind," Johnny said.

"We gotta miss all the fun," Charlie said as they reluctantly went back to Johnny's room.

Soon Dr. Newberry arrived. He was a short plump man with white hair and a well-trimmed white beard and mustache.

"It's Sandy Claus!" Piped a little voice from the head of the stairs.

"Sh-h-h, Timmy," whispered Johnny. "That's not Santa. He's Dr. Newberry."

Meg, who had opened the door, glanced up and saw four little faces peering around the corner at the top of the stairs. She pointed her finger at them, and they disappeared.

The women made coffee and sandwiches in the kitchen while the doctor examined Dan.

"Dan has pneumonia and needs to be in the hospital," Dr. Newberry said. "I'll call the ambulance and the hospital."

In five minutes the ambulance from Parker Funeral Home in Oak Grove arrived with lights flashing and siren wailing. The two attendants quickly loaded Dan on the stretcher and placed him in the ambulance. Joe got in beside him.

"I have to go with him," he said. "I'm his only relative."

At the first sound of the siren, the four little boys dashed back downstairs. They watched the proceedings with open mouths and were too excited to go back upstairs to play.

"Supper is ready, boys," Mom said. "Come into the kitchen and have a sandwich and a glass of milk."

Meg lay in bed that night thinking about Joe and his uncle. Theirs was a strange relationship. They seemed to hate each other, yet were drawn together by invisible threads. Perhaps it was because each had loved Aunt Peg.

CHAPTER VIII

The next day, after a hearty breakfast, the guests departed with lots of hugs and kisses and thanks all around.

Mom and Dad were sitting at the breakfast table with a second cup of coffee congratulating themselves for escaping any damage from the boys, when Meg came down and announced that her red fingernail polish was missing.

"Poor Uncle Harry. I can imagine what the back seat of their car will look like by the time they reach home," she said.

"Your Grandpa was sitting back there with them. Maybe he can control them," Mom said.

Dad grinned and said, "He'll probably be asleep before they get out of town."

"Have you seen the bathroom?" Bob came in asking. "The boys squirted toothpaste all over the place."

"I thought it was a mistake when Babs sent them up there by themselves to brush their teeth," Dad said.

Bob drove to the hospital in Wolfeton to stay with Dan and let Joe come home to rest. While he was gone, the phone rang.

"It's for you, Meg," Mom said.

Meg talked a few minutes and then said, "Mom, Don Anderson wants to take me to the party at Amy's house."

"You know that you can't date yet," Mom replied.

"It isn't a date! He lives further out than we do and this is on his way. He's picking up others also."

"Who else is he taking?"

"Sue and Brock and I don't know who else."

"Sounds like a double date to me."

"If I can't go with them, I won't go!" Meg stormed. "I positively refuse to be driven to a party in that old truck, and Bob has our car since his went kaput."

"Joe will bring the car back before you have to leave," Mom said. "I'll talk to your dad about it. The Andersons are good friends of ours, and I'm sure that Don is reliable."

When Joe came home, he reported that Dan was not doing well

and was in an oxygen tent. He ate breakfast, and then went to bed.

Dad came home for lunch, and Mom told him about Meg's invitation to ride with Don to the party.

"I don't see any harm in it as long as others are going and its on his way," Dad said.

When Joe awakened later in the day, he took a bath and shaved. "I'm going back to the hospital and let Bob come home," he said.

"Wait until after you eat," Mom said. "Sam will be home early tonight, and he wants to stay with Dan."

"No, he's my responsibility," Joe objected.

While Joe ate, Dad came home.

"I'm staying with Dan tonight," he said, "so you and Bob can go to the party at Betty Connor's."

"No, I can't let you do that."

"I want you and Bob to spend all the time you can with your friends. It may be a long time before you see them again."

Finally Joe agreed, but said, "I'll go with you to see how he is doing and then ride home with Bob."

Meg sat before the mirror of her dressing table and brushed her hair until it shone. Her eyes were bright with anticipation. She was going to a party with Don Anderson, the most popular boy in school. No matter what she said to her parents, she felt like it was a date. Her new red dress hung on her closet door in readiness, and the gold locket gleamed in its velvet nest. Putting the brush down, she picked up the locket and stroked it lovingly against her cheek. "I'm going to put Joe's picture in you," she whispered as she fastened it around her neck.

As she came down the stairs in the new dress with the locket fitting perfectly in the scooped neckline, Joe and Bob walked in the front door.

"You're going to wow all the boys tonight in that outfit!" Bob exclaimed.

Meg glanced quickly at Joe and caught a strange look in his eyes, almost of longing. It passed so quick that she wasn't sure it had been there as he congratulated her on how nice she looked.

Mom came in and said, "Your supper's waiting on you, Bob."

"I've got to eat fast and get ready for the party at Betty's," he said.

"I'm going up and change," Joe said.

A few minutes later the doorbell rang. It was Don Anderson looking well-groomed and handsome in his Sunday suit.

"Hello, Don," Mom said. "You look nice."

"Thank you, ma'am," he said. "Ready to go, Meg?"

"Yes," she said, taking his proffered arm.

"Now you drive carefully and come straight home when the party is over," Mom said.

"Yes, ma'am," Don replied.

When they got to the car Meg said, "Oh, your parents let you drive their new Dodge! It's beautiful!"

As they drove into town they talked mostly about how they had spent Christmas Day. They picked up Brock first and when they came to Sue's house, Brock went to the door and escorted her to the car.

Sue started talking excitedly. "Did you know that we're going to dance tonight? Amy told me, but I didn't dare tell my parents. They wouldn't let me go if they knew."

Alarm and surprise registered on Meg's face. The Baptist church of which she and Sue were members disapproved of dancing. Amy's father was a Methodist deacon, and she didn't think they approved of dancing either. What should she do? Her parents would not have let her come if they had known. Besides, she didn't know how to dance. Well, she would just have to learn in a hurry because she didn't want to sit and watch the others all evening.

Colored lights twinkled on the bushes outside Amy's house, and a glow radiated from all the windows. Mrs. White welcomed them at the door and took their coats to the front bedroom. The living room and dining room rugs had been rolled back and all of the furniture lined up against the walls. No one was dancing yet, and the young people sat in groups talking. They greeted the newcomers enthusiastically, and Sylvia came over to talk with Meg.

"Are you going to dance tonight?" she whispered. "I am. It'll be fun."

Meg was still troubled about this, but when Mr. White put a record on the phonograph, and the strains of Glenn Miller's "Moonlight Serenade" filled the air, she was ready. Don took her in his arms and showed her a few steps, and with her natural rhythm, she was soon following his lead as if she had done it all of her life.

For the rest of the evening she had no dearth of partners. As Jimmy Lester whirled her around the floor, she imagined herself in Joe's arms. "He's probably dancing with some other girl right now," she thought.

Occasionally, her conscience troubled her when she thought of her parents, but she reasoned that they had urged Joe to go to Betty's party, and it was probably a dance, too. Besides, the Whites were good Christian people, and if it was okay with them, there couldn't be any harm in it.

It was nearly midnight when the party broke up. Don took Sue and Brock home first and then drove to Meg's house. The porch light and her parents' bedroom light were on.

"Thank you for the ride to the party," Meg said as she started to open the car door.

"Just a minute," Don said. "How 'bout a kiss first?"

"Do you require payment for the ride?" Meg asked.

"Of course not!" Don was indignant. "You look so pretty that I just wanted to kiss you."

Meg was surprised and touched, but she still said, "No."

Don was disappointed, but he didn't insist. He opened the car door for her and walked her to the front door.

"See you later," he said.

Inside the living room Meg whirled around humming softly.

Mom called down the stairs, "Is that you, Meg?"

"Yes, Mom," Meg said, and quickly climbed the stairs.

Her mother followed her into her room, full of interest and wanting to find out all about the party.

"Who was there?" she asked.

"Oh, the usual bunch," Meg replied.

"Did you play games?"

"Y-yes. Lots of games."

"You seem tired. Did you have a good time?"

"Oh, yes," Meg sighed. "I had a wonderful time."

"I'll let you get to sleep now. Maybe we can talk about it in the morning," Mom said. "I'm glad you had fun."

As Meg climbed into bed that night, she felt guilty. It was the first time she could remember lying to her mother.

CHAPTER IX

After the party Friday night, Joe went to the hospital and insisted that Sam go home. On Saturday the oxygen tent was removed, and Dr. Newberry announced that Dan was out of danger. Joe called the Mitchells and told them the good news and that no one need stay that night. Bob went to pick him up, and Joe never went to the hospital again. However, Sam went every day to visit Dan and to see if he needed anything.

On Saturday night Bob had a date with Betty. He tried to get Joe to ask a girl out to double date, but Joe declined. He claimed that his short nap after returning from the hospital had left him feeling rotten, and he wouldn't be good company on a date.

After Bob left Meg said, "We never did finish the puzzle. Want to help me with it?"

"Sure," Joe said. "We need to finish it before I leave."

Once again Meg took pleasure in the closeness of Joe as they bent over the puzzle. She felt that he enjoyed it also.

Dad finished reading the paper and said, "Hey, Joe, how about a game of checkers?"

"Okay," Joe said. Meg wondered if he was as disappointed as she. He gave no indication of it though as he cheerfully got the checker board and checkers from the hall closet.

On Sunday morning the Mitchell family and Joe went to Sunday school and church together. The regular pianist was ill, so Mom played the piano for the church service. Meg and her dad sang in the choir and Bob and Joe sat with their friends. Johnny sat with his usual gang. Meg and Jimmy Lester sang "The Holy City" as a duet with the rest of the choir joining them on the chorus. Jimmy's beautiful tenor voice blended well with Meg's soprano. Several "Amens" filled the church when they finished. Meg glanced at Joe, and he was looking at her with a special light in his eyes. She lowered her eyes in shy happiness.

In the afternoon Bob, Betty, and several others went to Wolfeton to see a movie. Joe said he had seen that one and didn't want to go.

"Want to walk to town and get a Coke?" he asked Meg.

"Yes," she answered happily and went to get her coat.

The sun shone brightly and Meg enjoyed the walk in spite of the cold. They talked about the past and the future and everything except the war and the fact that Joe was leaving in a few days. When they reached town, Joe suggested the Main Street Café instead of the drug store.

"It isn't as crowded on Sundays," he said.

The café was deserted except for a few older men drinking coffee at a round table. Doc Sheffield and Jack Higgins sat with them. Scout lay quietly under the table but wagged his tail when he saw Meg.

"Hi there, Meg and Joe," Doc greeted them. "What brings you to town?"

"Is that Meg Mitchell who just came in?" Jack asked. "I want to thank you again for Christmas dinner."

Meg said, "Hi. We were glad that you were able to come. The pickles and pecans were sure good."

Joe went over to shake hands with them and meet the other men. Meg was looking at the selection on the juke box when he got back.

"What would you like to hear?" he asked.

"I like 'Blueberry Hill,'" she said.

He put a nickel in the slot, and pressed her selection. They walked over to a booth and sat down. Sally Ray came over to wait on them.

"Hello, Joe and Meg. What'll you have?"

"Hi, Sally," Joe said. "We just want Cokes."

They sipped their Cokes while listening to the strains of the Glenn Miller rendition of "Blueberry Hill."

When it ended Meg said, "That's my favorite song."

"Mine, too," Joe said. "I think I'll play it again, unless you'd rather hear something else."

"No. I could listen to it all day."

Meg watched him as he put the money in the slot and then headed back to the table. She loved looking at him. He was so handsome. If only he would sit beside her and put his strong arms around her! But, no, he resumed his place opposite her.

"I see you're wearing the I.D. bracelet I gave you," she said. She reached over and picked up his hand ostensibly to look at the bracelet, but in reality she just wanted to touch him. He covered her slim fair hand with his larger brown one.

"I'm going to miss you, Maggie," he said and looked deep into her eyes.

Her heart turned over. "Oh, Joe. I wish you didn't have to go. Can't you wait awhile?"

Joe smiled into her face and said gently, "Is this the girl who was so eager to go to war a short time ago?"

She pulled her hand back and dropped her eyes. "That was before you came home," she said quietly.

Later at home, they worked the puzzle again until Mom called them to eat sandwiches and then get ready for evening service at church. Bob had not returned, but Joe went to church with them and sat beside Meg.

Following the church service, Meg, Joe, Dad, and Mom played dominoes while Johnny read one of his Zane Grey books.

On each of the next two days Bob and Joe went hunting. In the evenings Bob went over to Betty's house while Joe stayed home with the Mitchells, working the puzzle with Meg or playing checkers with Dad.

On Wednesday, Meg asked Joe if he was coming to the New Year's Eve Watch Night service at the church.

"I'd like to go," he said, "but our high school class is having a New Year's Eve party at the Fields' house. It will be a farewell event for all the boys going into the service, and Bob is determined that I go."

Meg turned her head away to hide her disappointment. She wanted to spend every moment she could with him before he left. On Sunday afternoon he would catch the bus for Oklahoma City where he would enlist in the marines on Monday morning.

Joe sensing her distress, lifted her chin gently with his forefinger and brushed her lips with his. "We'll still have a few more days together," he said softly.

CHAPTER X

On Wednesday evening at seven the Mitchells made their way to church for the covered-dish supper and Watch Night service. It was a frosty cold night, and the well-lighted church was a welcome sight.

"Come in, come in, Mitchells," the pastor, Brother Cunningham, welcomed them. He was a dignified gentleman with white hair and twinkling blue eyes. The delicious aroma of hot cooked food assailed their nostrils as they entered the church basement.

Mrs. Cunningham, a short rotund woman, bustled up to greet them. "Let me show you where to put your dishes," she said. Her round cherubic face always seemed to be smiling.

Mom stayed in the kitchen to help the other women put the food on the serving tables while Meg, Dad, and Johnny mixed with their friends in the dining area.

After supper the tables were folded and put away, and the chairs were lined in rows for the funny skit that the adults put on. Meg was embarrassed at first when her dad came out admiring himself in a hand mirror. He was Handsome Harry, the hero, and her mom was Sweet Sue, the heroine, in the melodrama of the wicked landlord and the girl who couldn't pay the rent. It was a lot of fun, and they got a lot of laughs out of it.

When the skit was over they broke up into age groups to play games, charades, and Bible quizzes. Some of the elderly preferred to play dominoes or checkers.

"Meg," Sue whispered, "have you noticed that Brock always chooses me to be his partner?"

Sue Gregory was a pretty girl with black curly hair and large brown eyes. She usually wore a small bow on each side of her hair in colors to match her sloppy-joe sweaters. Any bright color looked good on her, and she had a large variety of sweaters with matching plaid skirts. These clothes with white bobby socks and penny loafers or saddle oxfords made any high school girl right in fashion.

"Don has been choosing me," Meg said. "I think we're making progress in the art of flirting."

During the evening festivities they took a break for coffee, hot chocolate, spiced tea, and desserts. At eleven-thirty everyone gathered in the auditorium and prayed together until midnight.

At the stroke of midnight Dad took Mom in his arms and kissed her and then hugged Meg and Johnny. Friends and neighbors all around them hugged and wished each other a happy new year.

Mrs. Johnson, the pianist, began playing "Blest Be the Tie That Binds," and everyone joined hands in a circle and sang.

The service concluded as Brother Cunningham prayed one more time for God's blessings on the new year and for a quick ending to the war and for peace throughout the world. Then he dismissed them to their homes.

The babies and young children asleep in the pews were gathered up by their parents, wrapped in blankets, and carried to the waiting cars.

New Year's Day remained cold and blustery. After breakfast they gathered in the living room before the fireplace for a second cup of coffee.

"Are you going any place today, Bob?" Dad asked.

"No," he replied. "Think I'll rest from the hectic week I've had. Besides, Betty is going to visit her grandmother."

"Let's finish this puzzle," Meg said.

Everyone pitched in until the picture was completed. The colors blended together to form an old sailing ship tossed about on a rough sea.

"I'm going to frame this to remember the good times we had working on it," Meg said.

"Will it remind you of Bob and me when we are overseas?" Joe asked.

"I'll think of you every time I look at it," she said.

Friday morning after chores were done and breakfast was eaten, Bob said, "Joe, I'm working with Dad in the store today. He let his help off for the weekend. Want to come?"

"Do you need me?"

"Not really. Business will be slow."

"Since I'm leaving Sunday, I think I'll hike around the countryside. Want to come, Maggie?"

"Sure!" Meg answered happily. "After I do the dishes."

Joe dried while she washed, and soon they were through. By the time they dressed in their warmest clothes, the sun had come out from behind the clouds. Instead of taking the path to the river, Joe headed south into the hills. There was no trail, but he seemed to know where he was going. Meg had trouble keeping up with him.

"Wait, Joe," she pleaded.

"I'm sorry, Maggie. I forgot you couldn't keep up with my long legs."

When they reached the top of the hill, Joe led the way along the ridge until they came to a bare knoll overlooking the Poteau River. On the other side of the river the cliffs were not so high. The undulating terrain of hills and valleys swept off into the horizon.

Meg gazed in wonder at the breath-taking view.

"It's beautiful!" she exclaimed.

Joe looked off into the distance and said, "Someday I'm going to build a house on this spot."

"I can't remember coming to this place before," she said.

"Bob and I came across it a long time ago while hunting. He wasn't as impressed with it as I, though."

"Look, the ground is covered with wild blueberry bushes. You could call it 'Blueberry Hill' like the song."

Joe took her by the hand and led her to a boulder. "Sit here in this chair. You are the first guest in my new home."

"Thank you, sir. Your furnishings are exquisite. They must have come from Paris."

Joe sat down on the ground beside her and took one of her hands in his. He removed the glove and studied her palm.

"Are you going to tell my fortune, sir?" she asked.

"Yes. I see a long life, a happy marriage, and many children."

Meg snatched her hand back. "Ha! You're just saying that because I'm a girl. Maybe I'll be a doctor or a lawyer or-or even the President of the United States and not get married at all!"

Joe retrieved her hand and studied it with concentration. "Nope! This capable little hand shows a loving and caring person. You'll make some man very happy one of these days."

He held her hand and seemed to be in deep thought. Meg looked down on his glossy black hair as he lay sprawled beside her and was filled with love for him. Her hand in his large firm one gave her an exhilarated feeling.

"Maggie, how old are you?" he asked suddenly.

"I'll be sixteen in June."

Slowly he replaced the glove on her hand. "That's what I thought. You are so young and sweet and innocent, Maggie. I-I care a great deal about you, but I have no right to say what's in my heart. Time and war change many things. Please stay as good and pure as you are now. This is how I'll remember you." He rose and held out his hand to help her to her feet. "It's getting late. We'd better go home."

Meg didn't know what to say, but he didn't seem to expect a response. They picked their way down the hill toward home. "I'll always love only you," she thought.

On Saturday Joe went to town with Dad and Bob to help unload boxes of merchandise and stock the shelves. In the afternoon he visited friends, and in the evening he went with Bob to another party. Meg helped her mom clean house and bake apple pies for Sunday. She wished she could have spent the day with Joe.

On Sunday morning during the worship service, Meg sang "The Old Rugged Cross." Joe looked at her as if he was trying to memorize her features and her voice. It saddened her because this was the day he was leaving, and she didn't know when she would see him again.

In the afternoon they all went to the bus station to see Bob and Joe off. Bob was returning to the University of Oklahoma at Norman, and Joe was going to Oklahoma City to enlist in the marines.

"See you in a few weeks, Mom," Bob said as he hugged her. He shook hands with Dad, waved casually at Meg and Johnny, and boarded the bus.

Joe shook hands with Dad, tousled Johnny's hair, and hugged Mom. "Thanks for everything," he said. "I'll write."

Meg held out her hand for him to shake, but he ignored it and took her in his arms. "I love you, Maggie. Wait for me," he whispered in her ear.

"I will, I will wait for you, Joe," she said softly.

He released her and quickly boarded the bus.

CHAPTER XI

War was raging in Europe and in the Pacific in the spring of 1942. America was in the process of building the largest war machine in the history of the world, but all was quiet in the tiny town of Oak Grove, Oklahoma. The only signs of the conflict were the red stars in the windows of several homes, representing the sons, fathers, and brothers in the service. So far there were no gold stars denoting one who had given his life for his country.

One sunny afternoon in early April, Meg took a peanut butter and jelly sandwich and a canteen of water into the woods. The hunting dogs, Buck and Duke, accompanied her. They seemed to know that she didn't hunt, so they ran hither and yon on their own business. Dogwood and redbud trees and plum bushes bloomed in profusion, making a beautiful sight against the dark bare oak trees. Meg thought the dogwood blossoms looked like butterflies flitting among the somber background. Soon the blossoms would be gone, and the oaks would leaf out, and the woods would look like a green fairyland. Dead leaves covered the ground now, but already scattered patches of green grass and wild flowers peeked out. Before long berry bushes would be blooming and bearing fruit to feed the small woodland animals and birds.

"The black bears are probably out of hibernation," Meg thought. "Hope I don't meet a mother with cubs." Dad had told them the bears wouldn't bother them if they left them alone. It was rare to see bears, but Meg had seen a cinnamon colored one once. She knew that they were classified as black bears also.

Wild turkeys inhabited these woods, and in the fall Dad and Bob hunted them. However, Dad bought farm-raised birds for Thanksgiving and Christmas dinners.

She reached the top of Joe's hill and stood among the blueberry bushes gazing at the beautiful view. Since Joe left she had been up here several times. It made her feel closer to him. One early morning recently there had been fog in the valleys. The sky was blue-gray and the dark ridges of the hills rose out of the gray layers of mist. It was a panorama of different shades of blues and grays. Today, however, the sun was shining, the sky was blue, and the hills were greening.

Filled with the peaceful scene, Meg sat on a rock to eat her lunch. It was the rock that Joe had seated her on when he had brought her here. She liked to pretend that she was sitting in a chair in the house that Joe built for her. This was her favorite place to think about him. The locket that he had given her hung around her neck. She only took it off to bathe. Now she opened it and looked at Joe's picture. It was cut from a snapshot taken on Christmas Day. How handsome he was! In her eyes a halo surrounded him. Stroking her cheek with the open locket, she said a little prayer for the Lord to protect him. He was still in training in California, but she had heard tales about the dangers they faced in training. The marines had to be tough.

A few weeks later, Meg sat in her history class looking out of the window. Her mind was closed to the droning voice of the teacher as she fondled the gold locket around her neck and thought of Joe. Briefly she noticed the riot of colorful flowers in Mrs. Overton's garden across the street and the green of the lawn next to it. She glanced up at the clear blue sky and wondered what the weather was like in California. "Maybe I'll hear from Joe today," she thought as the dismissal bell rang.

Meg and her three best friends walked out of the school together.

"Let's go to the drugstore for ice cream before we go home," Amy suggested. She was a petite blonde girl with green eyes in a fine-boned, oval-shaped face. A slight over-bite marred her otherwise perfect classical beauty and gave her a human quality that added to her charm. Her mother made all of her clothes, and the materials were always dainty prints in pale hues. Even in winter she wore pastel skirts and sweaters.

"I can't," Meg said. "The Cunninghams are coming for dinner, and I have to get home to help Mom."

"Meg wants to go home to see if she has a letter from Joe Sullivan," Sylvia remarked.

Meg's face turned scarlet. Her feelings for Joe were so special that she had not shared them even with her three best friends. But Sylvia had guessed! Sylvia was not a beauty, with a long, narrow face and mousy brown hair, but her sharp gray eyes missed nothing. "She always needles me," Meg thought. "She has an uncanny way of putting her finger on the right spot and rubbing it the wrong way."

"I told you the reason," she said, and ran to catch her bus.

When Meg reached home she could hear her mother in the kitchen.

"Hi, Mom! I'll go change and wash up and then be down to help you. Any mail?"

"On the dining room table," Mom replied. "We didn't hear from Bob, but you got one from Joe."

Meg hastened to the table, glad no one was in the room to see her flushed face and the excitement in her eyes. She snatched the letter and hurried upstairs to her room, savoring the feel of it. Flinging herself on the bed, she tore it open and began to read. The letters she had received in the past had been friendly, but noncommittal. He had told her about boot camp, the drill sergeant, and his new friends who called him "Chief." They always call Indians "Chief," he had written.

Each letter had been treasured, not so much for its content, but for the bold handwriting, and the paper that he had touched. She kept them in the music box her father had given her for Christmas. Often she took them out, wound the music box, and reread them to the strains of "Always." Just to touch them and to see his handwriting brought him closer to her.

When she finished reading this one, though, she had a stunned look on her face. She couldn't believe the words that she had read! She read them again slowly.

Dear Maggie,

This is a hard letter to write, but I feel that I must write it. I hope I did not leave you with a wrong impression of my feelings for you. You are very dear to me, and I love you as a sister. If I left you with any other thoughts, I'm sorry. Our outfit is getting ready to pull out for overseas duty, and I want to leave with a clear conscience and no strings attached.

You are a lovely girl and I want you to date and enjoy your high school years as much as I did mine.

Your friend,

Joe

Meg's heart sank! What was this? She read the letter again. He couldn't mean it! But he did. Her first impulse was to tear the letter to pieces and do the same with all of the others. Instead she put this letter with the rest, took off the locket and carefully placed it on top, shut the lid, and hid the box on the highest shelf in her closet behind her other possessions.

Throwing herself back on the bed, she burst into tears. So this was the end of her first love and fine dreams for the future. How could he be so cruel when she loved him so much? Had she misread his feelings? She felt like a fool. He wanted her to date high school boys! Those babies! Okay! She would be sixteen in June, and that was the age her parents had set for her to begin dating. She would flirt outrageously and date every boy in school!

"Oh, Joe," her heart cried out, "You're the only one I want to be with! Why can't you love me as I love you?"

CHAPTER XII

June twelve marked Meg's sixteenth birthday. Mom baked a cake and decorated it with candles. She had asked her earlier if she wanted a party, but Meg had said, "No!"

After lunch Meg said, "I'm going hiking in the woods, Mom. See you later."

She dressed in her oldest slacks and shirt and took the dogs with her. As she climbed Joe's hill, she remembered the happy times she shared with Joe when she thought he loved her. If only she could stop loving him! This was her first hike to the hill since she had received that letter. She looked at the view and then sat on the rock and daydreamed about what might have been.

It was no use thinking about the future. She had lost Joe. Maybe she could be a missionary and go to Africa and devote her life to serving others. Would she need to take nurse's training or go to college and be a teacher? What did missionaries do besides preach to the natives? She would ask Brother Cunningham. The shadows had lengthened while her mind wandered deep in thought.

"Here, Buck. Come on, Duke," she called. "It's getting late, and we have to go home."

As she approached her house, she saw two horses and a wagon load of hay standing by the barn. "I didn't know Dad ordered more hay," she thought.

"Mom," she called as she entered the kitchen, "did Dad order more hay?"

There was no answer, so she went on through the house to the living room.

"Surprise! Happy Birthday!" shouted a room full of her schoolmates, all grinning at her.

"Oh, no," she cried. "Mom, how could you? Look how I'm dressed!"

"It's okay, Sis," Johnny said. "We're going on a hay ride!"

"I'm dressed for that, all right," she said.

"Then let's go," Dad said. "Everyone on the hay wagon."

They all ran and climbed upon the hay. Several boys wanted to sit by Meg.

"Where are we going?" Meg asked.

Mr. Potter, the driver and owner of the wagon, said, "We're going out to my farm. There's a good place to build a fire so you can roast wieners and toast marshmallows."

On the way they sang old songs such as "I've Been Working on the Railroad" and "She'll Be Coming 'Round the Mountain." It was great fun, and Meg found herself enjoying it.

While they roasted the wieners, Tommy Riggs asked Meg if she could date now. A handsome boy in a florid sort of way, he was the elected captain of the football team for the coming year. She told him she would have to ask her parents.

Sylvia overheard them talking and shouted, "Sweet sixteen and never been kissed!"

Meg remembered Joe's kiss and blushed in the darkness. "How dared he!" she thought. He hadn't loved her but had led her to think he did.

"Meg," Jimmy Lester said at her elbow, talking in a low voice as if he didn't want to be overheard, "I'm leaving next Monday to join the 45th Division. It would mean a lot to me if you would go to the show with me Saturday night."

Meg looked in his face and saw in his eyes that he was afraid she would refuse. Her heart melted. Jimmy had always been a good friend. She knew that Sylvia would tease her because her first date would be with him, but she didn't care.

"I would like to very much, Jimmy. What's playing?"

Jimmy grinned his relief and said, "White Cliffs of Dover."

Saturday night Jimmy showed up in his father's old Ford. He had washed and polished it until it shone. Mom invited him in for apple pie, but he refused, saying, "If Meg is ready we had better go."

As he drove he seemed nervous and talked a lot. Meg wondered if it was his first date also. He bought Cokes and candy when they went in, then kept asking her if she wanted anything more, until people around them began to complain that they couldn't hear the actors.

Meg whispered, "You don't have to try to impress me, Jimmy. I've known you since you were a snotty-nosed little brat."

"And I can remember you at church with baggy wet pants," he whispered, and they both laughed quietly.

On the way home Jimmy pulled over to the side of the road and turned off the motor.

"What's the matter–out of gas?" Meg quipped.

"No, Meg," Jimmy was serious. "I just want to tell you how much I've always liked you and how much I've enjoyed singing with you at church and in the glee club."

"Don't forget the medals we won at Enid during the TriState Band Festival. That was fun," Meg added.

"Yes, we had fun at Enid, didn't we? All those kids from different states and the carnival rides in the middle of the courthouse square."

"Wish you could be there with me next spring," Meg said.

"Me, too," he answered. "I also remember how you stood up for me when the other kids teased me about my red hair, freckles, and teeth. Even though you were just a little thing, you shouted at them to leave me alone."

"I was quite a tomboy in those days."

"You could never stand cruelty to people or animals."

"Especially animals," she said with a smile. "I wish I were as good a person as you paint me. Say, why don't we ask if we can sing a duet in church tomorrow?"

"I would like that."

"When this war is over and you're home again, we'll sing together often."

"Meg, may I kiss you?" he asked. "I've wanted to for a long time, and this may be my last chance."

"Well..." she said with indecision.

"Please, Meg."

Meg gave her consent, and he took her in his arms and kissed her with more fervor than she expected. Instead of releasing her, he kissed her again and again, and she found herself kissing him back. Though awkward, at least he was sincere.

On the first day of school in the fall of 1942, the junior girls met in the gym. Meg and Sue sat on a bench near the top of the bleachers talking. Amy joined them and asked, "Are you all going to try out for cheerleader?"

"Yes, we are," Meg answered.

Sue groaned, "I'll never make it. I don't have Meg's pep."

"I'm trying out also," Amy said. "What about Sylvia?"

"What about Sylvia?" Sylvia was climbing the bleachers to sit with them.

"We're all going to try out for cheerleader," Sue said. "Are you?"

"No! I'd rather join the debate team."

Meg said, "I think you would make a good debater. You can out-think, out-talk, and out-guess anyone."

"Thanks. I'll take that as a compliment," Sylvia said dryly.

"Let's go out for basketball, also," Meg said. "The girls team, I mean. We always have gone out for the boys team."

"Meg!" Amy was shocked. "What's gotten into you?"

"I don't know," Meg shrugged. "Moment of truth?"

"I think Meg got carried away with her successes this summer," Sylvia said. "She had more dates than anyone else."

"Yes, but it was the best summer we ever had, and Meg did plan most of the outings," Sue responded.

It was true. Meg felt as if she had to keep busy to forget Joe. The summer had been filled with picnics, hikes, swimming, skating parties, watermelon feeds, ice cream socials, and hay rides. She had to admit that she had enjoyed the summer more than she had thought she would. Now she intended to squeeze in all the school activities she could and still have time to study. Pep club, glee club, drama, and basketball were on her agenda.

"Any mail, Mom?" Meg called as she banged into the house and dropped her books with a thud on the dining room table.

"We got a letter from Bob, and you got one from Jimmy."

Bob was training to be a pilot in the Naval Air Force. Meg scanned his letter and then took the one from Jimmy up to her room.

This letter was similar to the others she had received from him. Although he never mentioned it, she felt the homesickness in his letters. He always expressed his love for her, and she feared he presumed too much from their kisses that night. The thoughts of his leaving and the dangers he might face, plus the hurt and longing for Joe, caused her to respond with more fervor than she should have. Now she didn't have the heart to write him a letter such as the one Joe had written to her. Even though she kept her letters light and friendly, he was not discouraged. She had sent him a picture of herself as he had requested, and he told her how much the other men in his unit had admired "his girl." At the end of this letter he wrote that they were shipping out soon and he wanted her to pray for his outfit. "They are a great bunch of guys," he wrote. "By the way, I received a sharpshooter medal. I told them that where I came from, all the boys were sharpshooters."

"Oh, Jimmy," she cried to herself with a sudden fear for his safety. "I will pray for you daily."

For a few days after receiving this letter, she was more subdued than she had been for a long time.

A week later she stood in the musty hall of Oak Grove High putting her books in her locker, when Brock Vandenberg came by and said, "Congratulations, Meg, I hear by the grapevine that you made cheerleader."

Meg answered, "Amy and I are the two juniors chosen. We are excited! After school we're celebrating at the drug store. Want to come?"

"I never miss a celebration. See ya later."

"Brock is the handsomest guy in school," Meg thought as she watched him walking down the hall. "He has that all-American prep look." Still tanned from the summer, his skin blended with his brown hair and hazel eyes. His classical features were perfect from the high brow and straight nose to the firm chin that had a trace of a cleft in it. A well-proportioned athletic physique added to his attractiveness. However, his affections were easily engaged and just as easily changed. "Like a bee in a flower garden," she thought.

On the way to the next class Amy caught up with her.

"Meg," she said breathlessly, "Tommy Riggs asked me to go steady with him."

Meg replied, "I'm glad. You like him a lot, don't you?"

"He's wonderful!"

"You can really cheer him on in football this fall."

"Can't I, though!"

Meg was happy for Amy. Amy loved someone who returned her love.

"Why can't I love someone who loves me?" she thought sadly.

CHAPTER XIII

The loaded school bus, smelling of wet raincoats and damp books, wended its harrowing way through torrents of rain on an April afternoon in 1943. Meg stared gloomily out of the window. "This has got to be the worst spring ever!" she exclaimed.

"I hope it doesn't rain on our Senior Day picnic," Mary Anderson said. "It's just my luck that it will. Have you heard from my brother lately, Meg?"

"No. I'm due for a letter from him and Jimmy Lester. Maybe I'll hear from one of them today. Well, here's where I get another soaking," she said as the bus pulled up in front of her house.

Buck and Duke bounded down the path to greet her.

"Down, boys! Don't you dare get me muddy!" she said as she dashed for the front door with the dogs at her heels.

When she opened the door, they bounced in ahead of her and shook water all over the entry hall. She was exasperated, but couldn't help but laugh at them.

"You sly dogs! You know better than to come into the house wet like that. I can't turn you back out into that deluge, though."

In the living room she found her mother slumped on the couch with a sad expression on her face and traces of tears on her cheeks.

"Mom, what's wrong?" she cried. "I'm sorry about the dogs."

Mom replied, "It isn't the dogs, dear. Come and sit down. We've received bad news."

Meg was terror stricken. "Nothing has happened to Bob, has it?"

"No, it isn't Bob. Mrs. Lester called today. It's Jimmy."

"Jimmy?" Meg asked, uncomprehending.

"Oh, Meg, dear, Jimmy has been killed in North Africa. The Lesters received word today."

"No! I don't believe it!" Meg cried. Mom took her in her arms, and they wept together.

When their tears abated some, Mom said. "I'm taking a roast and some vegetables over to the Lesters. It was to be our dinner, but we can eat leftovers. Do you want to come with me?"

"No, not now. I can't bear it. I don't want any supper!" she said and fled upstairs to her room.

She lay on her bed, and her tears flowed freely. Different pictures flooded her mind of Jimmy, grinning at her from behind the soda fountain, winking at her from under his head covering as he played Joseph to her Mary, singing with her in different competitions and at church. She was glad that they had sung together at church on the Sunday before he left.

Since the Lesters also attended the Baptist church, she had known Jimmy all of her life. She remembered the little red-headed, freckle-faced boy of her childhood. The impish grin, the determined look as he swung a baseball bat, even the bloody nose he received as he defended his red hair against an aggressor.

"Oh, God," she cried out in anguish, "why didn't you keep him safe? He was barely nineteen. You let him down!"

The next day Meg accompanied her mother to the Lesters' house to offer condolences. Numerous friends and relatives were there. Jimmy's fifteen-year-old brother Billy and twelve-year-old sister Kathy sat side by side on the couch with reddened eyes. Four-year-old Angie didn't understand, and she kept shyly peeking around a door and smiling at them. With her mop of red hair and little freckled face, she reminded Meg of Jimmy.

Mrs. Lester put her arm around Meg and took her into the bedroom.

"Meg," she said, "before Jimmy left he told me that if anything happened to him, he wanted you to have this medal. It matches the one you got when you two won first place in the duet division at the Enid Music Festival."

"Oh, I can't take it, Mrs. Lester. I know you want to keep everything in memory of him."

"I have other things, and he specifically requested that I give this to you. He loved you very much, Meg."

Meg began crying, and Mrs. Lester put her arms around her and comforted her.

On the way home, Meg remembered and was glad that she had let Jimmy kiss her on that first and last date. Jimmy had loved her, and she was proud of it. She was grateful that she had not disillusioned him by telling him that her feelings were not as strong for him as his were for her. The medal would rest with her own in her box of treasures.

Memorial services were held for Jimmy in the Community Building. The whole town turned out to honor him. Businesses closed, and school let out for the day. He was the first from the community to die in this war. War had come home to Oak Grove. Meg looked around at the faces and thought, "They are afraid now. It might be one of theirs next."

The mayor, town council members, and two U.S. Army officers were there. Eulogies were given for the benefit and comfort of the bereaved family. Then Brother Cunningham, Jimmy's pastor, spoke. He told of Jimmy's conversion at the age of eight and the faithful life he had led.

"We don't know why God chose to take him at this time, but we do know that even now he is with God, and some day we shall see him again. Paul wrote in Romans 8:35,37-39, 'Who shall separate us from the love of Christ? Shall tribulation, or distress, or persecution, or famine, or nakedness, or peril, or sword? Nay, in all things we are more than conquerors through him that loved us. For I am persuaded, that neither death, nor life, nor angels, nor principalities, nor powers, nor things present, nor things to come, nor height, nor depth, nor any other creature, shall be able to separate us from the love of God, which is in Christ Jesus our Lord.'"

Brother Cunningham paused and looked at the family, and said, "We know that Jimmy was a child of God, and that God was with him on the battlefield, When he was mortally wounded, God's angels led him up to heaven, and Jesus Christ himself was on God's right side to welcome him."

Meg was comforted by these words. In one of Jimmy's letters he had mentioned that the chaplain had read scriptures describing how God was with them in battle. This realization had taken away most of the fear and had given him peace.

CHAPTER XIV

In March of 1944 Meg, Sue, Amy, and Sylvia sat in Glass Drug Store drinking cherry Cokes and discussing their upcoming high school graduation. On the juke box Vaughn Monroe sang, "When The Lights Go On Again."

"That's my theme song now," Meg said. "I'm so tired of this war!"

"Me, too," Sue chimed in, "but we have it easy compared to the rest of the world."

"I'm tired of all the shortages," Sylvia put in. "Especially the man shortage."

"Yes," Sue quipped. "Nothing but high school boys and old men around here. Remember when we were freshmen? The senior boys seemed mature, wise, big, almost men. Even when we were sophomores it gave us a thrill to be noticed by a mighty senior. When we were juniors they were so-so. But now that we are seniors, the boys in our class are so immature. Why is that?"

"Tommy graduated last year, and he never was immature!" Amy said.

"Oh, sure, he's an exception," Sylvia said. "However, I agree with Sue. There are no exceptions in the class of 1944."

The music had stopped on the juke box, and Amy jumped up and said, "I'm going to choose the next song." She put a nickel in and the strains of "I'll Be Seeing You" filled the air.

"I got a letter from Tommy today," she announced as she breezed back and took her seat.

"How unusual," Sylvia mocked.

"You get one nearly every day," Sue added.

"He has completed twenty-five bombing missions and is coming home on furlough and will be stationed in the States for a time."

"That's great news, Amy," Meg said.

"He'll be here for our graduation and...." Amy paused, her face beaming and her eyes shining with excitement.

"Don't keep us in suspense," Sue said. "And what?"

"We are going to get married!"

Her three friends stared at her in amazement.

"Married!" they exclaimed in unison.

"Yes, married. I want you three to be my bridesmaids."

"How wonderful for you, Amy," Meg said. "Tommy is a nice guy, and I think he is really lucky to get you."

"I'm happy for you also," Sue added. "It is a surprise, though. I'll be glad to be your bridesmaid."

"Little Amy. I can't believe it. You will be the first one in our class to be married," Sylvia said, "and my first time to be a bridesmaid. Thank you for asking me."

They spent the next hour discussing the wedding, her bridal gown, and their bridesmaids' dresses.

"Let's look in McCall's pattern books to get an idea for my gown and your dresses," Amy said.

A few days later when Meg came home from school there was a letter from Bob on the dining room table.

"Mom," she called into the kitchen, "I'll be in to help you after I read this letter from Bob."

March, 1944
Dear Family,

Received a batch of mail and thought I'd answer it right away. Wish I could be there for your graduation, Meg. What will you do after that? Johnny, keep up the good work in baseball. Dad, you and Mom don't work too hard in the store and garden.

I had a happy surprise the other day. When we came into port, some marines were sprawled on the dock waiting to ship out. One of them looked familiar and, sure enough, it was Joe! He looked tired, but when he saw me, the weariness vanished. His eyes lit up in that old way of his, and he grinned from ear to ear. We were so glad to see each other that we hugged and back-slapped like crazy!

When he asked about all of you, I told him that you would like to hear from him. He said he had been kept busy. I know the marines see a lot of action, and he is a sergeant. The men with him seemed to think a lot of him.

Meg, send me another grad picture. I showed mine to Joe and he kept it.

Love to all,
Bob

So Joe had her picture! What did he want with it? Maybe to show everyone what his "sister" looked like. She knew he didn't write to her because she wouldn't write to him, but he should write to her parents. They had always been good to him.

She went into the living room, took her graduation picture off the mantel and scrutinized it. Her eyes stared back under smoothly arched eyebrows, and her lips curved up at the ends in a slight smile. The feather-cut hair style flattered her face, and the black off-shoulder drape caused her to appear more mature. Why did he want her picture?

She placed the picture back on the shelf and went into the kitchen to help her mother with dinner.

"Isn't it wonderful that Bob ran into Joe over there?" Mom asked. "It's like a miracle."

"Yes, it is unusual," Meg agreed.

"I don't understand why Joe doesn't write to us. When he was in the States he wrote regularly."

"Do you want me to peel the potatoes?"

"Did something happen between you and Joe?"

"No. Why do you ask?"

"I don't know. You seemed so close when he was here, but now you don't even correspond."

"He thinks of me as a sister. Maybe sisters aren't important."

"You're too young for him to think of you as anything else. Yes, please do peel the potatoes."

Two weeks later Meg was reading in the living room when the doorbell rang. "I'll get it , Mom," she called.

She opened the door and a uniformed Western Union employee

stood there with a yellow envelope in his hand. Her face blanched, and she backed away. "No, no!" she cried. "You must have the wrong address!"

"What is it, Meg?" Mom said as she hurried into the room. She stopped short when she saw the man at the door, and her face paled.

"I have a telegram for Samuel Mitchell," the man said. He looked as if he would rather be anywhere but where he was at that moment.

"I-I'll sign for it," Mom said. After she had signed her name, he gave her the envelope and left in a hurry.

Mom sat down as if her legs could hold her no longer. She held the envelope limply in her hand while tears slid down her face. Meg stared at the envelope in horror.

Finally Mom opened it and read the message and then handed it to Meg, who read it silently.

"We regret to inform you that your son, Captain Robert S. Mitchell, is missing in action."

"Oh, Mom. He isn't dead, he's only missing! I know he'll be found!"

"We must call your father," Mom said. She was still in a state of shock.

Meg called Dad and told him that they had just received word that Bob was missing in action. "Mom needs you," she cried.

Dad closed the store and came home immediately. Mom sat silently twisting her hands until he walked in the door, and then she flew into his arms and wept openly. Dad held her close until her tears subsided, and then he said, "Let's pray about it, Sarah." Johnny had come in, and Meg had quietly told him that Bob was missing. Dad kept one arm around Mom and held out his other one for them to come into the circle. Then he prayed for the safe return of their son and brother.

"I'm going to call Brother Cunningham so that he can ask our church family to pray for Bob and for us," Dad said.

It wasn't long until the telephone began to ring and people came with food and to offer prayers and comfort for them. Mrs. Lester was one of the first to arrive with a cooked ham. She put her arms around Mom and prayed with her.

"Oh, Opal," Mom cried, "I don't see how you have stood it. I wish I could be as brave as you!"

"You are, Sarah, you are. I was devastated, but the Lord helped me and He'll help you. I know I'll see Jimmy again one day. When I get to heaven he'll be waiting for me. Have faith that Bob will be found."

A few days later, Dad answered the door to receive another telegram. With trembling hands he opened it, while the rest of the family stood by tense and apprehensive. A smile broke out on his face, and he laughed with joy. "He's been found! He's alive! It's a miracle! Praise the Lord!"

Mom broke into tears again, but they were tears of happiness and relief. They all hugged and kissed each other and thanked the Lord.

"I'll call Brother Cunningham so he can tell our church family the good news," Dad said.

After he finished, Mom called Opal Lester to tell her the good news and to thank her for her prayers and words of encouragement.

The next day an officer, Captain Louis Oldham, came from the naval recruiting station in Oklahoma City to give them the details.

"Let me tell you what happened, and then I'll answer any questions you may have, as far as I'm able," he said. "Your son, Captain Mitchell, had been in a dog fight with the enemy and was shot down. He parachuted from the plane and landed on a rocky plateau of a small island. His left leg was fractured with an open wound. Some natives saw him coming down and took him to their village deep in the jungle. Two of them went by boat to a nearby island where a radio man was stationed. He contacted the nearest American base, and a PT boat was sent to rescue him. There were marines on the base, and one of them volunteered to go with them.

"The PT boat came near the island and put the marine ashore. He was led through the jungle to the village by a native guide. With two natives' help, Captain Mitchell was then carried to the PT boat and taken to the base hospital.

"They had a little trouble on the way. Five Japanese soldiers were put ashore on the opposite end of the island, but your son and the marine took care of them and made their escape. Any questions?"

"How bad is Bob's leg?" asked Mom.

"I don't know. He is in the hospital on the base. They plan to send him to Fitzsimmons Hospital in Denver, Colorado. You will be able to see him there."

"What is the name of the marine?" Dad asked.

"A friend of your son from this town, Joe Sullivan."

"Praise the Lord! I thought it must be Joe."

"You did?" Captain Oldham seemed surprised.

"Bob mentioned seeing him in his last letter," Dad replied.

"Joe deserves a medal," Mom said.

"He is up for the silver star, and your son will receive the purple heart."

After Captain Oldham left, Meg went up to her room to think about all that had happened to Bob, and Joe's part in rescuing him. She got the music box from the closet, took the locket out, opened it, and gazed on his face. This was the first time she had opened the box since she had put it in there. Her heart overflowed with love and gratitude. She kissed the picture and whispered, "Thank you, Joe"

News of Bob's rescue by Joe spread swiftly through the town. The Oak Grove Weekly News ran the story on the front page and suggested a parade to honor them when they came home.

Mom laughed when she read the article. "They would both hate it. Especially Joe."

Dad came home from town and shared the latest, "Dan O'Brien is strutting his stuff since he found out that Joe is a hero."

"He would!" Meg said.

"You must admit that Dan has greatly improved since he stopped drinking," Mom said. "The Candlelight Inn seems to be doing well, although I can't agree with the drinking and dancing that goes on there."

"It has a reputation for good food and romantic candlelight suppers. Dan even greets his guests in a tuxedo," Dad said, and winking at Meg, he added, "I've been thinking about taking you there for our anniversary. There is a small orchestra, and we could dance to 'All This and Heaven Too.'"

Mom laughed and said, "Thanks, but no thanks."

"It's strange," Meg said. "People in this town who wouldn't touch Dan with a ten-foot pole a few years ago now flock out there and act honored to be greeted by 'The Owner.'"

"Your mother is right, Meg," Dad said. "Dan has improved since he quit drinking. I'm glad to see people accepting him. Wish we could get him in church, though."

"He has improved his house and yard, too," Mom said. "Mrs. Etheridge, who cleans for him, said that he repainted and repapered the inside and bought new furniture. An interior decorator helped him with the inside, and Josh at the nursery helped him with his lawn and shrubs. His boots are hand-tooled leather and his suits are Hart, Schaffner, and Marx."

"You ladies wouldn't gossip, would you?" Dad asked teasingly.

Mom tossed her head and said, "It's only gossip when you say bad things about others."

"I hate it when he tips his hat to me on the streets," Meg said. "He may be changed on the outside, but he's probably as mean as ever on the inside."

"Is Meg gossiping, Mom?" Dad asked innocently.

CHAPTER XV

Graduation Day finally arrived. Meg floated down the stairs in her royal blue gown and mortarboard. The blue and white tassel on the right side of her cap swung back and forth as she moved.

"How do I look?" she asked

"Like you're going to graduate," Johnny said, and shrugged.

"Nice," Mom said.

"You look like your mother did twenty-some years ago," Dad said with admiration.

"Grandma and Grandpa Mitchell will be here and will spend the day with us," Mom said. "Aunt Barbara and her family can't make it, though."

"Too bad," Meg said, tongue in cheek.

The ceremony went well. Sylvia graduated valedictorian of the class of 1944 and delivered a fitting farewell speech.

Meg looked around at the flushed and excited faces of her classmates and pondered where each would be this time next year. More than likely if the war continued, the boys would be serving overseas and the girls would be working or attending college. She intended to go to Oklahoma City and work in the war plant there. Sue and maybe Sylvia would be going also, but Amy planned to marry and go with Tommy to the air base in Tampa, Florida. They would miss her.

Meg glanced back at petite and dainty Amy. "She seems too young to be married," she thought. Tommy, sitting there in his Air Force uniform, looked at Amy with adoration in his eyes. Although he was a gunner on a B-24 and had completed twenty-five missions, he still appeared boyish.

The day after graduation, Meg awoke with the sun streaming through her bedroom window. "What a beautiful day for Amy's wedding," she thought. She smiled to herself as she thought about Amy's happiness. However, she knew their friendship would change somewhat, and it might be a while before she would see her friend again.

The ceremony was scheduled for two o'clock at the Methodist

church with a reception following in the church garden. Not only was Meg to be a bridesmaid, but Amy had also asked her to sing "Always" before the ceremony and "The Lord's Prayer" at the end. After the reception the young couple planned to take the four o'clock bus to Oklahoma City where they would spend the night. The next day the short honeymoon would continue with a train ride to Tampa, Florida.

She looked appreciatively at her bridesmaid dress hanging on the closet door. It was a floor-length pastel blue organdy to be worn over a matching satin slip. The style was princess and had a sweetheart neckline and puffed sleeves. All of the attendants' dresses were styled alike, but in different pastel colors. Sue chose yellow and Sylvia, green. Beth, Amy's married sister and the matron-of-honor, was to wear pink. Each had a matching broad-brim sun hat and wore a necklace which was a present from the bride. Amy's white bridal gown was made from the same pattern, but her mother had made the skirt fuller with lots of lace trim.

At one o'clock Meg and the other bridesmaids arrived at the church to help Amy get ready in the room set aside for these occasions. The girls, swarming around her, helped her into her gown, veil, and long white gloves. Then they handed her the white Bible and mixed spring flower bouquet that she was to carry. Her mother stood to one side looking on critically. When they finished, she walked over to where Amy was standing in front of the floor-length mirror, tweaked at her skirt in several places and readjusted her veil.

"That's better," she said with satisfaction.

When she was ready, the photographer stepped in and posed the bride and attendants in various positions for pictures. As soon as Meg finished posing, she left to sing while the photographer took pictures of Amy with her parents and siblings.

"My feet are killing me," Amy complained. She put the flowers and Bible down to run her fingers around the backs of her new pumps.

The strains of the wedding march began, and Amy suddenly panicked. "I'm not ready!" she cried. "Where are my flowers? Where's my Bible?"

"Here's your Bible," Sylvia said.

"And here are your flowers," Sue said.

"You're ready," her mother said. "You look beautiful."

Her father took her arm, and the party moved to the vestibule to begin the walk down the aisle.

Tommy looked handsome as he proudly waited for his bride at the altar. Four fellow crew members stood with him.

After the pastor pronounced them husband and wife, the wedding party proceeded to the garden for the reception. Everyone agreed the bride was beautiful and the ceremony lovely. Before she left to change, Amy threw her bouquet to the single girls, and Sue caught it.

"It seems that I'm the next one to be married," she said with a smile, "but I haven't found him yet."

She received offers from all of Tommy's friends, but she laughed and turned them down.

Mr. Riggs brought his car around to take them to the bus station. The windows were soaped with congratulatory messages and paper streamers and tin cans were tied to the back bumper.

"I should have kept a guard on the car," he said.

"Too late now," Tommy said. "We need to get moving to catch the bus." He helped Amy into the back seat amid a shower of rice, and then climbed in after her.

Mr. Riggs put the car in gear and took off with the tin cans rattling and the guests cheering.

Meg spent the next week preparing for her move to Oklahoma City. She contemplated when she should leave.

"Why don't you wait until we hear from Bob and find out how he is," Mom said.

That afternoon Meg went out to the mail box and found a letter postmarked Denver, Colorado, with a return address of Fitzsimmons Hospital. She rushed into the house calling her mother, "Mom, Mom, we got a letter from Bob!"

"Don't open it until I call Dad. He'll want to be here when we read it," Mom said. "Call Johnny in."

Dad left the store in charge of his assistant and rushed home. They gathered around while he opened the letter and read aloud:

Dear Family,

I'm back in the States sooner than I expected to be, but it's a lot better than being in a Japanese prison. As you have probably heard, I owe it all to Joe. He's a great guy! A hero! But he wouldn't appreciate being called that.

My plane was put out of commission in a dog fight over the Pacific. I tried to make it to my carrier, but finally had to abandon the plane and bail out. Landing on rocky terrain on a small island, I fractured my left tibia and fibula. It was a bad break as the bones came through the skin.

I passed out from the pain, and when I came to, I was surrounded by a group of small brown men. They gibbered in a foreign language, and at first I thought they were Japanese, but they turned out to be friendly islanders. Was I ever grateful. They made a splint out of reeds and carried me to their village. A couple of them rowed over to another island where there was a radio operator who sent a message to a nearby base for help.

Although we couldn't understand each other, we communicated with signs. Several of them had afflictions that I thought could be cured with modern medical treatments or surgery. Some day I hope to return there to help them.

Two days after I got there they signed to me that a patrol of five Japs had landed on one end of the island, and one American from a boat had landed on the other side. They sent a guide for the American.

When I heard a whippoorwill in the jungle, I couldn't believe my ears. I had to laugh. I knew it had to be Joe. That had been our signal as boys when we got separated in the woods at home.

We had to leave in a hurry to get to the PT boat before the enemy soldiers got to us or discovered the boat. The islanders had made a litter out of two poles and a mat, and two of them carried me while Joe walked beside us with his carbine ready. We hadn't gone far when we unexpectedly came upon a Japanese soldier. Joe raised his gun automatically and fired, killing him instantly. They hid me in some bushes, and the guides quickly disappeared. Joe left me with a handgun while he went after the rest of them. The hunted became the hunter.

I heard one of them moving through the underbrush getting nearer and nearer to me. Holding my breath, I waited until he crept into my sight, and then I shot him. It shook me up to see a man that I had killed sprawled in front of me. In hand-to-hand combat you have to get used to that, I guess. Joe took care of the other three. It didn't seem to bother him. Sure was glad that Indian was on my side. The guides came back, and we reached the boat without further trouble.

My leg became infected, but they are about to get it cleared up with that new wonder drug, penicillin. My poor hips feel like pin cushions from all of the shots. At least that's what they call the place where they give them. Ha!

I may be here for a long time. Come see me, please.

Love,

Bob

"Oh, Sam," Mom said, "when can we go to see him?"

"As much as I would like to go right now," he replied, "we will have to wait a while. With spring planting here, I need to be at the store."

"I'd like to be a marine like Joe and shoot all those Japs!" Johnny exclaimed.

"No, Johnny," Dad said, "Joe doesn't enjoy shooting people. He had to do it to save his and your brother's lives."

"It takes a brave man to do what Joe did," Mom said. "We must keep praying for his safety. I pray also that the Holy Spirit will lead someone to witness to him and that he will accept Jesus as his Savior."

"We should have been bolder witnesses to him while he was growing up here," Dad said. "Instead we just tried to get him to go to church and hoped he would come to know Christ there."

Meg went upstairs to her room, took the locket out of her music box, and opened it. She gazed at Joe's picture for a long time. With bowed head, she prayed for his safety and for his salvation.

CHAPTER XVI

Meg was packed and ready to move to Oklahoma City. She had mixed emotions about leaving home, but she was excited to get out on her own and try her wings. Sue and Sylvia were going with her, so she wouldn't be entirely friendless in a strange town. They had arranged to stay with Sue's uncle and aunt until they could get jobs and find an apartment of their own. Jobs were plentiful during war time, but apartments were scarce.

Mom came into her room and watched her apply her make-up.

"Meg, dear," she said, "are you certain you are doing the right thing? You could stay here and work for your father in the store."

"I know I could, but I feel stifled in this small town," Meg replied. "I need to get out and see more of the world even if it is only Oklahoma City."

"You will continue to go to church, won't you?"

"I'll not slip into sin," she said with a twinkle in her eye. "If they'll have me, I'll even sing in the choir."

"If you have any problems, you will call us?"

"Mom, it's going to be okay."

"Meg, darling." Dad had entered the room while they talked. "You will be meeting all kinds of people in a large town like that," he said, "and you must be very careful with whom you associate. Be kind to everyone, but only get close to other Christians. Do you understand?"

"Yes, Dad. I'll be careful."

At the bus stop, Dad kissed her, and Meg could see the concern in his eyes.

"I'll take care, Dad. Don't worry about me — please."

The Gregorys and the Ashleys also talked earnestly with their daughters. It was a relief for the girls when it was time to board the bus.

"You'd think we were going to Sodom and Gomorrah," Sue complained as the bus pulled out onto the street.

"I hope we can get on at the defense plant," Meg said.

Sue agreed, but Sylvia said, "I have no intention of applying there. No assembly line for me. Rosie the Riveter I am not. Work in an office will suit me better."

It seemed to take forever to get to the city. The bus stopped at every small town on the way. At one stop they bought Coca Colas to drink as they ate the sandwiches from home.

Finally, from a distance they saw the skyline of Oklahoma City sprawled out on the prairie. Three tall buildings stood out with clusters of smaller ones around them. Sue had been to the city many times to visit her relatives, and she knew the names of the tall ones.

"The two close together are the Ramsey Tower and the First National Bank and that one over there is the Biltmore Hotel," she said.

"How tall are they?" Sylvia asked.

"Oh, I don't know," Sue said. "Thirty stories at least, I guess."

As the bus wended its way through the busy streets, the girls sat wide-eyed. Their heads swivelled this way and that with so much to see.

When they entered the bus station they were amazed at the number of people there. All ages were represented, from the elderly to the newborn. Young mothers with babes in arms and little ones clinging to their skirts, and servicemen from every branch of the armed forces filled the small area. Not a seat was empty. They all had one thing in common: tired, strained faces. Brightly painted walls and large windows tried to make up for the drab chairs and dirty, scuffed floors. Smoke filled the air, and cigarette butts littered the room.

Porters came and went with all kinds of luggage. The girls retrieved their bags, tipped the porter, and looked around for Sue's uncle.

"I don't see Uncle Chad any place," Sue said. "Let's find the lounge and freshen up."

They were directed upstairs to the lounge, and even this room was crowded. An elderly lady slept on a plastic couch, and a young mother sat in a chair nursing her baby. Women of all ages combed their hair or reapplied their make-up in front of the mirrors over the lavatories. At last the girls got their turn to freshen up at one of the wash basins, and they washed their faces, put on fresh make-up, and combed their hair.

When they descended the wide stairway, Sue squealed, "There's Uncle Chad!"

She rushed to him and he kissed her on the cheek. When she introduced Meg and Sylvia, he smiled and shook their hands heartily. "Welcome to Oklahoma City," he said. "Let me help you with those bags."

The girls found the drive through the downtown area exciting. It was Saturday afternoon and the streets were thronged with people. Servicemen were everywhere, in groups or paired with girls. Lines formed in front of restaurants and the three movie theaters.

"There are the Midwest, the State, and the Criterion theaters," Sue said pointing them out. "I've been in all of them when I visited Uncle Chad in the past."

Tracks lay down the middle of Main Street with streetcars clanging up and down them. At every stop they unloaded and loaded passengers. City buses, crowded with people, moved through the traffic also

"Why are there so many sailors and marines here?" Meg asked.

Uncle Chad laughed. "It does seem strange, since we are so far from the oceans. There are two naval bases in Norman, only a few miles away. They offer technical training. Most of the airmen are from Tinker Field, others are from Mustang or Enid where there are cadet pilot training programs. The army comes in from Ft. Sill and other bases in Oklahoma."

Sue's uncle and aunt, Chad and Laura Gregory, lived in a three-bedroom brick house in the northeast area of the city. The girls settled in and felt welcomed. Uncle Chad and Aunt Laura showed them how to get around on the streetcars and the buses. Meg and Sue applied for work at the Douglas Defense Plant and were hired immediately. It took only two more weeks to find an apartment.

"It's nice to have our own place, even if it is small," Meg said, looking around the dirty, cramped living room containing a daybed, two over-stuffed chairs, and two end tables with lamps. The bedroom was furnished with a double bed, a chest of drawers, and a bedside table with a small lamp on it. A small closet and an old-fashioned bathroom each opened off the bedroom. The kitchen was also sparsely equipped with an ancient stove, a refrigerator, and a rickety table with four mismatched chairs. A few well-used dishes and odds and ends of silverware, glasses, and pots and pans were in the cabinets.

"I'll bet Uncle Chad and Aunt Laura are happy to be rid of us," Sue remarked. "We crowded them too much."

"I'm glad we got hired so quickly at the Douglas Plant," Meg said. "I wonder if Sylvia has found a job yet."

As if in answer to her question, Sylvia bounded into the room. "I've found the perfect job at last!" she exclaimed. "It isn't much to start with. The pay is only fifty a month, but the potential for advancement is great."

"What kind of job is it?" asked Sue.

"I'm employed by the law firm of Abner, Milton, and Carter as a clerk typist, but I can attend night school and learn to be a legal secretary! Isn't that exciting?"

"Sounds boring to me," Meg said.

"Not as boring as an assembly line!" Sylvia retorted.

"But we are helping the war effort!" Meg replied.

"Good for you!" Sylvia said, "But I'm not mechanically inclined, and civilian life must go on as well."

"You're right, Sylvia," Sue said soothingly. "Meg was only joshing you."

"I think everyone should do their own thing, even if it does seem boring to others," Meg said with a grin. "Let's get busy with soap and water and clean up this cockroach-infested place. We won't get rid of the cooked cabbage odor until we paint. If we hurry we can get it done before Monday."

Sue said, "There's no use washing these filthy curtains. They would just fall apart. Aunt Laura said that we could use her sewing machine to make new ones."

"Who's sleeping on the daybed?" Sylvia asked.

"We can draw straws and rotate every month," Meg said. "Isn't it exciting to be on our own in a large city?"

CHAPTER XVII

On Sunday morning Meg woke up and stretched. The sun streamed through the freshly washed windows, causing them to sparkle. The newly painted apartment looked cheerful in the early morning light. "We did a good job," she thought contentedly. She quietly made up the daybed and went into the kitchen to start the coffee perking. While it brewed, she slipped through the bedroom, past the sleeping girls, and into the bathroom to take her shower. After her shower, she returned to the kitchen and took out the bacon, eggs, and milk. The bacon sizzled in the pan while she mixed the pancake batter.

"Rise and shine," she said as she opened the bedroom door and allowed the aroma of the bacon and coffee to waft in. "The Mitchell special breakfast, pancakes and bacon, will soon be ready. Time to eat and then get ready for Sunday School."

"Sunday School! You've got to be kidding!" Sue said in a muffled voice.

"No. I promised Mom," Meg replied.

"Let's just go to church services," Sylvia said sleepily.

"It's easier to meet people and make friends in a class," Meg said. "I want to find out about the choir, too. Trinity Baptist is in walking distance. We'll try there first."

After the morning service Meg met the choir director, Mr. Baker, and informed him that she was interested in singing in the choir. They went into the choir room and Meg sang the first verse of "Amazing Grace."

"Beautiful," he said. "How would you like to sing at the Baptist Servicemen's Club?"

"What's that?" she asked.

"It's a place downtown in the old Huckins Hotel where servicemen can relax when they are on pass. All of the Baptist churches in this area support it. We offer food and games, and provide rooms where they can read or write letters. On weekends we try to have some kind of entertainment."

"May my friends come with me?" she asked.

"Sure. Our Baptist youth are hosts and hostesses, and we would be glad for them to serve."

Friday evening the three girls took the streetcar to the address given them by Mr. Baker. A friendly, matronly woman greeted them at the door. "Welcome," she said. "I'm Mrs. Connely."

Meg introduced herself and the other girls.

"Oh, yes," she said. "Mr. Baker said you were coming. He had high praise for your voice. We look forward to hearing you sing. Come on in and make yourselves at home."

She led them into a room filled with servicemen and girls. Some stood around talking, while others played games such as darts, Ping-Pong, and shuffleboard. Across the back of the room was a counter with stools where sandwiches, cookies, and soft drinks were served.

"Mingle for a little while, and I'll let you know, Meg, when it's time to start the entertainment," Mrs. Connely said and fluttered off.

"Hi, Beautiful." Meg turned around to see a young sailor grinning at her. His curly black hair framed a pair of merry brown eyes and puckish face. "My name is Pat Antonelli. What's yours?"

"Meg Mitchell."

"Now that we're acquainted, let's blow this joint and go somewhere to dance. I just came in here to eat," he said.

"First, it's against our policy to meet here and date," she said with a twinkle in her eye. "Secondly, I don't dance, and thirdly, I'm part of the entertainment."

"I'll hang around and catch your act," he said.

"There you are," Mrs. Connely squeaked as she fluttered up to Meg. She led her over to the piano where a young airman was playing. "You two get together and plan your numbers," she said and fluttered away again.

"I'm Jerry," he said with a smile.

Meg returned his smile and said, "And I'm Meg."

"What would you like to sing?" he asked. "I can play most anything."

"How about 'It Had To Be You' and then ask for requests?"

"I think I can handle that," he said, and played a few bars of the song.

Meg sang for an hour as requests kept coming. When her voice grew tired, she took a break. Pat was at her elbow as soon as she stepped away from the microphone.

"Sit down with me and talk," he said as he led her to a couch in the corner. "Did anyone come with you?"

Meg pointed out her friends. Sue was playing Ping-Pong with a soldier, and Sylvia was throwing darts with a marine.

"Are you from this city?" he asked.

"I'm from a little town in eastern Oklahoma," she replied. "Where are you from?"

"Scranton, Pennsylvania," he replied.

"You're going to have to do the talking," Meg said. "I need to rest my voice."

"Gladly," he replied, and for the next fifteen minutes he entertained her with amusing incidents from his life in the navy. "Haven't seen an ocean, yet," he said, "but if I ever get there I'll know how to swim. We have to take lessons and pass a test. 'Course, I hope I'll never have to use that ability in a real ocean."

An airman came up and asked Meg to sing, "Don't Sit Under the Apple Tree With Anyone Else But Me."

"Okay," she said, and turning to Pat, she added, "my public calls."

After she finished that song a sailor shouted, "Anchors Aweigh!" A marine shouted, "No! 'From the Halls of Montezuma.'" Then pandemonium broke out as men from each branch of the service shouted out their songs.

Meg, laughing and waving her hands, finally got their attention. "We'll sing each song and, when your song is played, sing with me."

They cooperated while she ran through all the service songs, then when she started singing "God Bless America," they all joined in.

When they finished the song, she said, "That's all for tonight. Thank you for helping me."

"Thank you, Meg!" they shouted.

Pat had stayed all evening listening to Meg sing.

On Saturday morning the girls cleaned the apartment. They divided the work and alternated jobs every weekend. Meg looked longingly out the window as she dusted the furniture. The bright sunny day reminded her of picnics at home.

The phone rang, and she answered it. "Hi, is Meg Mitchell

there?" a boyish voice asked.

"This is she."

"This is Pat Antonelli. I met you last night at the Baptist Servicemen's Club, remember?"

"I remember you, but how did you get my phone number?"

"With a little sleuthing and a lot of charm."

"I thought they didn't give out phone numbers there."

"I found out which church you were from and called them, pretending to be an out-of-town relative. They gave it to me, and here I am talking to you. How about going to the Lincoln Park Zoo this afternoon? Before you say 'no,' I have two buddies who would like to escort your roommates. They met them last night. Out in the open we couldn't possibly seduce you girls. Is it a deal?"

Meg laughed and said, "You are persistent. I'll ask my friends and if they want to go, I'll go."

She talked it over with the others, and at first they were doubtful, but finally agreed it might be fun.

"It's better than sitting around here bored," Sue said.

"We'll go," Meg told Pat. "I've been thinking this is perfect weather for a picnic. How 'bout we bring a picnic lunch?"

"My mouth is watering already."

"Great! What time will you be here?"

"We'll be there on the twelve o'clock streetcar, sharp."

Meg fried the chicken that she had bought for their Sunday dinner, while Sue and Sylvia made potato salad and cut up carrot and celery sticks. They packed all of this in a picnic basket along with three cans of pork and beans and a loaf of bread. Paper plates, cups, napkins, a can opener, silverware, and a table cloth went into another basket. Sylvia squeezed lemons for lemonade and poured it into a jug.

"This scrawny little chicken might not be enough for three growing boys," Meg said, remembering her brothers voracious appetites. "I'll just throw in this left-over ham."

By twelve o'clock they were ready, and a few minutes later, the doorbell rang. When they opened the door, three sailors in dazzling white uniforms stood grinning at them.

"Ready?" Pat asked as he took the basket of food from Meg and gave her his arm. "I know you couldn't forget me, but I'm Pat

Antonelli, in case your friends have. The fair-haired, blue-eyed Anglo-Saxon-type Italian is Phil Nardoni, and the dark husky Sicilian is Tony Marco. They were with me last night."

The girls remembered them and Phil took Sue's arm and the other basket, while Tony took Sylvia's arm and the jug.

"Hope you brought a lot. I'm hungry," Pat said.

"Smells good," Phil said with a smile.

It was fun riding the crowded streetcar with the boys. They kept up a steady stream of nonsensical, but hilarious, comments and the girls responded in kind. Twice they had to transfer, and these cars were also packed with people going to the park. When they finally got there they were jostled and pushed about as everyone got off at their destination.

"Do we still have the same baskets of food?" Tony asked.

"I'm not sure we even have the same girls," Phil said.

They all laughed and then hunted for a place to eat.

"I think everyone in town decided to picnic here today," Meg said.

Finally they found an empty table, spread the cloth, and laid out the plates and food. It was Meg's custom to thank the Lord before meals, but when she started to bow her head, she noticed the boys filling their plates. Not wanting to embarrass them, she followed suit.

"I don't believe they feed you guys at the base," Sue said as the last piece of chicken and morsel of food disappeared.

"Not like this," Pat replied. "Now I know for sure that when I marry it will have to be a girl from Oklahoma."

"That's not what you said when we left boot camp at Great Lakes Naval and you ate home cooking," Tony said. "Then the girl had to be from Illinois."

"Can I help it if I'm fickle?" Pat quipped.

"Now that we've eaten, let's go to the zoo," Phil said.

Inside the entrance of the zoo they stopped to watch the antics of the monkeys on Monkey Island. Meg glanced across the island and saw a tall dark marine staring at her. Joe! Her heart skipped a beat and her face paled. On closer observation she saw that she was mistaken. It wasn't him after all.

"Meg, are you okay?" Pat asked. "You look ill."

"I'm fine," she said. "It's just the crowds and the heat."

"We'll find some shade and rest a minute," he said.

He led her to a shady spot under some trees where other couples rested on the grass. Some of them embraced and kissed so passionately that Meg blushed. She turned away quickly and asked Pat to take her back to their friends.

Pat laughed and said, "I like modesty in a girl."

Darkness surrounded them by the time they alighted from the streetcar at their stop. Pat took the basket in one hand and placed his other arm around Meg's waist as they walked the few blocks to her apartment. It seemed natural and Meg didn't object.

"I had a lot of fun today," she said.

"What do you want to do tomorrow?" Pat asked.

"In the morning we're going to Sunday school and church at Trinity Baptist. Do you want to go with us?"

"We'll probably go to early mass at St. Joe's. What about the afternoon?"

"Sue's aunt invited us over for homemade ice cream."

"I sure do like homemade ice cream."

Meg turned around and called, "Sue, do you think your aunt would appreciate three extra guests for ice cream?"

"Sure, she likes to 'do her part for our boys in service.' I'll call her when we get home. Do all of you want to come?"

"Count us in," Tony said.

"Yeah," Phil agreed.

When they reached the apartment, they asked the boys in while Sue called her aunt.

When she hung up she turned to them and said, "My aunt said she would love to have you all come."

"What time shall we pick you up?" Pat asked.

"One o'clock would be fine," Meg answered.

They exchanged farewells, and the sailors left.

The heat from the day settled in the walls of the tiny apartment and the sultry night air stifled Meg. Even the small fan didn't help. Sleep eluded her and she tossed and turned on her bed. Her thoughts were tormented by that brief glimpse of someone who resembled Joe. Why did it give her such a start and make her heart palpitate? Hadn't she recovered from that puppy love years ago? No. In spite of everything she still loved Joe. With closed eyes she could see Joe's face clearly, feel his arms around her and the passion of his lips on hers. "I do love you, Joe," she thought. "Are you safe tonight, or are you in combat somewhere in the Pacific? Are you in danger right now?" She whispered a prayer for him and finally dropped off to sleep.

CHAPTER XVIII

Everyone termed the ice cream party a huge success, and the sailors made a date for the next weekend.

"Let's go dancing tonight," Pat said when they arrived on Saturday.

"No dancing for me," Meg said. "But if you want, you're free to go without me."

"I'd rather be with you," Pat said. "How about a movie?"

After much discussion they agreed on "Meet Me In St. Louis," which was playing at the Criterion. The wait in line was so long that Meg decided movies weren't worth it.

On Sunday the girls invited them for lunch and then challenged them to a game of tennis. At the crowded park, they stood in line for their turn at the courts.

Later in the week Meg received a phone call from a lady who introduced herself as Mrs. Callahan from the Catholic Servicemen's Canteen.

"Some of the boys told us that you sing at some of the other canteens," she said. "Could you sing at ours this Saturday night?"

"I'd love to," she replied, surprised by the invitation. "Could I bring my two roommates? I don't want to come alone."

"That will be fine. See you at eight o'clock Saturday."

The following Saturday the girls arrived at the canteen a few minutes before eight. They gave their names at the door and entered. Three familiar smiling sailors met them.

"So you all are the ones responsible for our invitation," Meg said. "I should have guessed."

A large buxom woman rushed up to them like a ship in full sail. "Which one of you is Meg Mitchell?" she asked.

"I am," Meg replied, awed by such a magnificent presence.

"Follow me," she said. "You other two, circulate."

"Yes ma'am," the three said in unison.

A small band waited to accompany Meg. They produced a list of popular song titles and asked her to choose the melodies she wanted to sing. Meg selected several and handed it back to them. She enjoyed the band and sang with gusto. After several songs they told her she was great. "You make me sound good," she said, "but I need a break."

As soon as she left the bandstand, Pat took her in his arms and danced her out on the floor.

"Where are Sue and Sylvia?" she asked.

"Somewhere on the floor dancing," he replied. "For someone who doesn't dance, you're very good."

In spite of herself, Meg took pleasure in dancing with Pat. Before long another sailor tapped him on the back and danced off with her. The next half hour she danced with different ones and then decided it was time to sing again. At that moment a tall, handsome, black-haired airman approached her. His intense brown eyes looked her over, and then he smiled at her with dazzling white teeth.

"May I have this dance?" he asked, and not waiting for her response, he pulled her into his arms and danced out onto the floor with her. His embrace was so tight that she could hardly breathe.

"Let me go," she said. "You're holding me too close. Besides, it's time for me to sing again."

"You like it and you know it," he whispered in her ear.

"Please don't hold me so tightly," she begged, but he didn't release her until the music stopped, and then he had the audacity to ask her for a date.

"Are you out of your mind?" she retorted. "Not only is it against the policy of the canteen to meet here to make a date, but it's against my policy to date anyone who holds me too tightly and won't let go when I ask." With those words she turned on her heel and swiftly walked to the bandstand.

When she finished for the night, Pat came up to her and asked her if she were having fun.

"You know I am," she replied.

"How about some 'Boogie'?" he asked as the band began playing "Mairzy Doats."

"I'll try," she said.

"You learn fast," he said breathlessly as the dance ended.

Later in their apartment Sue announced, "I don't see anything wrong with dancing. I think it's a lot of fun."

"My parents dance, and they taught me." Sylvia said.

"Mine are against it," Meg said. "They believe that dancing may lead to sexual temptation. After dancing with that one airman tonight, I can believe it! He held me too close, and I didn't like it, but he acted as if I should be thrilled and fall all over him."

The alarm sounded on schedule the next morning, but Meg pressed the button and went back to sleep. Her last thought was that she would skip Sunday School and go to church. When she next opened her eyes the mid-morning sun shone brightly in the room.

"Oh, no!" she exclaimed, "It's ten-thirty. We'll never make it to church on time."

Sue said sleepily, "It won't hurt to miss this one time."

As they ate a leisurely brunch, Pat called. "We just got out of mass. What would you like to do this afternoon?"

"Every place is so crowded. Why don't you all come here for dominoes, or we could walk in the nearby park," Meg said.

By pooling their funds, the girls had bought an ice cream freezer, and they wanted to surprise the boys. Meg blended milk, cream, vanilla, eggs, and sugar together and poured this mixture into the metal container. Then Sue placed the container in the wooden bucket, put the paddle in, the lid on, and hooked the crank to it. Next Meg and Sue layered the crushed ice and ice cream salt around the metal container while Sylvia turned the handle. It was ready to be churned when the boys arrived.

"We've done our part, now you all can do the rest," Meg said.

"Okay, we 'all' will," Pat said with a laugh.

The sailors took turns at the crank until the ice cream hardened, and then covered it with a towel to let it set.

"It's such a pretty day, let's walk in the park," Sue said.

When they returned they ate the ice cream with relish and agreed it was the best they had ever tasted.

Before they left that evening, Pat said, "We hate to tell you but our course ends in two weeks, and we're shipping out."

"Where will you be stationed?" Meg asked.

"On a ship, I hope," Tony said, "but we don't know yet."

"We'd like to take you girls out to a nice restaurant to pay you back for all you've done for us," Pat said.

"Yes, and maybe dance a little," Phil added.

"Sounds great," Sue said.

"What about you, Sylvia?" Tony asked.

"I would like it very much," she replied.

"Meg?" Pat asked anxiously.

"If the others are for it, I'll go," Meg said. "I don't want to be a wet blanket."

"The place where we have reservations is formal," he said.

"You were sure of yourselves, weren't you?" Meg joked.

"If you had turned us down, we could have canceled," he said. "I know you will like it, though."

The next Saturday night the girls were excited as they dressed for the occasion. Meg had purchased a blue formal with an off-shoulder drape, tight bodice, and long flared skirt. Around her neck she wore a silver and blue topaz necklace with matching ear rings. The flashing blue stones in her ears reflected in her sparkling blue eyes. Her short hair curled softly around her face.

"I give up! Fasten this clasp for me, Meg," Sue said, and handed her the offending necklace. Meg admired Sue's green formal with its vee neck, small puffed sleeves, and full skirt. As usual little green bows adorned each side of her curly black hair.

"Do you like my new hair style?" Sylvia asked.

"It looks great on you," Sue replied as she appraised Sylvia's short brown bouffant-style hair. "Broadens your features."

"That's what the beauty operator said it would do. She showed me how to apply my make-up, also."

"That rose taffeta dress brings out your coloring," Meg added.

Promptly at seven o'clock the three sailors rang the doorbell. They whistled when they saw the girls in their finery.

"I can't believe you're ready," Pat said. "Didn't your mamas teach you that you should always keep a man waiting?"

"I forgot that along with her admonition not to dance," Meg said wryly.

"This is for you, Sylvia," Tony said shyly and handed her a white carnation corsage.

The other two pulled white carnation corsages from behind their backs and handed them to their dates.

"We didn't know what color your dresses would be, so we figured white would go with anything," Phil said.

The boys pinned the flowers on their dresses and said, "Let's go."

"Where are we going on this wonderful occasion?" Meg asked.

"To the Shepherd Supper Club," Pat said. "Ever been there?"

"No. Of course not," Meg answered.

"It's an old Georgian-style mansion on an estate a few miles out of the city, made into a fancy dining and dancing club. We've never been there either, but we've heard it's great."

"We borrowed a car from one of our buddies to take you there in style," Tony said.

"Hope he doesn't miss it before we return it," Pat said.

"Pat!" Meg exclaimed.

"Gotcha!" he said, "I was kidding. He loaned it to us."

"What I will miss most when you're gone is your sense of humor," Meg said.

When they drove up to the entrance of the mansion, a valet took their car to park. This impressed the girls, but they were even more awed when they entered the dining room. White linen cloths and matching fluted napkins covered the tables which encircled a small dance area and bandstand. Crystal and silver gleamed in the dimmed lights, and a rose in a cut-glass vase graced the center of each table. Soft music played by a small orchestra floated across the room.

Pat gave his name to the maitre d' who signaled a waiter to show them to a corner table. After the waiter had seated them and left, Pat said, "This isn't exactly the ringside table that I asked for."

"It's fine," Meg said.

"A corner table is cozier," Sue said.

"At least it isn't by the kitchen door," Phil added.

"Oh, dear, the menu is in French and I took Spanish in high school," Sylvia said. "Can any of you read French?"

"No, but it's in English on the next page," Tony said.

"We're going to live it up and have the prime rib, if it's agreeable with everyone," Pat said.

While she ate, a feeling came over Meg that she was being watched. She looked up to find a pair of brown eyes staring at her. They belonged to the airman who had danced too closely at the canteen. She dropped her gaze, but every time she glanced up, his eyes remained steadily fixed on her. It made her feel uncomfortable. Another airman and two girls sat at his table, but he ignored them.

After the delicious meal, Pat invited Meg to dance. The floor wasn't as crowded as the canteen, and the music had a slower beat. With her eyes closed she floated around the room in Pat's arms. They danced through two numbers and then returned to their table. While the others remained on the floor, Meg and Pat took the opportunity to talk over the good times they had together during the past few weeks.

"May I have this dance?"

Meg looked up in surprise. It was the tall handsome airman who had stared so rudely. She glanced at Pat and saw him compress his lips.

"I came with Pat and I'm only dancing with him and his friends," she said.

"Maybe I'll catch you later," he said and moved off.

CHAPTER XIX

Two weekends later Meg's parents and Johnny came through Oklahoma City on their way to Denver to see Bob. Sue and Sylvia spent two nights with Sue's uncle and aunt so Meg's family could stay with her.

"How's Bob?" was Meg's first question.

"Doing fine," Dad said. "We don't know when he'll be able to come home, so we thought we'd go there to see him. Your mother was also anxious to see how you were getting along."

"Everyone's been asking about you girls," Mom said. "And I wasn't the only one wanting to come." She looked expressively at Dad.

"I wanted to come to the city, too," Johnny said. "It's too big, though. Wouldn't want to live here."

"The Lesters let us have some of their gas ration coupons," Dad said. "Otherwise we wouldn't have been able to make the trip to Denver."

"We're looking forward to going to church with you in the morning, Meg. Will you be singing in the choir?" Mom asked.

"No. I want to sit with you," was her evasive reply. She didn't tell them that she had stopped singing in the choir. Of course she'd rather sit with them, anyway. That wasn't a lie.

The evening passed quickly as they exchanged news. Meg told them that she sang sometimes at the Baptist Servicemen's Canteen and sometimes at the Catholic one. She neglected to tell them that she also danced with the men at the latter.

When bedtime arrived, Meg made a pallet on the floor for Johnny. Her parents slept in the bedroom, and she slept on the daybed.

In the morning, after a leisurely breakfast of bacon, eggs, and toast, they attended the church service.

"Your choir is wonderful," Mom whispered. "You must love singing with them."

"Yes, I do," Meg replied. That was a lie, she hadn't sung in the choir lately.

After the services they went back to the apartment for lunch. Meg had prepared a cold meal ahead of time consisting of ham, potato salad, a green salad, and cake for desert. In the afternoon they walked in the nearby park and talked.

That evening, after a supper of sandwiches and fruit, they again attended the services at church. The young women's choir called "The Silver Belles" provided the special music.

"Meg, that was beautiful!" Mom whispered. "Why don't you sing with them?"

"I'll tell you later," Meg replied, and then spent the rest of the hour trying to think of a good excuse. She couldn't disappoint her mother by telling her that she didn't want to take the time to practice with them. The truth was that too many new and exciting experiences filled her life, and church was no longer her first priority. Service to God and then to others had always been important to her mother. She often told Meg that her voice was a gift from God and she should use it for His glory whenever the opportunity arose.

At the end of the service Meg said, "See those dresses they're wearing? I'll join as soon as I can afford one." Another lie!

"I'm going down there to tell them how much I appreciated their singing," Mom said.

The next morning after an early breakfast, the Mitchells left for Denver and Meg went to work.

Meg's conscience, triggered by her mother's inquiries, worked overtime when she thought about how much time she spent at the canteens, while neglecting church and choir. The following Wednesday evening she went to prayer meeting and choir practice and started singing in the choir again. On most Fridays she sang at the Baptist canteen, and occasionally she sang at the Catholic one on Saturday and danced with the servicemen. Sue and Sylvia went with her. Even though she tried to convince herself that this wouldn't interfere with church, there were times when she was too tired to get up on Sunday morning. She soothed her conscience by telling herself that it was important to entertain the servicemen. "After all," she told herself, "most of them will go into danger soon, and I'm helping them to relax and have fun before facing battles." At the same time she pushed away thoughts that she was neglecting God.

CHAPTER XX

"It's been over a month since the boys left, and I still miss them," Sue said one evening as she filed her fingernails.

Meg looked up from the book she was reading and said, "They seem to like ship duty, but it's a shame they couldn't stay together."

"Yes, they were together through boot camp and the training at Norman and had become good friends," Sue replied. Then she mused, "I wonder who this new date of Sylvia's is?"

Sylvia had not accompanied them to the canteens on the last two weekends as she had dates with a special new friend.

"I haven't met him, but she has a date with him this evening. He must be able to get off on more than weekends."

"Are you hungry?" Sue asked. "I am. Let's walk over to Carl's Café and get a hamburger."

"Okay. As soon as I get my shoes on," Meg answered.

The girls walked the three blocks to the small café on Classen Boulevard. A full moon lit up the warm clear night like daylight, and a million stars shone brightly. The aroma of fried hamburger and onion permeated the air as they approached the well-lighted building. Inside a counter and plastic covered stools lined the back wall, while plastic and chrome booths looked out the large glass windows on the front.

"Why, there's Sylvia!" Sue exclaimed as they entered.

Sylvia sat in the last booth, facing them. A black-haired man in an Air Force uniform sat across from her with his back to them. She looked at him with adoration in her eyes as he caressed her hands and talked earnestly to her. When she heard Sue, she looked up and blushed.

They walked down to her booth to meet her date. He stood up and turned to face them. Meg gasped. It was the rude airman who had held her too tightly and had stared at her at the supper club.

"You!" she exclaimed involuntarily.

"Hello again," he said and gave her his brilliant smile.

"Have you met?" Sylvia asked.

"Not officially," the airman said smoothly.

Sylvia introduced them, "Meg and Sue, this is John Hook."

"Won't you join us?" he asked.

"No, we're going to take our hamburgers home to eat," Meg said. "Nice meeting you. See you later, Sylvia."

On the way home, Sue glared at Meg. "Why did you say that we were going to take our hamburgers home to eat? I wanted to eat there."

"I don't think Sylvia wanted us to stay," Meg said.

They were still awake when Sylvia breezed into the apartment. "Isn't he the most charming man you ever met?" she asked. Her face glowed and her eyes shone. Meg thought she had never looked prettier.

"I don't know about charming, but he is handsome," Sue replied. "Almost as handsome as Brock Vandenberg."

"He's very good-looking," Meg agreed. She didn't add that she didn't like him or trust him.

A few nights later Sylvia and Sue went to a movie. Meg stayed home to shampoo her hair. When she finished, she came out of the bathroom in her robe with a towel wrapped around her head. The doorbell rang and, without removing the chain, she opened the door a crack. John Hook stood there.

"Sylvia isn't home," she said.

"I know," he replied. "I came to see you."

"What do you want to see me about?" she asked.

"It's about Sylvia," he said.

"What about her?"

"I don't want to stand out here in the hall discussing her. It will take only a few minutes of your time."

"Wait until I get dressed," she said reluctantly and shut the door. She dressed in her oldest and least attractive dress and left the towel around her head.

"What about Sylvia?" she asked as she opened the door and let him in.

"Nice little apartment," he said. "May I sit down?"

"Yes, of course, but what do you want to tell me about Sylvia?"

"Sit down so I don't have to strain my neck to see you." He patted the seat next to him on the daybed, but she took the chair farthest away and waited.

"That towel is very becoming around your head," he said.

"My patience is exhausted. What do you want?"

"You."

"What?"

"You. Ever since I first saw you at the canteen and then again at the supper club, I've dreamed of you. I didn't realize that Sylvia was with you that night at the club. You blinded me to everyone else and now I've finally met you. What rotten luck that you happen to be Sylvia's roommate."

"If that's all you wanted to tell me, you may go now."

"Can't we meet some place without Sylvia knowing?"

"No, I'm not that sort of person, and even if you were not dating Sylvia, I wouldn't go with you. Didn't I make that clear to you at the canteen?"

"Why? What's wrong with me? I could like you a lot."

"Please go!" Meg went to the door.

"Meg, I know you like me. Sylvia is standing in the way, isn't she? She means nothing to me. I'll end it with her if you will go out with me."

"John, your ego knows no bounds. I promise you that whether you go with Sylvia or not, I'll not date you. If you feel the way you say about her, you should do her a favor and break off with her." Meg opened the door and waited for him to leave.

John walked slowly across the floor until he stood next to her.

"Meg," he said and took one of her hands in both of his, "I can't help the way I feel about you. You are so beautiful. The first time I saw you I felt that we were meant to be together." His eyes took on a soft warm glow as he gazed into her face.

For a moment Meg was tempted to believe he was sincere. He drew her tenderly into his arms and bent his head to kiss her lips.

"No!" she said and pushed him away. "Leave now!"

His expression changed instantly to one of mockery. "Are you going to tell Sylvia that I was here?" he asked.

"I should."

"You know she won't believe you, and if you do tell her, I'll say that I forgot that she wouldn't be home, and that you flirted outrageously with me."

"You are despicable! She will find you out on her own sooner or later."

Meg locked the door after him and gave a sigh of relief. A troubled frown crossed her face as she pondered the problem. She had been right not to trust John Hook. He could certainly turn on the charm and be appealing and persuasive, she admitted to herself. Sylvia was in love with him and wouldn't believe her if she told her the truth about him. It would only make her angry. She shrugged her shoulders. "Sylvia is an intelligent girl. Let her find out for herself what kind of man he is," she thought.

The days passed swiftly for Meg, but she still had time to get homesick. She hadn't seen her family since their visit in July. They spent only one night with her when they returned from Denver. It was now August. In the last letter she had received from her mother, she had wanted to know when Meg was coming home.

"I'm going home this weekend," she announced to her roommates. "Anyone want to come with me?"

"Yes, I do," Sue replied. "I've been planning to go soon."

"Guess I'll go, too," Sylvia said. "I hate to leave John, but my parents won't like it if you come home and I don't."

Meg spent a happy two days at home. On Saturday she dressed in old slacks and a work shirt, then took to the woods. The dogs went along with her. They seemed as glad to see her as did her parents and Johnny. In spite of her resolve not to, she found herself climbing Joe's hill. She gazed at the restful view for a while and then sat on "her" rock and thought about Joe. How she longed to see his dear face again, feel his strong arms around her, and experience his loving kiss. He seemed closer to her here. "Oh, Joe, my love," she cried out, "my heart yearns for you. Please come back to me."

She recalled the day that he had first brought her here. He had taken off her glove and pretended to read her palm. Why had he mentioned a happy marriage? When he remembered that she wasn't even sixteen, he had backed off. Yet, he had said that he cared a great deal for her. He had asked her to stay the same as she was–good and pure–and unmarried?

Yes, Joe did love her! He had held his feelings back as long as he could, but he had broken down and admitted it at the bus stop! "I love you, Maggie. Wait for me," he had whispered. The words still rang in her ears.

He had written that letter to release her so she would participate in school activities and date rather than sit at home and wait for him. If only she had kept writing to him! She didn't have his address now, but she would keep praying for him, not only for his safety, but also for his salvation.

Could she marry him if he didn't become a Christian? The Bible warned Christians not to be yoked with unbelievers. Why would the Lord let her love him if he wasn't the one He intended for her to marry? Some day the war would end, and he would come home. Then she would know for sure.

On Sunday Meg was asked to sing a solo at church, and she sang "In The Garden." After the service people told her how much they missed her singing. Later Mom asked her if she had joined the "Silver Belles" and she had to tell her, "No."

In the afternoon her family took her to the bus stop where she met Sue and Sylvia for the trip back to the city.

A week after their visit to Oak Grove they received a letter from Amy. Tommy's unit had been sent back to Europe, and Amy would be moving back home.

CHAPTER XXI

State Fair Week in Oklahoma City fell during the last week in September. It rained most of the week, but by Friday the sun shone bright and clear. Sylvia had a date with John that evening, and Meg and Sue decided to spend time at the fair rather than the canteen. They rode the streetcar out Northeast Eighth Street to the fairgrounds on Eastern Avenue. The crowd pushed and shoved as they got off and surged toward the gate. Their hard-earned dollar bought them entrance and they passed through the turnstile.

"Where do you want to go first, Sue?" Meg asked.

"I don't want to see the animals, but I would like to see the arts and crafts," she said.

After an hour of browsing through the exhibits, they emerged from the building to a darkened sky and a neon-lit midway. They stopped to look at the large stuffed animals on display at the games-of-skill booths. Barkers called through their megaphones to entice customers to see the freak shows or girlie revues. Ahead of them bright lights twinkled on the rides, and the music blared from the merry-go-round calliope.

"Let's ride the Ferris wheel first," Sue said.

From the top of the ride they could see the entire fairgrounds. The loud noises so overwhelming below were now muted, and the twinkling lights gave the area the appearance of a fairy land. Fair goers continued to file through the turnstiles.

"I think there are a couple of airmen staring at us," Sue said.

"Yes, I see them," Meg answered. "What should we do?"

"We'll play it by ear," she said.

The Ferris wheel stopped and started as passengers got off and new ones came aboard. Soon their ride ended, and the two airmen approached them as they stepped off.

"Hi! Are you enjoying the fair?" a sandy-haired young man asked Sue. "I'm called Sandy, for obvious reasons, last name is Moore, and this is Dick Ramsey. Could we walk with you?"

Sue glanced at Meg and shrugged her shoulders. "It's a free country," she said.

"My name is Sue Gregory and this is my friend Meg Mitchell."

Meg felt an immediate attraction to Dick. He was slender and boyish-looking with a delicate fine-featured face, green eyes, and slightly curly brown hair. A shy smile made him even more appealing.

"Where are you stationed?" Meg asked.

"Right here on the fairgrounds," he said. "See that brick building at the back of the grounds? We have preflight classes there and have been coming to the fair free every evening."

"You're going to be a pilot?"

"If I make it through preflight and then through training, I will."

"My brother was a Navy pilot. His plane was shot down in the Pacific and he is now in the hospital waiting to be discharged."

"That's too bad. He'll probably miss flying. I'm anxious to get my wings and start."

"Would you girls like some cotton candy?" Sandy asked.

"Sure," Sue answered. "It's been years since I tasted it."

Not even the gentle mist that had begun to fall dampened their spirits. Dick tucked Meg's hand in the crook of his arm as they walked and asked her if she liked poetry.

"Sort of," she replied. "We had to memorize several poems in high school. Do you know 'The Raven'?"

As he began quoting from it, she joined in. They quoted several more poems as they walked in the rain. It was an enchanted evening for Meg.

At ten o'clock Sandy said, "I hate to leave, but it's our curfew time. We are free weekends. May we come to see you tomorrow afternoon?"

"Sure," Sue said and she gave them their address and phone number.

A month later as Meg put the finishing touches on her make-up, she thought of the last time she wore her blue formal. The engagement party for Fran Simmons, a coworker at the plant, promised to be just as fancy. Fran's fiancé, a major stationed at Ft. Sill, had been on active duty in the war in Europe. However, after suffering a bad injury, he was reassigned to a desk job stateside. Originally from Oklahoma City, he and Fran had known each other most of their lives. They had both grown up in Nichols Hills, a wealthy section of the city. Their parents were hosting the event in the ballroom of the Biltmore Hotel.

Not even the anticipation of attending such an elegant affair relieved Meg's depression. Three weeks before, the girls had returned home for a memorial service for Tommy Riggs. On the first bombing mission of his second tour, his plane was shot down over Germany. All the crew were killed.

Amy, waif-like in black with her pinched pale face and red swollen eyes, seemed too young to be a widow, just as she had seemed too young to be a bride in her white gown. Meg's heart ached for her.

Again the services had been held in the Community Building with all the military and community officials and townspeople present. The schools had again been let out for the day and businesses had closed. A second son of Oak Grove had given his life for his country.

Meg had sobbed all through the service, remembering Jimmy as well as Tommy. How many more would die before peace was restored?

Tonight her roommates were gone, and she was alone in the apartment. Sue's parents were visiting in the city, and she was staying with them at her uncle's house. Sandy was to be there to meet them, and they were all going out for dinner. Sylvia was in Dallas to attend a cousin's wedding. She had been excited about it and had bought new clothes for the occasion. John had taken her to the train station.

Meg was fond of Dick and tried to shake off the depression before he arrived to escort her to the party. He would be leaving soon for the next step of his pilot's training.

When the doorbell rang, she was ready. The late October weather had turned cold and windy. She opened the door for Dick and then let him help her into her coat. All the way out to the taxi she chattered gaily. He handed her in and then got in beside her.

"Biltmore Hotel," he instructed the driver.

He settled back in the seat and put his arm around her. "Now, what's the problem?" he asked.

"What makes you think there's a problem?" she countered.

"Meg," he said softly, "I know you well enough now to sense

your moods. Are you still thinking of your friend who lost her husband?"

Meg looked into his gentle face, and her heart turned over. She wondered if she was falling in love with him. Always courteous and tender, he handled her like glass. When she was with him she felt cherished and protected.

"I'm sorry," she said, "I don't want to spoil the party for you."

"You could never do that," he said and tipped up her face with the forefinger of his free hand and kissed her gently on the lips.

They entered the hotel, checked their coats in the cloakroom and went to the entrance of the brightly decorated ballroom. Fran greeted them warmly and introduced them to her fiancé, both sets of parents, and others in the receiving line.

Once in the ballroom a passing waiter offered them champagne, but before Meg could refuse, Dick handed one to her and took one for himself.

"This will help lighten your mood," he said.

She took a sip and said, "Ugh! Does one get used to this horrible taste?"

"After the fourth one you don't care anymore," he said with a laugh. "Just kidding."

When they had finished their drinks he asked her to dance. The orchestra was playing "Tangerine," one of her favorites, and the champagne helped lighten her mood, so she gave him her hand and said, "Yes, let's."

Dick was a good dancer, and Meg found it exhilarating to whirl around the ballroom in his arms. During the evening she danced with many men, and it seemed as if someone constantly handed her a drink. However, she would only take a sip before being claimed for another dance. Her spirits soared and she laughed gaily at the playful banter of her partners.

Finally Dick corralled her and, taking her firmly by the arm, led her to the cloakroom to retrieve their coats.

"I had better get you home while you can still maneuver on your own," he said.

"I haven't told Fran what a good time I had," she objected.

"Write her a note tomorrow," he said.

Outside the cold wind hit Meg's face and she felt dizzy.

"Whoosh! I must have drank too much champagne," she said with a giggle. Suddenly nausea overcame her and she leaned over and threw up into a potted tree.

Dick loaned her his handkerchief and hailed a taxi. He helped her in, climbed in after her, and put his arm around her. She went to sleep immediately with her head on his shoulder and didn't wake up until they arrived at her apartment. When Dick paid the driver, he dismissed him and half carried her upstairs.

"You need some coffee," he said as he set her down on the daybed and went into the kitchen to make some.

While he was in the kitchen, Meg got up and turned the radio on. Strains from Glen Miller's "Moonlight Serenade" drifted through the air, and she began dancing around the room with an imaginary partner. Dick came in, took her in his arms and began dancing with her, holding her close. Meg looked up at him through half-closed eyelids, and he bent down and kissed her hungrily on the lips.

They stopped dancing and stood swaying, locked in an embrace. He moved his hands gently up and down her back, and Meg lost herself to his touch. Vaguely she sensed the danger of the situation but didn't want him to stop. The alcohol that had at first lifted her spirits had gradually caused her to sink back into depression. Slowly they moved toward the daybed and he gently pushed her down.

"No," she said, but his insistent lips covered hers, and she sank further among the pillows.

The jarring ring of the telephone caused them both to jump. It rang again with a shrill, discordant note.

"Let it ring," Dick said hoarsely.

"I can't," she said as it rang for the third time.

She pushed him away, got up, and stumbled across the room to answer it. "Meg," the voice of her father immediately sobered her. "I've been trying to get hold of you all evening. Your mother has been injured in a car accident."

CHAPTER XXII

Terror gripped Meg's heart. Frantic thoughts raced through her mind. What was Dad saying? He couldn't mean Mom!

"Meg?" Dad said. "Do you understand what I said?"

"How bad is it?" she finally asked, trying to grasp the situation.

"It's serious, darling. You need to come home immediately. I contacted Jack Gregory at his brother's house, and he will bring you home tonight as soon as you call him. Meg, do you hear me?"

"Yes, Dad, I'll call him." Slowly she replaced the receiver in its cradle and stared at it as if it were alive. Tears coursed down her cheeks.

"What's the matter, honey?" Dick asked with concern.

"It's-it's my mom. She's been seriously injured in a car wreck. I must go home at once. Sue's parents will take me. You'd better leave."

Before he could respond the phone rang again. Meg lifted the receiver and heard Mr. Gregory's voice. "Meg, we've been trying to reach you. Have you talked to your father?"

"Yes. I'll be ready by the time you get here." In a daze she hung up the phone.

Dick came out of the kitchen with two cups of coffee. He placed one of them in her hands and said, "Drink this. It'll help clear your head."

Silently, they drank their coffee and then she asked him to go.

"I'm not leaving you alone," he said. "Now go change your clothes and pack."

In a trance like state, Meg disappeared into her bedroom. While she prepared to leave, Dick washed the coffee pot and cups and put them away.

She came out of the bedroom dressed in a gray wool suit with her suitcase in her hand. Her face was white and strained. Taking the bag from her, he set it by the door and helped her into her coat. Then he drew her into his arms and kissed her gently on the top of her head.

"Meg," he whispered, "I'm so ashamed of the way I behaved

tonight. I never meant for that to happen. Will you forgive me?"

"It's as much my fault as yours," she said. "I don't know if I'll even be able to forgive myself." She turned toward the window. "I think I hear their car."

He picked up her suitcase and followed her out into the hall, locked the door behind them, and handed her the key.

When they reached the car, Mr. Gregory opened the trunk and put in her suitcase. Dick opened the car door for Meg and she got in next to Sue in the back seat.

"I'm going with you," Sue said, explaining her presence. "I called the night manager at the plant and told him that we wouldn't be there Monday and that I wasn't sure when we would be back."

Meg nodded numbly at her.

Mr. Gregory told Dick good-bye, started the motor, and drove down the street.

"I'm sorry that we couldn't reach you sooner, Meg," he said. "We were out to dinner when your dad first tried to get hold of us. After we got home and got the call from him, we called the Biltmore Hotel, but you had already left."

All the way home Meg sat in a corner of the back seat with her mind in a turmoil. Outside, the wind whipped gusts of rain against the windows, but she stared out with unseeing eyes. She prayed silently for her mother. "Oh, God, hear my prayer for my mother. Forgive me for my sins and hear my plea. Don't let her suffer. Relieve her pain and heal her. I'm the one who has sinned, not her. I should be the one lying there in pain. She is so good, and she doesn't deserve this. Please don't let her die!"

When they arrived at the small Wolfeton hospital, the Gregorys went in with her. Bob waited for them in the lobby.

"Bob!" Meg said as she ran into his arms, "How is Mom?"

Bob shook his head sadly, "Not good, Meg. She has regained consciousness, however, which may be a good sign. I've been waiting for you here. Come, I'll take you to her."

"We'll be in the waiting room if you need us," Mr. Gregory said. "Please let us know if there's any change."

Bob led the way on his crutches down the shadowy hall. A strong antiseptic odor permeated the air. The only light shone from a lamp on the nurse's desk. Dr. Newberry stood at the desk with a chart in his hand talking to a white-clad nurse. He glanced up as they approached and, laying the chart down, came to Meg with outstretched arms. She collapsed against him sobbing. He patted her on the back and said, "Meg, I'm sorry."

"Is there any hope?" she asked.

"I'm afraid not," he said. "We can only pray and leave her in God's hands. I'll take you to her."

He showed her into the room across the hall from the desk, where her mother lay swathed in bandages. Intravenous fluid slowly dripped into her right arm. Her face was pale except for the dark circles around her closed eyes. Shallow breathing was the only sign of life in the still form. Dad sat beside her with bowed head, holding her hand.

Fearfully, Meg approached the bed and touched her father's shoulder. He rose immediately and hugged her, then indicated that she should sit in the chair he had vacated. She took the listless white hand in hers. Mom opened her eyes drowsily and focused them on Meg's face. A look of joy brightened them for a moment. Meg leaned over and kissed her cheek lightly. A smile flickered across her face before she closed her eyes again in sleep.

Dad left the room with the doctor. Meg sat beside her mother, holding her hand, and Bob took the chair on the other side of the bed.

Tears slid down Meg's face as she watched her mother. She thought of all the lies she had told her the past few months. Her mom would not have approved of her dancing and erratic church attendance. She sang in the choir sometimes, but they couldn't depend on her. Last night she had let alcohol rob her of her better judgement and had come close to giving in to lust.

Dad came in with a thermos of coffee and offered her and Bob a cup. Meg shook her head. She felt as if she would choke on it.

"Johnny is asleep in the lounge," he said. "Poor kid. It's been tough on him."

"How did you get here so fast, Bob?" Meg asked.

"The hospital gave me a few days leave, and I came today to surprise the folks."

At five in the morning Mom roused again and attempted to say something to Dad.

"Don't try to talk, dear. We are all here. Meg, get your brothers."

Meg hurried out to the lounge. Bob and the Gregorys were drinking coffee and talking in low tones. Johnny slept on the couch and Sue dozed in a chair. Meg motioned for Bob to follow her and he woke Johnny. Silently they hurried down the hall to Mom's room. Dad was bent over kissing her when they came in.

They gathered around the bed, and she tried to smile. Love for them shone out of her eyes. With great effort her lips formed the words "I love you" before she lapsed into a coma.

Dr. Newberry came in and examined her. He looked up at the anxious faces and sadly shook his head. "It's only a matter of time," he said.

Half an hour later she was gone.

"Why was she out on such a bad day?" Meg cried. "I bet she was on an errand for someone else, wasn't she?"

Johnny responded bitterly, "It was for you! She went to Wolfeton to get some material for a stupid choir dress!"

Meg's face blanched, "Oh no, no, no!" she cried.

Dad put his arm around her. "Johnny is just upset, Meg. She went for other things, too. If she had known the storm was coming, she wouldn't have gone. She slid off the road on a sharp turn. They think she may have been dodging an animal. It isn't your fault!"

CHAPTER XXIII

Meg spent the next two days in her room sobbing quietly into her pillow. Dad and her brothers tried to entice her with food, but she could not eat. Grandma Mitchell and Aunt Barbara tried to comfort her, but she could not be comforted. She wished they would just leave her alone.

In spite of what Dad had said, guilt consumed her and she felt responsible for her mother's death. All her lies had led to this. Why hadn't she just told her mother the reason she hadn't joined the choral group? She selfishly didn't want to put the time and effort into practicing and traveling around singing in other churches. Was her mother's death God's way of punishing her for her sins? Would Dad and her brothers hate her if they knew she had lied and Mom's trip had been for nothing?

She tried to pray for God's forgiveness, but felt she couldn't reach Him. How could He love her after the way she had lied to her mom and caused her death? If the phone hadn't rung when it did, would she have gone all the way? She shuddered at the thought.

The day of the funeral was cold and rainy. With an effort Meg got up and dressed. If only she could just stay in her bedroom. She wished she had a black hat with a veil to cover her face.

When the family car from the funeral home came to take them to church, Dad rapped gently on her door. Numbly, she took his arm, went down the stairs, and climbed into the car. In spite of the bad weather, the church was packed, and a canopy was hastily erected outside to protect the overflow crowd. Every able-bodied person in town came to pay their respect for Sarah Mitchell. In one way or another they had all been touched by her.

Meg, deep in her own misery, wasn't conscious of the music or the words of comfort from Brother Cunningham until he read the scripture from Proverbs 31:10-31. A virtuous woman. How well it described her mother! "She stretcheth out her hand to the poor; yea, she reacheth out her hands to the needy." And then the last few verses. "Strength and honor are her clothing; and she shall rejoice in time to come. She openeth her mouth with wisdom; and in her tongue is the law of kindness. She looketh well to the ways of her household, and eateth not the bread of idleness. Her children arise up and call her blessed; her husband also, and he praiseth her. Many daughters have done virtuously, but thou excellest them all. Favour is deceitful, and beauty is vain; but a woman that feareth the LORD, she shall be praised. Give her of the fruit of her hands; and let her own works praise her in the gates."

The words "strength and honor" stayed with Meg all the way to the cemetery and for days to come. If only that could be said of her!

Letters of condolence and flowers continued to arrive long after the funeral. Everyone had loved Sarah Mitchell. Despite all the kindness, Meg could not shake off her depression. Guilt coupled with her loss hung heavy on her shoulders.

Bob returned to the hospital in Denver for further treatment. Meg resigned her job at the plant. Her place was at home now, seeing after the needs of her father and Johnny. Although she would rather not, she attended all of the church services with them, but she wasn't able to sing in the choir yet. She prayed for forgiveness but felt none.

One blustery Sunday evening in early December Meg sat in church only half listening to Brother Cunningham's sermon. His topic centered on "The Prodigal Son." How many sermons had she heard on that scripture? Plenty! Her attention was caught, however, when he said, "While the son was a long way off the father saw him and had compassion for him, and ran to meet him, and embraced him. The father was waiting for him to come home and ask for forgiveness. Our heavenly Father is always ready to forgive us as soon as we ask. God remembers our sin no more. The slate has been wiped clean."

The truth dawned clear and new to Meg. God had already forgiven her and she had only to accept it. Her burden of guilt melted. The relief was so great that she could hardly contain herself. She felt God's love wash over her and, in return, she felt an inexpressible love for Him. Later, she could tell others of God's love and forgiveness; but, for now, she could only hug the newfound happiness to herself.

Instead of reading the Bible casually, now she read it with a deep thirst. Never before had she known God's love so real and personal. In turn her prayer life filled her with great joy.

A short time later, Meg felt compelled to confess to her dad and ask for his forgiveness. Johnny had gone up to bed, and Dad sat reading the newspaper.

"Dad," she said, "I need to tell you something."

Dad laid aside the paper and said, "What is it, dear?"

"I lied to Mom. It wasn't that I couldn't get the choir dress, it was that I didn't want to take the time to sing in that choir. Mom's approval was important to me, and I didn't want her to think less of me. Please don't hate me for causing her death." She choked back sobs as tears streamed down her face.

Dad immediately got up and put his arms around her and said, "Meg, I could never hate you. You are my daughter and very precious to me. It wasn't your fault! Please stop blaming yourself. Your mother had other things to shop for and would have gone anyway. Because of gas rationing, she never went to Wolfeton unless she had several things to buy."

Meg buried her face in his shoulder and said in a muffled voice, "Th-that's not all, Dad. I've not been going to church regularly, and I've been d-dancing at the canteens. The night you called about Mom's wreck, I had been dancing and drinking champagne at a party, and I-I d-drank too much, and I-I almost..."

Dad took her by the shoulders, and looked anxiously in her face. "You weren't harmed, were you Meg?"

"No, Dad," she answered.

"Thank the Lord," he said and kissed her on the forehead. "We should never have let you go to Oklahoma City alone. You were too young to be out from under our protection."

Though the loss of her mother still saddened Meg, the guilt was gone. She not only started singing in the choir again, but also sang around the house as she worked.

Soon after her mother's funeral, she had received a letter from Dick. He again apologized for his actions and expressed sorrow at the death of her mother. Sandy and he were training to be pilots at the Enid Air Force Base in northwest Oklahoma. Sandy corresponded with Sue and she had sent Meg's address at Dick's request.

Now that she was in better spirits, she decided to write to him. She told him that she forgave him and hoped that he would forgive her. "God has forgiven me, and I have been able to forgive myself." she wrote. "I apologize for leaving you standing in the street without a word of thanks or a good-bye. My only excuse is that I was so upset about my mother that I couldn't think of anything else. You and I had some good times together, and I will always remember you with appreciation."

She signed it, "Your friend, Meg."

CHAPTER XXIV

On New Year's Eve, 1944, Sue invited her three best friends to a slumber party at her house. She and Sylvia arrived in Oak Grove before Christmas to spend the holidays at home. All four of them, Meg, Sylvia, Amy, and Sue, lounged on the bed in Sue's rose and chintz bedroom. Her parents and two younger brothers, Thad and Doug, had gone to the Watch Night service at the Baptist church.

"I'm glad you all could come," Sue said. "Remember the fun we had at slumber parties when we were younger?"

"It seems strange not to have parents here to chaperone us," Amy said with a laugh.

"We got used to no chaperones in our apartment in Oklahoma City," Sylvia said. "It was a slumber party every night."

Sue asked, "How is your dad, Meg?"

"His cold is hanging on," she answered. "I didn't think I should leave him tonight, but he urged me to come. It's our first New Year's Eve without Mom, and I know how hard it is for him. Bob and Johnny are there, though, and they plan to pop corn and make hot chocolate and listen to the celebrations on the radio. Dad said he would probably go to bed early." She turned to Sylvia. "How are things in the city, Sylvia?"

"Fine, but I won't be there much longer."

"Are you coming home?" Amy asked.

"No, I'm going to Chicago to work for two well-known lawyers as a legal secretary, and I will study law at night. My bosses recommended me."

"Oh, Sylvia!" Meg exclaimed. "That sounds exciting! Imagine living in Chicago! Sue will be in Oklahoma City, and Amy and I will be stuck here in Oak Grove."

"Not me, Meg," Amy said. "I've been accepted in the school of nursing at University Hospital in Oklahoma City. I start in February. Nurses are needed, and it will help keep my mind off losing Tommy. I'll be in the Cadet Nurses program, and the government will pay for my training."

"That's wonderful!" Sue said. "I've got some news also."

She went to her dresser and took out a small box and, opening it, held it out for all to see. A diamond ring sparkled on a plush cushion.

"An engagement ring!" they all exclaimed together.

"Sandy?" Meg asked.

"Why aren't you wearing it?" Amy asked.

"Yes, it's from Sandy, and he sent it by mail from Enid. He wanted me to have it but couldn't get to the city. I want to wait until he can put it on my finger himself. What do you girls think?"

"Wear it!" they answered with one voice.

"He wants you to wear it now or he wouldn't have given it to you yet," Meg said.

"He might be afraid that some other guy would capture your heart," said Amy.

"No chance of that happening," Sue said.

"When do you plan to marry?" Sylvia asked.

"As soon as he gets his wings. He will have a few days off. You all have decided for me," she said and put the ring on the third finger of her left hand.

They hugged and expressed their congratulations and best wishes for much happiness. Meg glanced at Amy and noticed a wistful expression on her face in an unguarded moment, so she said, "I'm starved. Let's eat. Isn't that what you are supposed to do at slumber parties?"

All agreed so they trooped down to the kitchen and made toasted cheese sandwiches, hot chocolate, and popcorn. They took this food along with some apples into the living room to eat in front of the fireplace.

"Poor Sandy," Sylvia said. "This will probably be the only kind of food he'll get after they are married."

"You know better. I'm a great cook, aren't I, Meg?"

"How would I know? Sylvia and I did all of the cooking. Are you staying in the apartment by yourself?"

"No. I'll move in with my uncle and aunt."

When they finished eating Sue said, "Let's liven this party up!" She put on the record, "The Boogie Woogie Bugle Boy From Company B," grabbed Amy's hand and started dancing her around the room.

"Come on, Meg!" Sylvia said. "Let's boogie."

While they were dancing, Sylvia's face paled and she broke away from Meg and dashed out of the room. They followed her into the bathroom where they found her throwing up into the toilet.

"Sylvia, what's the matter?" Sue cried anxiously.

"I'm okay now," she said. "I shouldn't have bounced around so soon after eating."

They went back to the living room and sat before the fireplace and watched the leaping flames.

"Do you remember Christmas and New Year's Eve of 1941?" Sue asked dreamily. "The war had just begun and we were all so excited. The boys were ready to quit school and join the armed forces, and lots of them did."

"Most of us girls wished we could go, too," Meg added. "We were so innocent."

"We had no idea how terrible war is," Amy said. "Now I only wish it were all over and the men were home. It'll never be the same without Tommy, though." Tears came to her eyes.

"No, things will never be the same," Sylvia said sadly.

"I was glad that your grandparents were able to come to your house for Christmas, Meg," Sue said.

"I heard that the 'Lonely Hearts Club' came also," Sylvia added.

"I should never have called them that," Meg said ruefully. "They are really dear, sweet people. A few days before Christmas, I met Miss Patty in the grocery store. She told me how much she missed my mother and looked so woebegone that I impulsively asked her to Christmas dinner. Then I called Doc and Jack and invited them, too. With all of them there I felt my mom was there with us, smiling her approval."

"Your mother was a wonderful person," Sylvia said. "I bet you could tell her anything, and she would understand and forgive you."

Tears came to Meg's eyes. "Yes, Sylvia, I could, but I didn't. I didn't tell her the truth about the way I was living in Oklahoma City, and I regret it now. Even when I was in high school I lied about the dancing at the parties. When she died in that car wreck she was going to get material for a dress so I could sing with the Silver Belles. I didn't tell her the reason I wasn't singing with them was because I didn't want to."

"I did something worse than lie," Sylvia said, "and now I'm

pregnant and can't tell my parents."

Three pairs of eyes stared at her in shocked surprise. Meg was the first one to find her voice.

"But, Sylvia, you have to tell your parents. What else can you do?"

"It has already been decided. I'm not going to a wonderful job in Chicago, but to a home for unwed mothers. The lawyers I mentioned are going to handle the adoption for me. They offered me a job after the baby comes. So you see, I have it all worked out."

"Are you sure you want to give up your baby?" Amy asked. "If your parents knew, wouldn't they help you keep it?"

"You don't know my parents! It would kill them if they knew I had sex before marriage. Mother thinks I'm perfect, and Father thinks of me as his innocent little girl. It's hard being the only child. If you fail, they have no one else."

"Who is the father of your baby?" Sue asked. "Or would you rather not say?"

"As long as I'm confessing, I might as well tell all. It's John Hook. He talked marriage, and fool that I was, I believed him. That weekend I went to Dallas we were supposed to be eloping. It was to be a big surprise for everyone. We drove down there after I got off work on Friday, and it was late when we got there, so we stayed in a hotel. I was surprised when he booked just one room, but he said that since we were to be married the next day it would be okay. Of course you can imagine what happened that night. The next day was Saturday, and he claimed that we couldn't get a license. We stayed another night and then came home Sunday. He said we would get married in Oklahoma City." Sylvia paused and wiped the tears from her eyes.

"Several days passed, and I didn't hear from him. I ran into a friend of his and found out that he had been shipped out. He told me not to expect anything from John, because he 'wanted to dance but didn't want to pay the piper,' as he crudely put it."

Meg had suspected what kind of a man John was, but it was too late to mention it to Sylvia now, and she probably wouldn't have believed her then. She had been too much in love.

Sylvia blew her nose and wiped her tears away and said, "Meg, it was the same weekend that your mom had her wreck."

Meg remembered how excited Sylvia had been and the new clothes she had bought in anticipation. It hadn't been for a cousin's wedding, but for her own. Her heart went out to her, and she put her arms around her.

"I'm a terrible person," Sylvia said. "I know none of you would have been so foolish. I'll probably go to hell for my sins."

"No, Sylvia," Meg said. "I'm as big a sinner as you are. I got carried away that Saturday night and almost went all the way with Dick. We had been to Fran's engagement party, and both of us had too much to drink. We were on the daybed when the phone rang. It was Dad telling me about Mom. I don't know if we would have come to our senses and stopped or not, but I am so glad we didn't go through with it."

"That's just it!" Sylvia cried. "You didn't go all the way, and we did!"

"Jesus said that if you have lust in your heart, it's the same as adultery," Meg said, "but He also said that if you confess your sins and turn from them, He will forgive you. That's what I did, and it was as if a load had fallen off my shoulders. God loves you, Sylvia, and wants the best for you."

"I do want forgiveness but I still believe I should give up my baby. My parents may not be as forgiving as God. Anyway the baby would be better off with a married couple who truly want one. What could I offer it? I would be stuck here in Oak Grove with a bad reputation, or if I left, I couldn't get a job that paid enough to support us both. My mind is made up. It will be hard, but I must give up my baby."

"I think you're very brave," Sue said.

"There's no need for my parents to know about it. It would only upset them. Promise you won't tell anyone."

"Of course we won't tell," Sue said, and the other two nodded in agreement.

"I didn't mean to turn this into a pity party," Sylvia said. "It's nearly midnight. Let's turn on the radio and listen to Guy Lombardo."

At the stroke of midnight they hugged each other and sang "Auld Lang Syne" with the radio. They went out on the porch to listen as the whistles blew and bells rang out all over town.

“Happy New Year, world!” they shouted together.
“And may the war end this year,” Meg added.

CHAPTER XXV

June 2, 1948
Oklahoma City, Oklahoma

Darkness closed in as Joe crept through the jungle. He couldn't see his men, but he knew they were there. The overgrowth was so thick they had to cut their way through. Suddenly lights flashed as machine guns rained bullets into them. Ambush! His men fell all around him. Screams of agony tore from the throats of the wounded and dying. Hordes of Japanese soldiers surrounded them. By the flashing lights he saw a raised hand with a grenade, and he opened his mouth to shout.

"Oklahoma City."

Joe awakened with a start. Sweat poured from him, and he was trembling. The jungle on the faraway island gave way to a bus pulling into the station in Oklahoma City. Reality reminded him it was June 2, 1948, not July of 1945. The woman across the aisle looked at him strangely. He was glad that no one shared the seat with him.

This was the first time the nightmare had occurred in a year. At first the dreams had happened frequently but with time and therapy, they had gradually diminished. He had hoped they were gone for good.

"It must be caused by tiredness," he thought to himself. The past week he had stayed up late every night studying for finals at Oklahoma A and M University. Shortly after the bus had left Stillwater he had dozed off, but it had not been a restful sleep. Then the dream had started.

After the other passengers left the bus, he stood up, stretched cramped muscles, rubbed his sore neck, and retrieved his kit and book pack from the overhead rack. When he stepped off the bus, he found that his suitcase had been unloaded. He picked it up and went inside the station. It was noon, and the bus for Oak Grove wouldn't leave for another hour, so he headed for the small lunchroom.

"Joe? Joe Sullivan?" It was more of a question than a statement.

He looked down at the attractive young woman in the booth. She was slender with a narrow face expertly made up. Mascaraed lashes framed a pair of wide gray eyes over a slightly tilted nose and a small mouth. A stylish blue suit with a matching hat perched on short well-coiffed brown hair. A ruffled white blouse, white pumps, and a white handbag completed the picture.

"I'm sorry, but do I know you?" he asked, puzzled.

"I'm Sylvia Ashley. You don't remember me, but I'm a friend of Meg Mitchell's."

"Oh, yes, I do." He remembered the skinny, sharp-tongued girl in the group of Maggie's closest friends. "You look so sophisticated that I didn't recognize you."

"Thanks, I guess," she said with a laugh. "I've spent the last few years in Chicago. I only get home twice a year to see my parents. They wrote me about the death of your uncle. I was sorry to hear it."

"Thank you," he said. "May I?" he asked, pointing to the seat across from her.

"Sure, sit down," she invited. "How often do you come home?"

"I haven't been back to Oak Grove since I left for the marines," he replied. "Everything must be changed. Most of the people our age have probably moved on to bigger and better things."

"Not everyone. Meg is still there. Did you know that her mother was killed in an automobile accident in the fall of 1944?"

"No!" Joe was stunned! He sat silently remembering Sarah Mitchell. She had been like a mother to him while he and Bob were growing up. The Mitchells had wanted him to live with them, but he had felt he couldn't leave his Aunt Peg to the mercies of his Uncle Dan.

"How are Mr. Mitchell and the rest of the family doing?"

"It was hard on them, but they are doing fine now. Meg quit her job in Oklahoma City to keep house for her dad and take care of Johnny. She helps in the store also."

The waitress approached with pad and pencil ready.

"I'll have a chicken salad sandwich and a Coke," Sylvia said.

Joe glanced at the menu. "Make mine a ham and cheese with a cup of coffee," he said.

After the waitress left, Joe asked Sylvia what she was doing in Chicago.

"I'm a legal secretary to a firm of lawyers, and I'm studying law at night. What are you doing?"

"Last fall I started college at Oklahoma A and M on the GI Bill. I plan to teach history and coach football in a small high school. You can see that I'm not as ambitious as you. It's great that you want to be a lawyer. Since the war more women have gone into professions that were considered a man's domain."

"Did you know that Bob Mitchell is studying medicine?"

"I haven't kept up with Bob. Not surprised, though."

"Do you remember Amy White? She was in my class."

Joe nodded. He remembered the petite, pretty blonde who was a good friend of Maggie's.

"When she graduated from high school, she married Tommy Riggs. He graduated the year ahead of us and became a gunner on a B-24. On his second tour overseas, his plane was shot down. Everyone on board was killed."

"That's too bad. How is Amy doing?"

"Okay, now. After his death she went into nurses' training at the University Hospital in Oklahoma City. Bob is in medical school there, and they met at the hospital, started dating, and now they are engaged to be married."

"Here you are," the waitress said as she put the sandwiches and drinks on the table. "Enjoy."

They were silent for a while as they ate. Trying not to seem too anxious, Joe asked, "Is Maggie married?"

"No, but I hear that she is practically engaged to Brock Vandenberg, the bank president's son. He's studying accounting, business administration, banking, or something like that so that he can one day take over for his father, who took over for his grandfather. His future is assured. Guess they will marry after he graduates. He works for the bank in the summer."

"You aren't married or engaged?" he asked.

"Goodness no. I'm much too busy trying to get an education to think about marriage and a family." She sounded independent, but Joe noticed a sadness in her eyes. "Guess I'm destined to be the 'old maid' of the bunch. Our friend, Sue Gregory, married a pilot she met in Oklahoma City. He stayed in the Air Force and is stationed in Germany. They have a baby."

When they finished eating, Sylvia pulled a package of cigarettes and a lighter out of her purse and offered Joe one.

"No, thanks," he said. "I did smoke. Cigarettes were so easy to get in the service, but the doc told me that if I wanted to live, I had better quit. So I did."

"I know I shouldn't, but it's a hard habit to break." Sylvia sighed. "Since I don't smoke in front of my parents, I'm going to have one now." She put the cigarette in her mouth, and Joe took the lighter and lit it for her.

She inhaled deeply, blew the smoke out and then asked, "Why did your doctor want you to quit?"

"Had part of a lung removed. Shrapnel." He changed the subject. "How did Mrs. Mitchell's accident happen?"

"She went to Wolfeton to do some shopping and a storm blew up. It was raining so hard that visibility was nearly zero. Somehow she skidded off the road on a curve. They didn't know if she didn't see the curve or if she dodged an animal at the last minute. She lived a few hours, and Meg and Bob were able to see her before she died."

Joe looked at his watch and said, "Time to go."

Sylvia stubbed out her cigarette and got up.

On the bus they sat together and talked. Sylvia updated him on everyone that she knew anything about, and it made the time go faster. Soon the bus climbed the curving mountain road that led to Oak Grove. When they reached the top, they could see the picturesque little town in the bend of the Poteau River spread out below them. Set among the oak trees, the charming white stone Methodist church with its steeple, the scattered houses, and the stores lining Main Street presented a tranquil appearance.

"It's still beautiful here," Joe said.

"I always enjoy coming home," she said. "It's nice to get away from the hurly burly life in the city occasionally."

They pulled up to the bus stop in front of the Main Street Café. Joe got their small bags and his book pack from the overhead rack and followed Sylvia off the bus.

"Now where are my parents?" Sylvia asked. "They were supposed to meet me."

"Sylvia!" A young woman hurried toward them. Joe's heart gave a leap. It was Maggie! A beautiful, mature Maggie. Dark brown hair curled softly around her oval face. Thick lashes fringed her remarkable deep blue eyes. Her nose was short and straight over a full, smiling red mouth. She was even lovelier than he remembered.

"Meg, what are you doing here?" Sylvia asked.

"Your mother called me at the store and asked me to meet you," she replied. "Your grandmother fell, and they took her to the emergency room at the Wolfeton Hospital. She's okay. Nothing broken, but they couldn't make it back in time to pick you up. I'll take you home."

"Thanks. Are you sure she's all right?"

"Yes. Your mother said she was just bruised and sore and for you not to worry. They were ready to start for home when she called."

Joe spoke up, "I'll get your bag, Sylvia."

"Do you know who this is, Meg?" Sylvia asked mischievously. "I picked him up in Oklahoma City."

Maggie turned and saw him for the first time. Joe felt a shock as their eyes met. Brilliant blue eyes locked with gray ones. Her face paled, but she recovered in a few seconds. Her hand trembled slightly as he took it in his. His heart pounded and it took all the will power he possessed to keep from sweeping her into his arms.

After an awkward pause he broke the silence and said, "Maggie, I just learned of the death of your mother, and I'm so sorry to hear it. She was a wonderful person. How are you and your dad and Johnny getting along?"

A shadow passed over her face. "It's been rough to lose her, but we are doing fine. Sorry about your uncle."

"Thanks," he said, and covered his emotions by reaching down and picking up Sylvia's suitcase. "Where's your car? I'll put Sylvia's bag in it."

"It's that blue Chevy in front of the drug store. Do you need a lift?"

"No. I'm going to see Mr. Vandenberg at the bank. He's the one who contacted me about the death of my uncle. Thanks anyway."

"Dad would love for you to come see him," Maggie said. "We are all so grateful to you for rescuing Bob."

"I heard about that!" Sylvia said. "It was a brave thing you did."

"I couldn't let the Japs get my best friend," he said with a grin.

"We'd best go, Sylvia," Maggie said hesitantly. "I've got to get back to the store before closing time to take Dad home."

Joe walked with them to the car and put Sylvia's suitcase in the trunk. He wanted to linger and talk with Maggie but somehow things seemed tense.

"Thanks, Joe. I enjoyed talking to you," Sylvia said.

"'Bye, Joe," Maggie said. "Come see us. You're always welcome."

Joe waved at them and went back for his suitcase and bags. It pleased him that Maggie didn't have a ring on the third finger of her left hand. He walked jauntily up the street to the bank on the corner and entered.

"I'm Joe Sullivan. Is Mr. Vandenberg in?" he asked the woman sitting at the desk in front of the president's office.

"Just a minute," she said and pressed a buzzer on her desk.

"Yes?" answered an irritated voice on the intercom.

"Mr. Joe Sullivan is here to see you."

"Send him in."

The secretary nodded to the door behind her desk, but before he could reach it, Mr. Vandenberg opened it and came out. He grabbed Joe's hand and shook it vigorously.

"Welcome home. We are all proud of you. Come in, come in," he said as he led him into the office.

Joe noted that the years had been kind to Mr. Vandenberg. He was still slim and handsome. Only a little gray showed in his hair and well-trimmed mustache.

"We are proud of all of our boys who risked their lives in that terrible war, but especially you," he said. "You put your life on the line to save one of our own. The town would like to give a celebration in your honor."

Joe winced. "Please don't, sir," he said. "I only did my duty. I'd rather forget about the war. You said in your letter that my uncle left a will?"

"Well, we certainly don't want to embarrass you, but we would like to show our appreciation. Yes, your uncle did leave a will. Bill Hamilton, our lawyer, is handling it. His office is in this building on the second floor. I'll call and let him know you'll be up."

A few minutes later Joe was ushered into Mr. Hamilton's law office. Joe remembered him. He was a large, friendly man with twinkling blue eyes and a receding hairline.

"Welcome home," he said. "We've been looking forward to your return. You're quite a hero around here."

"Thank you," Joe said quietly. "Mr. Vandenberg wrote about the death of my uncle. I'm sorry the message didn't reach me in time to make the funeral arrangements."

"We weren't sure how to get in touch with you. Brock, Sr., finally located you through the government. We expected you to come back when the war was over."

"I was in the hospital for a while and then started college last fall. My uncle and I didn't get along too well, so I didn't see any need to come back here."

"Your uncle was proud of you, Joe. I know he wasn't good to you while you were growing up, but he was sorry for it. After he quit drinking, he became a changed man. He left everything to you."

"Which probably doesn't amount to much," Joe muttered.

"On the contrary, he became well-to-do. He started a roadhouse out on Highway 102, and it has been very successful. Even people from other towns around here come to it. It's quite a show place."

Mr. Hamilton handed Joe a thick packet of papers. "Here is a copy of his will. You can take it home and read it. The gist of it is that you inherit everything he owned, which includes his house, acreage, car, and the Candlelight Inn, plus a hefty bank account."

Joe was stunned. "When I left all he owned was a rundown house, acreage, rattletrap Ford truck, saloon, still, and my five hundred dollars," he said stiffly.

"That five hundred was a down payment on the roadhouse that became the Candlelight Inn," the lawyer said with a smile. "Best investment he could have made. He stopped drinking and became a respectable businessman. He wanted you to take over the Inn."

"I'd rather get rid of it," Joe replied.

"We were hoping you would settle here in Oak Grove and run it. I don't think you will have any trouble selling, however. It's a going concern. Crowded every night."

"What kind of shape is the house in? Is it livable?"

"It's in excellent condition. Your uncle had it painted and redone inside and out. Bought new furniture and everything. Had a housekeeper, too. She's willing to work for you, if you like."

"You mentioned a car?"

"A brand new 1948 Ford. Paid cash for it. Bought it shortly before his fatal heart attack. It's in the garage at the house. Want a ride out there?"

"Yes, thanks." Joe would rather have walked the one and a half miles to stretch his legs but not with his suitcase and books.

When they arrived, Joe was pleasantly surprised. Trimmed bushes and a manicured green lawn complemented a freshly painted house. Gone were the run-down barn and sheds. A garage stood on the side by the kitchen door.

"Uncle did well for himself," he said.

"Yes, after he joined Alcoholics Anonymous, he became an upright citizen," Mr. Hamilton said. "Here are the keys to the house, car, and Inn. Would you like for me to go out there with you tomorrow to meet the help and look around?"

"Yes, sir, I would. What time shall I meet you?"

"We could go at four. That's when the help gets there. The bar opens at five, and dinners are served from six until midnight. A band with a woman singer starts playing at seven."

Joe shook Mr. Hamilton's hand, climbed out of the car, and retrieved his suitcase and books from the back seat. "I'll pick you up at your office at four," he said. "And thanks."

"Fine," said Mr. Hamilton, and he backed out of the driveway.

Joe entered the kitchen from the side door and was astonished. Even though Mr. Hamilton had told him it was improved, he still wasn't prepared. There were new cabinets, sink, stove, refrigerator, and table and chairs. Fresh curtains hung at the window and a beautiful linoleum rug covered the floor from wall to wall. He opened the cabinets and saw new dishes and glasses. In another one were pots and pans in mint condition. The drawers held good silverware and fancy kitchen tools. A vase of roses graced the table.

The rest of the house was also newly furnished and tastefully decorated. Attractive wool rugs lay on all the floors. The spare downstairs bedroom had been made into a den with a leather-covered couch and a massive mahogany desk. A comfortable chair was drawn up to it.

Upstairs in the master bedroom a cherry wood bedroom suit with a queen-size bed, chest of drawers, and dresser filled the room. The drapes at the windows matched the bedspread. Expensive suits and starched shirts hung in the closet, and the drawers were stocked with underwear, socks, handkerchiefs, and Tee shirts. On the dresser were combs, brushes, and other personal items. A wedding picture of Aunt Peg and Uncle Dan had a prominent place there. Joe picked it up and gazed at Aunt Peg. How young and pretty she was. Nothing like the worn, haggard face with the watery red eyes that he remembered. It enraged him to think about the hard life she had endured. "I'll never forgive Uncle Dan for what he put Aunt Peg and me through," he thought.

He hastily put the picture down and went into his old room. Dan had not bothered it. The little cot under the window with the homemade quilt and flattened pillow were just as he remembered them. His battered chest and old desk were still in their respective corners. Everything remained just as he had left it eight years earlier, including old clothes in the drawers and hanging in the closet.

He pulled open the desk drawers and found pencils, erasers, pens, and paper. One drawer held his diploma, some high school programs, and other mementos. A bag of marbles and a baseball filled another. An old ball cap and a cowboy hat hung upon wall pegs, and his baseball bat and glove lay upon the dresser. Next to the desk a bookcase held a few well-worn volumes.

Placing his suitcase on the bed, he cleaned out a drawer in the chest for his underwear and hung his suit, pants, and shirts in the closet. He set his shaving kit in the remodeled bathroom. Examining his face in the mirror, he rubbed his hand over it and decided he didn't need a shave and went downstairs.

In the kitchen he looked into the refrigerator and the pantry. A little food was available, but nothing appealed to him. He walked out to the garage and examined the new black Ford. "Might as well try it out," he thought and reached in his pocket for the keys, got in, and turned the motor on. "Purrs like a kitten," he said to himself.

He drove to town and parked in front of the Main Street Café and went in. The waitress, a bleached blonde with a tired washed-out look, took his order. He ordered a large steak, rare. After a satisfying meal he got up and left a generous tip.

Before going home he stopped in the Ashley Grocery Store and bought a few staples. At home he put the groceries away and made a pot of coffee.

The doorbell rang and he opened it to Police Chief Jay Bundy. He was a bulldog-looking man of medium height with a barrel chest and narrow hips. Bulging brown eyes, thinning gray hair, and heavy jowls completed the picture.

"Hi, Joe," he said. "Welcome home."

"Come in," Joe said, "I haven't broken any laws, have I?"

"Not that I know of," the chief said, smiling.

"Want a cuppa coffee?"

"Don't mind if I do. Smells good."

Joe filled two cups, and they sat at the table reminiscing about old times.

"Do you remember the time I caught you delivering your uncle's bootleg whiskey to some of his customers?"

Joe nodded his head ruefully as the chief continued.

"I told him if he ever had you delivering it again, I would close his still down. He never did, did he?"

"No," Joe admitted but didn't add that he had received a beating for getting caught. He had been fourteen at the time.

"Now I want you to do something for me in return for that favor," the chief said.

"If I can."

"Bill Hamilton said that you mentioned selling the Candlelight Inn. Is that right?"

Joe nodded, "Yes, I don't want it."

"I would like for you to wait a while before you do," he said. "Some shady business is going on at the auto repair shop next to it, and we are on the verge of cracking the case wide open."

"What has that got to do with the Inn?" Joe asked.

"The bozos that run the shop rent that back room for card games, and that's where they do a lot of their business."

"I don't want to get involved in any trouble," Joe said. "I just recovered from the war and can't handle anymore problems."

"We don't want you to do anything," he replied. "Our own undercover man is on the job. You don't even have to be there. Dan had good help, and they've been taking care of the Inn since he died. He mostly just greeted folks and sometimes tended bar."

"Sounds like him," Joe said bitterly. "Passing the work off to someone else."

"He didn't know about the crooked business going on under his nose. I wouldn't have told you, but I was afraid you would offer it for sale. Don't want a bunch of people poking around out there looking it over. It might interfere with our catching these guys red-handed."

"I won't put it up for sale until I go back to college this fall. Will that help?"

"Yeah, I think we can close in on them by that time."

"The bar isn't doing anything illegal, is it?"

"Naw, just selling a little illegal spirits besides the legal 3.2 beer. We turn a blind eye to that as long as it isn't the homemade stuff. That bunch in the back room gamble, but I'm letting that go for bigger fish. By the way, that Mitchell boy works at the garage. Doesn't know anything about their real business, though."

"Do you mean that little kid, Johnny?"

"Yeah, he's sixteen and wants to be a mechanic. I've tried to warn Sam in a roundabout way, but he doesn't understand meanness in a small town like Oak Grove. They buy equipment from him and pay cash, so he thinks they're okay."

The clock struck eight-thirty as the chief left. Joe decided to see if the Mitchells were home. It was Wednesday night, but prayer meeting and choir practice should be over by now. He put on a light jacket and walked the short distance to their house.

When he arrived he saw two cars in their drive. One was a red Chevrolet convertible and the other was an older Buick.

"Company or not," he said to himself, "I'm going in."

He rang the bell, and a blond youth opened the door.

"Hello, Johnny," he said.

"Joe!" he exclaimed. "Dad, Joe's here!"

Mr. Mitchell sat at the small table where they had played dominoes and checkers many times. A stranger sat opposite him, and chessmen were on the board.

"Come in!" he said, rising hastily to shake his hand and give him a friendly slap on the back. "Meg said you were in town. Was hoping you would come over. Paul, this is our good friend and neighbor, Joe Sullivan. He's the one who rescued Bob from that island in the Pacific. Joe, I want you to meet our pastor, Paul Benton. Brother

Cunningham retired a couple of years ago, and we called Paul to our church."

Paul rose and shook hands with him. His grip was firm, and he smiled into Joe's eyes. They were equal in height, six feet, but Paul was thinner. He had brown hair, a wide forehead, blue eyes, high cheekbones, and a hawk-like nose over a firm mouth. Although his face wasn't exactly handsome, it was attractive, and he had an open, friendly manner. Joe judged him to be in his early thirties.

Maggie came in from the kitchen, followed by Brock Vandenberg. "Hi, Joe," she said. "You remember Brock?"

Joe nodded and shook his hand. "It's been a while."

"We were just making coffee. Would you like some?" Maggie asked.

"I just drank some, but, yeah, I'll have some more."

"Still drink it black?"

"Sure, I'm still a Southwesterner," he said with a grin.

Maggie and Brock disappeared into the kitchen.

"Have a seat, Joe," Mr. Mitchell said.

"I'm afraid I'm interfering with your game," he said.

"We can finish it later," Paul said. "Our games go on all the time. Do you play chess?"

"A little. I learned to play while I was in the marines."

"Paul taught me the game. He comes over after prayer meeting to challenge me. I haven't beaten him yet, but some day I will," Mr. Mitchell said.

"He's improving all the time," Paul said.

"How long have you been out of the marines?" Johnny asked. "Bob's been home a long time."

"I've been out about a year," he replied.

"Why didn't you come home then?" Johnny asked. "We've been looking for you."

Joe was saved from answering by the entrance of Maggie and Brock with a tray of cups and a pot of coffee.

While drinking his coffee and listening to the flow of conversation around him, Joe covertly studied Maggie. The long-legged tomboy with the sun-streaked blonde hair, braces on her teeth, and freckles across her nose was gone. Occasionally there was a glimpse of the darker-haired, vivacious teenager with the bright, dewy, blue eyes that looked expectantly toward the future. This Maggie was a serene, self-confident, beautiful woman who moved with grace and poise. He longed to be as close to this grown-up Maggie as he had been to the young Maggie. Not much chance, though, with the possessive, determined, and very eligible Brock Vandenberg hovering over her.

"They make a beautiful couple," he thought. Maggie looked at him and blushed when she caught his eyes on her.

Joe finished his coffee, got up and stretched, and said, "I've had a long day. I think I'll go home and turn in. Thanks for the coffee. Glad I met you Paul, Brock."

"I called Bob," Mr. Mitchell said. "He and Amy are coming home next weekend. He was excited when I told him you were here."

"I'll be glad to see him," Joe said.

"Come back, and we'll play chess or whatever you like," Mr. Mitchell said.

On the way home Joe thought, "Sure, I'll be back. But it won't be just for chess. I intend to win Maggie's heart!"

Later, as Meg prepared for bed, her thoughts turned to Joe. His face had grown older and harsher and his eyes had a sad, haunted look. That special light that had kindled in them when he looked at her had gone out. He seemed so distant. Did he not love her? For years she had waited for him to come home. She had dreamed of him, longed for his arms to hold her, yearned for his kisses. Why didn't he come home when he was discharged?

Johnny had asked that question. She heard it from the doorway, and saw Joe's look of relief when they entered with the coffee. It saved him from answering.

"Oh, Joe," she thought as she slipped into bed, "I don't know if you love me or not, but I find that I do still love you."

CHAPTER XXVI

Joe slept well that night and awakened Thursday morning to find sunlight flooding his room. He fried bacon and eggs and made toast and coffee for his breakfast. As he finished the meal, a timid knock sounded on the kitchen door. When he opened it, a small middle-aged woman with wispy gray hair and watery blue eyes stood there.

"May I help you?" he inquired.

"My name is Maude Etheridge," she said. "I was housekeeper for your uncle, and I stopped by to see if you needed me."

His first impulse was to say no, but when he looked into her anxious eyes, he couldn't do it.

"Come in," he invited. "What were the arrangements with my uncle?"

"I worked Monday through Friday from ten until two. Mostly I did light housekeeping. Made his bed, fixed his lunch, and did the washing, ironing, sweeping, and dusting as needed. Also I grocery shopped and kept the kitchen cabinets clean and orderly. He paid me ten dollars a week."

Joe looked around. The house was as neat as a pin.

"Those arrangements are okay with me," he said. "It will only be for the summer. I plan to go back to college this fall."

"Thank you," she said gratefully. "Maybe by then I can get another job."

At that moment the telephone rang.

"I'll get it," Joe said. "Go ahead and get started with your work."

It was Bill Hamilton, the lawyer. "Thought I'd check to see if you were still planning to go to the Inn at four," he said.

"Sure. I'll be by for you," Joe replied.

Promptly at four o'clock Joe drove up to the lawyer's office. He had spent the day going through his uncle's papers and the will. Mrs. Etheridge had prepared a delicious lunch. She beamed with pleasure when he told her she would spoil him with meals like that.

Before he could get out of the car to enter the bank building, Mr. Hamilton walked out to meet him.

"Hi, Mr. Hamilton," Joe said. "Hop in."

"Call me Bill," he said. "Follow the highway east of town about half a mile."

When they came to the Candlelight Inn, Joe was surprised. The white frame colonial-style building with gas lights on both sides of the driveway entrance made quite an impression. They pulled into the large paved parking lot and got out

"Wow! I didn't expect this," he exclaimed.

The dimly lit lobby was decorated in an early American style with wall sconces hanging on both sides of a cherry wood reception desk.

The receptionist came forward and said, "Hi, Joe."

"Sally Ray!" he exclaimed. "We graduated from high school together," he explained to Bill.

"It isn't Ray anymore," she said. "It's Bradford. Come meet my husband, Mel. He's the bartender."

In the barroom to the left of the lobby, a large blond man was wiping the counter with a wet rag. As they approached, he smiled and came around from behind the bar to shake hands with them.

"Hi, Boss," he said. "I've heard a lot about you from your uncle and my wife."

"All good, I hope."

"As a matter of fact, it was."

"You aren't from around here, are you?"

"No. I met Sally in the service. She was in the WACs, and we were stationed at the same army base. My home was in New Jersey, but we moved here to be near Sally's family. I'd rather live in a small town anyway."

"Let me show you the rest of the Inn," Bill said.

"Okay. See you later, Mel."

"The door behind the reception desk opens to the coat room," Bill said, "and the wide door on the right leads to the dining area."

Inside the dining room, Joe observed heavy rose-colored drapes hung over wide windows along the outside walls. Matching rose-colored candles enclosed in glass chimneys decorated each white covered table. At the far end of the room, a circular dance floor skirted a small bandstand.

Swinging doors on the inside wall led to the kitchen, situated directly behind the barroom. The chef and cooks were busy preparing the food. Bill introduced Joe to them, and then took him back into the dining area. Near the bandstand another door led into a hallway, with rest rooms and a dressing room on the inner side. Across from the dressing room, doors led to two rooms on the back side of the building. As Bill opened the door on the left, they walked into a game room with a round poker table, several chairs, and a cabinet that contained cards, poker chips, and other games. There was one window on the left side of the room but no outside door.

The other door opened into an office. It contained a large roll-top desk, a file cabinet, and two chairs. A door on the right side of the room led outside to the parking lot.

"Dan had that door put in so he could come and go easily," Bill said. "The Inn is closed on Mondays and on Monday evenings the bookkeeper, Ed Clifford, comes out here and takes care of the week's accounts. If you want to meet him here Monday to go over the books, I'll let him know you're coming. His office is in the same building as mine."

"Thanks. That'll be great," Joe said.

"We had better go now. I have a few more things to do at my office, and by the time I get through, my wife will have supper ready. She frowns on my being late."

Sally was placing napkins, silverware, and glasses on the tables when they came back through the dining area.

"I'll be back for dinner," Joe told her.

CHAPTER XXVII

At seven-fifteen that evening, Joe walked into the restaurant. An auburn-haired girl accompanied by a small band was singing. Most of the tables were full. Sally led him to a table near the band, handed him a menu, and said, "The waitress will be with you shortly, Joe."

A pretty young waitress brought him a glass of water and asked him if he would like anything else to drink.

"Iced tea," he said.

As he examined the menu, Sally walked by with three people. "Hello again."

Joe glanced up and saw Sylvia and her parents. He stood up and shook hands with Mr. Ashley and smiled at Mrs. Ashley.

"Will you join me?" he invited.

"Be glad to," Mr. Ashley said, and pulled out a chair for his wife. Joe pulled out one for Sylvia.

Mr. Ashley was a large florid man and his wife was a thin sharp-faced woman. "Sylvia will look like her one day," Joe thought.

"The steaks are great here," Mr. Ashley informed Joe.

"Sounds good," Joe said.

So the men ordered steak dinners, and the women ordered roast chicken.

"All the food here is excellent," Mr. Ashley said. "We come here often. Do you plan to stay in Oak Grove and manage it?"

"Just for the summer," he replied. "In the fall I plan to go back to school and will probably sell it."

"I wish Sylvia would move back here to stay," her mother said. "I worry about her living in Chicago."

"Oh, Mother, there's no place to work here that requires anything but endurance," Sylvia said. "I like the excitement of Chicago and the challenge of a job that takes more than muscle. I can use my intellect and advance as far as I'm willing to apply myself."

"Humph," Mrs. Ashley said. "You ought to apply yourself to marriage and rearing children, and leave that type of work to men."

"You're still living in the Dark Ages, Mother," Sylvia complained. "Women have more freedom today."

Mrs. Ashley opened her mouth to say something more, but was interrupted by the arrival of the waitress with the salads.

After they finished eating the delicious meal, Joe asked Sylvia to dance. She readily agreed, and they joined the few people on the dance floor.

"You dance well," she said.

"Thanks. You make me look good because you follow so easily."

When they returned to the table, Joe asked Mrs. Ashley to dance.

"Guess that means I must dance with my daughter," Mr. Ashley grumbled good-naturedly.

"I see where Sylvia gets her grace," Joe said as they glided across the floor to the strains of "Sentimental Journey."

Mrs. Ashley looked at him archly and said, "I see you have learned how to please the ladies."

Before the evening ended the Ashleys invited Joe to have dinner with them the following night.

At ten o'clock Mr. Ashley stated it was his bedtime and ushered his family out.

Joe went to the bar and ordered a beer.

"We have something stronger under the counter," Mel said with a grin. "The cops look the other way."

"So I heard, but this is enough for me tonight."

"Hello there."

Joe turned around and looked into a pair of beautiful brown almond-shaped eyes. The light caught a reddish glint in them that matched her auburn hair. It was the singer, Annie Graves. Under the heavy make-up, he could tell that she was older than she had appeared from across the room.

"Since we haven't met, I'll make the introductions," she said. "I'm Annie Graves, and I sing with this so-called band. You are Joe Sullivan, hero, long-time absent nephew, and present owner of this elegant restaurant. Right?"

"Everything except the hero part," he replied, holding out his hand.

Instead of shaking it, she took it in both of hers and said, "I hope you're as generous and kind as your uncle was."

"That depends on how generous and kind he was," Joe replied.

"He tried hard."

"I don't doubt it."

"For a start, would you buy me a drink?"

Joe signaled to Mel. "Give the lady what she wants."

"The usual," she told Mel. Turning back to Joe she asked, "How long have you been gone from this metropolis?"

"Since January of '42. How long have you been here?"

"Fourteen months too long," she replied.

Mel set a martini with an olive in it in front of her. She picked it up and sipped it. "I think I'm going to like you much better than your uncle."

Four well-dressed men passed the door. Joe noticed her eyes flicking over to them. She tossed down the rest of her drink, plopped the olive in her mouth, and said, "Gotta go. Need to get ready for my next number."

Joe had the feeling she didn't want them to see her talking to him. However, they didn't come into the bar, but headed into the restaurant. A few minutes later the phone rang. Mel answered it and then turned to Joe and said, "The guys from the garage next door are in the game room and want their bottle of booze. Want to meet them?"

"Might as well." He finished his beer and set the bottle on the counter before turning to follow Mel to the back room.

One of the men was getting cards and poker chips out of the cabinet as they entered. All of them turned and stared at Joe.

"This is Joe Sullivan, the new owner," Mel said as he set the tray with the bottle and glasses on a side table.

The man with the cards and chips set them on the game table before turning and shaking hands with him. "I'm Cal Blaine," he said. "Glad to meetcha." He was a large, flabby man with close-set blue eyes that were nearly lost in mounds of fat. His voice was surprisingly high pitched for a man of his size, and his plump hand was soft and limp.

"This is my partner, Jack Phillips," Cal said, indicating a small, slender olive-skinned man with slick black hair and black eyes that bore into Joe's gray ones. He didn't offer to shake hands, only nodded in acknowledgment of the introduction, and said, "We've been renting this room from Dan for quite a while and would like to keep the same arrangements."

Joe shrugged and said, "It's okay by me."

"These men are out-of-town business acquaintances of ours," Cal said. "Mr. Henniger and Mr. Walker."

They also merely nodded to him. In spite of the expensive suits they wore, they appeared tough.

"The chief's right," Joe thought, "they're up to no good." He would certainly leave them alone and let the police handle them. The war had given him enough trouble to last a lifetime.

CHAPTER XXVIII

On Friday morning Joe unpacked his books and took them into the den to study. By afternoon he was bored and decided to go to town to play pool. When he got there the usual bunch of "good old boys" were gathered at one end of the room playing on a couple of tables. At the other end an unusual sight in this previously all-male domain met him. Annie Graves, in shorts and a tight blouse, played at a table by herself. She looked up and saw Joe.

"Come play a game with me, Joe," she said. "These pantywaists are afraid I'll beat them."

"Women ain't allowed in here," one of the men growled and the rest started grumbling and agreeing with him.

"Now, boys, there's no law agin' it," said Matt Bailey, the man who had bought the saloon from Dan O'Brien. "I checked with the chief, and that's what he said, and I have to abide by it. Don't want no trouble with the law."

Joe winked at Annie and said, "Since all the tables are full, I guess I'll have to play with her."

She was good. He was hard pressed to beat her, but he wasn't about to let her best him in front of the other men.

After three games, she said she had to rest up for her performance that evening.

On the way out she linked her arm through Joe's and waved at the men. "Now that I let you beat me, maybe one of these guys will be brave enough to join me in a game," she called out with a mischievous grin and then added, "Are you coming to the Inn tonight, Joe?"

"Not tonight," he said. "I have another engagement. You played well. I bet you could beat half of those guys."

"I know I could. I've watched them play."

They were both laughing as they stepped outside on the sidewalk. Joe glanced up and saw Maggie! She had just come out of the hardware store next door. The shocked expression on her face made him conscious of Annie's skimpy attire and his closeness to her.

"Maggie–" Joe began.

"Hello," Maggie said and hurried on to her car.

Annie gave Joe a roguish grin and said, "Uh oh. Is that the girl friend? The next time I see her I'll explain to her that we just had an innocent game of pool."

"Don't bother, please," Joe said.

After he left Annie at her car, he walked down to the Main Street Café. Chief Bundy was about to enter the door.

"Come in, and I'll buy you a cuppa coffee," he said.

"Okay," Joe agreed.

After the waitress brought their coffee, the chief asked "What did you think of the Inn?"

"Very impressive," he said. "I was surprised."

"Did you meet your neighbors?"

"Yeah. Don't think much of them. Tough-looking bunch."

"You're right. I'm going to run them out of town or into jail as soon as I get my proof. Want you to stay out of it, though. My man is on the job."

"That singer, Annie Graves, is a looker. Does she have anything to do with them?"

"She's that dark, greasy little guy's girl. You don't want to mess with her. I hear he's the jealous type."

"He looks like the type who might carry a knife and not mind using it."

"I agree," the chief said.

That evening after a bath and a shave, Joe headed for the Ashleys'. Mr. Ashley owned the largest grocery store in Oak Grove, and the family lived in a large white house in the best part of town.

After a good dinner, Mr. Ashley suggested a game of cards. Mrs. Hadley, Sylvia's grandmother, had been dozing in her wheelchair, but at the mention of cards her eyes flew open and she eagerly rolled up to the table. While the others played Hearts, Mrs. Ashley knitted.

They played several hands with Mrs. Hadley winning most of them. When the clock struck ten, Joe said he had better go home and let them get to bed.

Before he left Joe took hold of Mrs. Hadley's hand and said, "You're a very sharp woman. I admire your skill."

"You gave me a lot of competition," she said. "Come back and we'll play again."

Sylvia accompanied him to the door and said, "There's a band concert in the park Saturday evening."

"Haven't been to one in a long time," Joe said. "Do you wanna go?"

"Yes," she said. "It starts at seven."

On the way home, Joe thought, "Sylvia trapped me into that one. I wish it was Maggie going with me."

CHAPTER XXIX

After breakfast on Saturday, Joe decided to inspect his old garden plot. Only weeds remained there.

"That's what I can do this summer," he thought. "Plant a late vegetable garden."

The old shed where the garden tools were kept had been torn down and he couldn't find any of them, so he went to town to buy some. He had forgotten how crowded the town was on Saturdays. Farmers and townspeople alike did most of their shopping on that day. Not only was it the end of the work week, but payday fell on Friday for nearly all the businesses around Oak Grove. He finally found a parking space a block from the hardware store.

Memories flooded his mind as he walked by the old stores: the five-and-ten where he had bought his Aunt Peg Christmas presents with his meager funds, Ashley's grocery store where he had helped her shop, and next to it, the barber shop where he had gotten his hair cut. As he passed the saloon and pool parlor he was thankful that his uncle had sold it. He would not have wanted to be saddled with it.

How he had hated his uncle! Especially the night he had come upon him hugging and kissing Maggie! He had been outraged at what he saw and was glad he had knocked him down. And then a frightened Maggie had thrown herself into his arms. How soft and trusting she had seemed as she had clung to him. He was ashamed of himself because he had not been able to resist the urge to kiss her with all the love he felt for her. She had returned the kiss with a passion that had surprised him. Before he left he had extracted a promise from her to wait for him. She hadn't even been sixteen at the time!

After receiving his overseas orders, he realized how selfish he had been. She was too young to sit at home and wait for him. How did he know if he would make it through the war? At her age she should be dating, going to parties and having a good time. It had been hard to write that letter releasing her from her promise. Harder still was knowing he had hurt her. She had never written to him again, and he had missed her letters. He shook the thoughts from his mind and entered the hardware store.

"May I help you?"

Joe turned from a seasonal display of tools at the front of the store and looked into the colorless face of a woman of uncertain age. Her brown hair was pulled back severely into a bun at the nape of her neck, and a pair of black-rimmed glasses covered her brown eyes.

"I need a few garden supplies. Rake, hoe, spade, seed, and fertilizer. You can tell I'm starting from scratch," he said with a smile.

"This way, please," she said leading him to the back of the store. In a middle aisle they came upon Maggie talking to a young red-headed man in mechanic's coveralls.

Joe said, "Hi, Maggie."

Maggie turned and saw him. "Hello, Joe. What are you doing here?"

"I don't have much to do this summer, so thought I'd plant a garden. Couldn't find my old tools. Guess Dan got rid of everything that resembled work."

The clerk had come back to where Joe had stopped.

"Alice, I want you to meet a good friend of our family, Joe Sullivan. Alice Waverly is our bookkeeper and clerk," Maggie said. "And, Joe, this is Alex Davis, chief mechanic in the shop where Johnny works. It's out by the Candlelight Inn."

"Glad to meetcha," Alex said, offering a large, callused hand.

Although Joe was suspicious of anyone working at that shop, he couldn't help but respond to the young man's friendly smile and warm handshake. Under his bushy red eyebrows a pair of blue eyes twinkled. He had a nose that appeared to have been broken at one time, and a wide mouth over a strong cleft chin. His short red hair was thick and curly.

"I better get back to work. Call me when that order comes in, Meg," Alex said. "Don't worry about Johnny. He has a natural aptitude for mechanics. See you around, Joe."

"I heard that Johnny worked at the auto shop next to the Inn. Does he like it there?" Joe asked Meg.

"Yes, he seems to. He wants to be a mechanic, and Alex is teaching him," she replied and turned to wait on another customer.

Joe followed Alice to the garden tools section. "Maggie must be upset with me," he thought. "She's cold and distant."

Mr. Mitchell appeared at the door of his office, saying, "Alice, did we order that–Joe! Come in here and visit a while."

Joe went into the cozy office with the battered roll-top desk, two chairs, and file cabinets.

"Looks just like I remember it," he said.

"Nothing has changed except a few more papers stuffed in the file cabinets," Mr. Mitchell replied. "Even have a high school student coming in to sweep up like you and Bob did."

"Johnny doesn't want to work here, I take it?"

"He would sooner work on cars. I'd rather he wasn't out there. Clem offered him a job in his garage in town, but he says they pay better there. The main reason, I think, is Alex. Johnny thinks he's the greatest."

"Alex seems a likable guy."

"That he is and a very good mechanic. Wish he worked for Clem. So how have you found things? Have you decided to stay?"

"Only for the summer. I'm going back to A and M this fall. My plans are to teach history and coach football."

"What about the Candlelight Inn?"

"I'll keep it a while."

Mr. Mitchell looked disappointed. Joe felt guilty. He knew that Mr. Mitchell was a strong Christian and a Baptist deacon who didn't believe in dancing or drinking alcoholic beverages. But if keeping the Inn open would help get rid of that gang and keep Johnny out of trouble, it would be worth it to Joe.

"Mr. Mitchell, I'm sorry if I upset you," he said.

"Isn't it about time you called me 'Sam'? We are both men now. You are old enough to know your own mind, and no matter if we agree or disagree on anything, we're still good friends."

"Thank you, Sam," he said. "It feels right to call you that. I'm grateful for everything you've done for me in the past and am proud to be your friend."

"If you aren't busy tonight, how 'bout coming over for a game of chess?"

Maggie had come into the office and looked questioningly at him.

"I'm sorry, but I've made other plans for the evening," he replied. "Give me a rain check on that offer."

Later at home he wished he hadn't gotten trapped into taking Sylvia to the band concert. Sam had been disappointed, and Maggie had shut him out.

He would have liked to explain to Maggie about Annie. What could he have said, though? Now he was going to the band concert with Sylvia when he would rather be with Maggie. How had his life become so complicated?

At six-forty-five, Joe rang the doorbell at the Ashley house. Mrs. Ashley opened the door and invited him in. Just as he stepped into the entrance hall, Sylvia came down the stairs.

"I'm ready. Are you surprised?"

"No. I thought you were the type to be on time and not keep a fellow waiting. You look nice."

"Thanks," she said. She had on a soft green dress and wore white sandals with hose. Her hair fluffed out around her face, and her make-up was flawless.

"Bye. Have a good time," Mrs. Ashley said.

They said good-bye and Joe followed Sylvia outside.

"I have my car here, or would you rather walk?" he asked.

"It's a beautiful evening and the park is near. Let's walk," she said. "In fact, everything is close in this town."

Joe offered her his arm as they made their way to the park. Others walked also and everyone greeted them and said they were glad to see them back. The band tuned their instruments in the gazebo as the crowd gathered. Joe and Sylvia found an empty bench and sat back to enjoy the music.

The first number, a Sousa march, was nearly over when Maggie and Brock came by. Maggie looked charming in a navy blue sailor dress and white sandals. Brock wore a navy blue sport coat, white open-collar shirt, and white trousers. Joe felt dowdy in his khaki shirt and trousers.

"Hi," Sylvia called out. "Want to share our bench?"

"Don't mind if we do," Brock replied.

Joe stood up as Maggie seated herself next to Sylvia. They sat quietly and listened to the music until the band took a break, and then Brock asked if they would like some lemonade.

"There's a stand on the other side of the park," he explained to

Joe.

"Lemonade sounds good," Sylvia said.

"I'd like some, too," Maggie added. So Brock and Joe went off in search of refreshments. When they returned, Maggie and Sylvia sat chatting about mutual friends.

"I'm glad Bob and Amy will be here next weekend," Sylvia said. "We must have a party for them."

When Joe walked Sylvia home after the concert, she asked him if he were going to church the next day.

"Hadn't thought about it," he said.

"We would like for you to go with us and eat dinner here," she said.

"That would be too much work for your mother."

"She loves to cook and told me to invite you."

"Okay. I really enjoyed her good home cooking."

The telephone was ringing when Joe entered his house. It was Ed Clifford. "I'll be at the Inn Monday evening at seven," he said. "If you'll come about eight, I'll go over the books with you."

Joe put on a small pot of coffee. While it perked he sat at the table and thought about the evening. Maggie still distanced herself from him. How could he get her to open up to him? He wished she was as friendly as Sylvia. Sylvia seemed glad for his company. But then there weren't many young people her age in town. Maggie worked days and Brock followed her around evenings and weekends.

"I have all summer to win Maggie back," he thought, "but things don't seem to be going very smoothly."

CHAPTER XXX

At ten-thirty the next morning Joe rang the bell at Sylvia's house. He wore his only suit with a dress shirt and a tie. Sylvia opened the door and let him in.

"I just have to put my hat on and get my purse," she said. "My parents and grandmother left earlier. They always attend Sunday School."

The sun shone brightly as they walked the few blocks to the Methodist church. Others also walked, calling out cheerful greetings as they met their friends.

"How can you bear to live in Chicago when small towns are so much friendlier?" he asked.

"My apartment is in a little neighborhood where there are small shops, delis, and markets. It's almost like a small town. You get to know your neighbors and the shopkeepers, but not too well, unless you want to. They don't know everything about you like in a small town."

As they arrived at the little, white stone church with a picturesque steeple, the bell began to toll. Sunday School ended, and small children spilled out into the sunshine. They painted a charming picture playing on the green lawn in their colorful clothes.

A friendly usher greeted them as they entered the wooden doors, and he seated them in the middle on the left side of the auditorium. Soft organ music filled the air.

"This is where my parents always sit," Sylvia whispered. "Pews aren't assigned, but everyone sits in the same place every Sunday."

"It would probably confuse the ushers and the preacher if the congregation changed places one Sunday," Joe whispered.

"They wouldn't know who was whom," she laughed.

"What's so funny?" Mrs. Hadley asked as her wheelchair stopped next to their pew. Since she was hard of hearing, she spoke loudly and people turned and looked at them.

Sylvia leaned across Joe and said, "We wondered what would happen if people sat in different pews from their usual ones."

"Humph," was all she said.

Mr. and Mrs. Ashley entered, and Sylvia and Joe scooted down to make room for them. The choir filed in, and conversations ceased as people got ready for the worship service.

Bright sunlight filtered through the stained glass windows, casting a rosy glow over the auditorium. Joe settled into the cushioned seat and thought of the hard wooden pews at the Baptist church. The windows there were plain glass, and the only color was the background painting in the baptistry behind the choir loft. It depicted a stream meandering through a wooded area.

While growing up, he had attended the Baptist church occasionally with the Mitchell family. The only time he had gone to the Methodist church was when he had dated Methodist girls.

Joe enjoyed the music and the singing. He also liked the sermon on the Christian life. "The world would be a wonderful place if people really lived that way," he thought. The preacher didn't raise his voice or pace as Brother Cunningham had done.

As they walked home the Mitchell's car passed them. They were returning from the Baptist church and Johnny was driving. He honked and waved at them. Sam sat beside him but no one was in the back seat. The next car to pass was a red convertible with the top down. Brock was driving and Maggie sat beside him. She smiled and waved.

After dinner Sylvia said, "Nothing goes on in this town on Sunday afternoon. Mother plans to make some ice cream. If it's okay with you, I'll call Meg and invite her and Brock over. You and Brock can turn the crank."

"Sounds like a good idea," he said.

Sylvia called Maggie on the phone and then turned to Joe and said, "They'll be here at two."

"Would you go to the ice dock and get some crushed ice, Joe?" Mrs. Ashley asked.

"Sure. Come on, Sylvia," he invited.

At two o'clock Brock and Maggie drove up. Brock wore casual slacks and an open-collar shirt, and Maggie looked lovely in a blue cotton dress with a full skirt. Sylvia had changed into pink slacks and a matching pink print blouse. Joe hadn't gone home to change, but had shed his coat and tie and rolled up his sleeves.

"Your time to turn the freezer handle," Joe told Brock with a smile. "It's nearly done."

"Glad to," Brock said good-naturedly.

When it was firm, Mrs. Ashley placed a thick towel over it.

"Why don't you young people play croquet while it sets," she suggested.

Sylvia picked the pink striped mallet and ball to match her outfit, so Maggie took the blue. Joe chose the green and Brock the yellow.

Joe played politely until Maggie's ball hit his at the third wicket. With great glee, she put her foot on her ball and hit it hard with her mallet, knocking his far away. After that they all played ferociously with much whooping and laughter until Mrs. Ashley called them in to eat the ice cream.

They sat comfortably in lawn chairs and talked while they ate. Joe smiled to himself, thinking Maggie hadn't changed that much after all. Underneath the polished exterior, existed the little tomboy he once knew so well. Brock was no match for her. He didn't have her fire and spirit, and Joe knew in his heart that she didn't love Brock. "But how does she feel about me?" he wondered.

Suddenly Maggie looked at her watch and said, "Sorry to eat and run, but I have to get ready for church. Thank you for inviting me. The ice cream was delicious, and the game was fun, even though it brought out the viciousness of some people."

"I can't decide who was the fiercest," Sylvia said.

"We all were," Brock said and added his thanks.

Joe stayed a little longer and then took his leave.

At home Joe's thoughts turned to Maggie. The more time he spent with her, the more attracted he was to her.

"I must get her alone and find out how she feels about me," he thought.

CHAPTER XXXI

Joe was up early on Monday morning to start his garden. He spaded the ground and added fertilizer. By the time he finished, Mrs. Etheridge called him in for lunch.

After he ate, he returned immediately to the garden to plant seeds and water. When the ground was well soaked, he went in to shower and shave. In the mirror he examined the scars on his bare chest. "I'll never be able to take my shirt off in public," he thought.

At five o'clock he walked to town to eat dinner. The day was beautiful, and he was glad for the chance to stretch his legs after all the bending and stooping he had done.

He had a good meal at the Main Street Café with the same tired waitress serving him. When she smiled at him, some of her fatigue seemed to vanish. Again he left a generous tip.

It was too early to go to the Inn, so he walked over to the pool hall. He looked around, but Annie wasn't there.

"Lookin' for your girl friend?" A grizzled old man said, and they all laughed.

"Don't see her. Guess I'll have to play with one of you," he said with a grin. "Who's ready to get beaten?"

After a couple of games, he left to walk to the Inn. A light shone from the office window. He knocked on the door. Ed Clifford let him in and introduced himself. Ed was a tall, rangy man with thick glasses and thin hair.

"Am I too early, Mr. Clifford?" Joe asked.

"Call me Ed," he said. "I'm just finishing. Have a seat."

Joe watched him as he recorded figures in a large ledger spread out before him.

"A profitable week," he said. He leaned back in his chair and stretched. "I didn't hear you drive up."

"I walked," Joe said. "That's the way I get my exercise."

They went over the books, and Joe decided that Ed was efficient and honest. When they finished, Ed offered him a ride to town, but Joe declined. He wanted to familiarize himself with the books a little better. He pored over the records until he got sleepy, and, closing the books, he switched off the desk lamp and leaned back in the chair with his eyes closed.

Thoughts of Maggie crowded into his mind. How attractive she was! She possessed more than physical beauty, although she certainly had that. Maggie glowed from within. She reminded him of her mother, who had displayed those same qualities. After their time together Sunday, he had decided she didn't love Brock, even though he seemed smitten with her.

He felt that she didn't show any partiality for him either. Had he hurt her so terribly with that letter, that foolish letter? On the other hand, maybe she hadn't loved him as he had loved her. Was there any hope?

He couldn't remember when he hadn't loved Maggie. When he first came to Oak Grove to live with his aunt and uncle, she had reminded him of his little sister, Callie, whom he had so recently lost. Granted, Maggie was as fair as his sister was dark, but they were nearly the same age. Callie had their mother's doe-like brown eyes and stiff black hair. She had been his only playmate most of the time. The sparsely settled area where they had lived, and the little country school they had attended, had few children.

Bob had objected to Maggie following them around, but he hadn't minded. To get away from her, Bob played many tricks on her or bluntly told her to get lost. Even though she was disappointed or hurt, she never cried. Joe had admired her defiant spirit.

"Enough of this reminiscing," he thought. "I'd better start for home. It'll be a long dark walk."

Before he could get out of the chair, he heard voices echo through the Inn. He sat back down when he heard an unfamiliar voice say, "Are you certain this is a safe place to discuss our business?"

"Sure." It was the voice of Jack Phillips. "No one's here on Monday nights after the accountant leaves. It was nice of ole Dan to give us a key."

"Yeah, we come here frequently on Monday nights to play poker," Cal Blaine said in his high-pitched voice.

"Business first," said the stranger as they entered the room next to the office. "And then we'll play poker."

Joe decided to sit quietly and listen to their business. He could hear them plainly through the thin walls.

They discussed how many cars they could expect and from where they were coming. Jack told the new man how many had been finished and shipped out. Joe wrote it all down on a piece of paper. He didn't know if it would be useful to the chief, but thought it wouldn't hurt.

"The boss is coming soon," the stranger said. "He wants to see this setup and how things are going."

"We'll be ready," Jack said. "Now let's play poker."

After they started playing, Joe got up to leave by the side door. As he pulled the door to, it squeaked slightly.

"What's that noise?" the stranger asked.

"I'll find out," Cal said.

As Joe hurriedly locked the outer door, he heard Cal rattling the locked inner office door. He sprinted across the parking lot while Cal ran through the Inn to the front door. Fortunately, the game room didn't have an outside door.

A large elm tree grew near the edge of the parking lot and Joe scrambled up into its sheltering branches. Cal walked around the parking lot and stood under the tree. Joe held his breath, but Cal never looked up.

The others came out and called to him.

"Nothing out here," he said.

"It must have been a mouse or a squirrel," Jack said. "Let's get back to the game."

Joe stayed where he was for a few more minutes and then swung down. He walked on the side of the road leading into town. When he reached the Baptist church, he saw car lights coming from the direction of the Inn. The doors of the church were unlocked, so he slipped through them while the car passed. He breathed a sigh of relief.

"May I help you?" Joe whirled around to face the pastor, Paul Benton.

"Hello, Paul. I was walking home from the Inn and thought I'd step in here to rest," he said lamely.

"Come into my office and rest, Joe. I like company," Paul said.

Joe followed him into the office. Well-filled bookcases lined the walls. The large desk top was covered with papers, books, and a Bible. A reading lamp shed light on an open book, and the desk chair was pushed back as if hastily vacated. Behind the desk, woven drapes covered a large window. Two comfortable leather chairs with a lamp on a table between them faced the desk. In a corner was a small table containing a coffee pot and several cups. Joe sat in one of the chairs.

"I just made a pot of coffee. Would you care for a cup?"

"Yes, thanks. Black."

Paul poured two cups of coffee and set them on the lamp table. He turned on the lamp and sat in the other chair.

Joe sipped the coffee and said, "Nice office."

"Thanks. The ladies of the church fixed it up for me. It's very comfortable."

They drank their coffee in companionable silence for a few minutes, and then Paul asked, "How long have you been out of the service?"

"About a year. I spent the last two years of my enlistment time in the hospital."

"Are you okay now?"

"Yeah, I'm fine now. Were you in the service?"

A brooding look came over Paul's face. "Yes. I was a chaplain in the navy. I was discharged in '46. Came here a few months later when Reverend Cunningham retired."

"You're not married?" Joe asked. "Never mind. None of my business. Shouldn't have asked."

"It's okay," Paul replied. "I was married. My wife died from complications of pregnancy. Lost the baby, also. I was at sea and couldn't be with her," he added sadly.

"That's too bad," Joe said. He looked down at his cup. He felt sorry for Paul. It must have been tough not being able to be there. What helplessness and grief he must have experienced. Words were inadequate, so he remained silent.

"Only my faith in Jesus Christ pulled me through. Are you a Christian, Joe?"

The unexpected question surprised Joe. "No. I've never gone to church much," he replied. "The Mitchells asked me to go with them every Sunday. Sometimes I did." He smiled ruefully. "I'm not good enough to be a Christian."

"If one had to be good enough, there would be no Christians,"

Paul said. "That's the wonderful thing about it. God loves us so much that He sent His only Son to die on the cross for us. He took all our sins away. Whoever believes on Him has eternal life. Do you believe that, Joe?"

Joe looked down and shook his head, "Haven't thought about it," he said. "I'm too much of a sinner."

"God is ready to forgive your sins. All you have to do is ask Him and then turn from them."

"You don't know how bad I've been. I can't change."

"Let me tell you a true story about two teenage boys who were so wild that they had a rough reputation in the small town where they lived. One night they got drunk on bootleg liquor, stole a car, and wrapped it around a bridge abutment. One of them was in a coma and not expected to live." He paused for a moment. "That driver was me, and the boy in the coma was my younger brother."

Joe sat in shocked silence.

Paul continued, "In the hospital I was so guilt-ridden that I wanted to die. It was the first time I had ever prayed, and I prayed to die. My parents were so upset that they wouldn't come to see me. I felt alone and unloved.

"My left leg was fractured and in traction, and my right arm was in a sling. I had a lot of physical discomfort with cuts and bruises, but the pain in my heart was the worst. I gave the doctors and nurses a hard time."

He paused with a faraway look in his eyes. "The hospital chaplain didn't give up on me. No matter how rude I was to him, he visited me every day and prayed for me. He told me that God loved me unconditionally. I didn't believe him at first. How could a perfect God love a person like me?"

Joe nodded his head in sympathy and understanding.

"He read Scripture to me and told me that God loved me so much that He sent his only Son, Jesus, to die on the cross for my sins. Soon I started listening to him and looking forward to his visits. I figured he must love me because he kept coming no matter how mean I was to him. Gradually, I felt God's love through the chaplain and it covered me like a warm blanket. One night I cried out for God's forgiveness, and He heard me! A great peace came over me. I was a new person. Everyone noticed the change in me and would ask me what had happened. I would tell them about Jesus and what He had done for me. Several accepted Christ through my words, and the Christians rejoiced with me."

Paul's eyes were alight and his face glowed.

"When my parents came to take me home, they couldn't believe I was the same son that had caused them so much pain and heartbreak. They weren't Christians, but when they saw the change in me, they accepted Christ. My brother finally regained consciousness, but it took months of therapy for him to overcome the brain damage. He does well now but still has residual weakness in his body. I'll always carry that sorrow with me. God has forgiven me, but it has been hard for me to forgive myself. However, Gary also became a Christian and doesn't hold the accident against me."

"Did you have to go to prison for stealing and wrecking the car?"

"No. I received a suspended sentence, and after three years it was erased from my record."

"That's good. You wouldn't have been able to go into the navy with a record. How did you become a preacher?"

"I was seventeen at the time, and when I returned to school I began to study in earnest. The teachers were amazed. Soon I felt God calling me to special service. At first I didn't know what His will was for my life, but I prepared myself. Went to college after high school and then to the seminary. God had called me to preach. He doesn't call everyone to full-time service, but He does call everyone to live for Him."

Paul sat in silent thought with his head bent down. Joe sat quietly gazing at the moths flitting around the lamplight.

Finally Paul lifted his head and looked at Joe and said, "No matter what you've done in the past, it can't be worse than what I did. Would you like to ask God's forgiveness and accept His salvation?"

"Not now," Joe replied. "I'll think about it. Better go. Thanks for the coffee. Appreciate your taking time to talk to me. Sorry about your wife and baby...also about your brother. Maybe we could talk again some time."

"You're welcome to come any time. Want a lift home?"

"No, I need to walk. I'll sleep better tonight."

The walk didn't help Joe sleep. He tossed and turned most of the night. He was certain the men at the Inn had been talking about stolen cars. First thing in the morning, he planned to go to town and tell Chief Bundy what he had overheard. He didn't want to phone, since there was no telling who would be listening. The undercover agent might have already told him about the 'Boss' coming soon.

His conversation with Paul troubled him also. It had been a long time since he had thought about God. During the war he had prayed to Him, but he didn't know if God heard him.

When his unit was ambushed and everyone was killed except him, he had given up on God. Why would God let that happen, especially when the war was nearly over? That last unnecessary battle, and the subsequent loss of so many lives entrusted to his care, had bothered Joe more than all the rest of the battles he had been in. At times he had wished he had died with his men. They told him he was more dead than alive when they found him, and his recovery had been long and painful. The dreams of that ambush had plagued him continuously, and he had suffered a nervous breakdown. "Battle fatigue" the psychiatrist had called it, and said it was caused by a culmination of all he had been through during the war. Still he was ashamed of breaking down, and the mental scars bore deeper than the physical ones.

Thoughts of Maggie flickered across his mind. He had dreamed of her while he was in the hospital. Sometimes it had been so real that he thought she was there, and he would wake up disappointed that it was only a dream. After his mental breakdown he had thought he wasn't good enough for her.

How beautiful she had looked in the blue veil that Christmas in 1941, and she had sung like an angel. He would rather have stayed for the reception, but Bob had rushed him off to a party with some of their classmates.

Finally, sleep claimed him and he didn't awaken until Mrs. Etheridge arrived at ten. After breakfast he went to town to find the chief. He was in his office alone, and Joe told him what he had overheard and gave him the paper with the figures on it. The chief hadn't heard that the "Boss" was coming soon.

"They must not have informed my man yet," he said. "This is what we are waiting for. We want to catch the leader of this bunch and then clean up the whole mess."

"Great," Joe said. "Then I can make arrangements to sell the Inn."

"Thanks for telling me this, but you stay out of it."

"Don't worry. It was an accident that I overheard them. Johnny won't be caught in the sweep up, will he?"

"No. We know he's innocent, and we'll make sure he isn't around even if we have to lock him up first."

Joe wasn't convinced that Johnny would be clear of danger. He would stay out of it unless Johnny needed his protection.

CHAPTER XXXII

The ringing of the phone echoed throughout the silent house and aroused Joe from his study. Setting aside his world history book, he moved to answer it.

"Hello, Joe. This is Meg." Joe's heart gave a lurch at the sound of her voice.

"Hi Maggie," he said.

"If you don't have other plans, we'd like for you to come for dinner tonight. Dad says he'll challenge you to a game of chess."

"Sure. What time?"

"We eat at six o'clock. Come earlier if you want."

Joe found concentrating on his book impossible after Maggie's call. Finally, he put it aside and went out to water his garden. By the time he finished it was time to shower and dress.

At 5:45 he knocked on the Mitchells' door. Sam opened it and stuck out his hand to Joe. "Come in, come in," he said. "Dinner is almost ready. Johnny had to work late tonight, but we won't wait for him. Meg prepared your favorites–pork chops, mashed potatoes, gravy, onions, fried okra, and lettuce and tomato salad. For dessert she baked a cherry pie."

"My mouth's watering already," he said.

A few minutes later, Maggie came in, greeted Joe, and announced that dinner was ready. Joe followed Sam into the dining room and they settled around the oval table with Sam at the head. After a prayer of thanks, Maggie passed Joe the platter of pork chops.

"I bet Dad told you what we're having," she said with a smile. "He never could keep a secret."

They were halfway through the meal when Johnny burst in. "Boy, am I hungry! Hope you saved some for me," he said on his way to the bathroom to wash up.

When he returned he loaded his plate and began eating.

"I believe this is Johnny's favorite meal, too," Joe said with a grin, observing the heaping plateful.

"It is, along with everything else Meg prepares," Sam said. "Or, for that matter, what anyone cooks."

"Sorry I'm late," Johnny said. "We got a car in at the last minute. Had to get it ready to be repainted. Don't know why. Looked good to me. Anyway, Alex said the owner didn't like the color. Must have more money than brains."

"Do you get very many cars that need repainting?" Joe asked.

"Yeah, that's what we do mostly. Body work and painting."

"I didn't realize so many cars around here needed repainting," Joe remarked.

"They aren't all from around here," Johnny explained. "Our shop has quite a reputation for quality work at reasonable prices. We get cars from everywhere, even as far as Oklahoma City and Tulsa."

When they finished eating, Maggie started clearing the table.

"Let me help you with the dishes," Joe offered.

"Thanks," she replied, "but Dad has been looking forward to a visit with you. Johnny will help."

Johnny groaned. "I'd rather talk to Joe."

"What do you want to play, chess or dominoes?" Sam asked as they got up from the table.

"Dominoes. My mind is drained after studying all afternoon. I don't feel like concentrating anymore," Joe answered.

Half an hour later, Meg and Johnny came in from the kitchen.

"All done," she said. "Soon as you are finished with that game, Johnny and I challenge you to a game of forty-two."

"Might as well stop now," Sam commented. "Joe's just letting me win."

"Don't know about that," Joe responded. "You're good."

"I'll be Dad's partner," Johnny said. "I know he's better than either one of you."

"If Joe doesn't mind," Maggie said, smiling at him.

Concentrating on the game gave Joe a real challenge with Maggie so near. He glanced at her often. How lovely she was! Her long eyelashes brushed her cheeks as she studied her dominoes, then there was a flash of blue when she looked up. Once she caught his eyes on her, and her face flushed slightly. Too soon ten o'clock came around.

"I'd better go and let you working people get to bed," he said. "The meal was delicious, Maggie."

"How come you call her Maggie?" Johnny asked.

Joe tilted his chair back and reminisced a moment. "When I first met your family, everyone called her Maggie. She's still Maggie to me."

"Then why don't we call you that?" he questioned his sister.

"When I was about ten, I read *Little Women* and one of the sisters in the story was called Meg, short for Margaret. I thought it sounded more dignified than Maggie, so I changed my name."

"You weren't very dignified at ten," Sam said with a laugh. "But you wouldn't answer unless we said 'Meg'– to anyone but Joe, that is."

"Would you rather I call you Meg?" he asked.

"No, Maggie is fine," she said lightly.

"Good. I don't think I could get used to calling you anything but Maggie. Could I take all of you out for dinner to repay you for this wonderful meal?"

"That isn't necessary, Joe. We enjoy having you," Sam said. "Bob and Amy will be here this weekend, so make plans to come over."

"You all come over to my house Saturday evening for a cookout," Joe said. "Dan added a patio with a built-in barbecue pit. Doesn't look like it has ever been used."

"What a great idea!" Maggie exclaimed. "We can invite Brock and Sylvia, if it is okay with you. Amy will want to see Sylvia."

"Of course. The more the merrier. I'll get steaks and have Mrs. Etheridge bake a cake Friday."

"Let's see, I could bring potato salad, baked beans, and slaw," Maggie said. "Since you said the more the merrier, let's invite our pastor, Paul, and Alice. They're both lonely people and I think they would enjoy a cookout."

"Invite as many as you like. There will be plenty of food," Joe said. "Good night. See you Friday, if not before."

After Joe left, Meg gathered the dominoes and placed them in the box. Johnny folded the bridge table and put it in the hall closet before going to bed.

"It was almost like old times having Joe here for supper," Dad said. "There is a sadness about him, though. It's hard for these veterans to come home and take up their lives again. They've been through so much." He paused with a pensive look on his face. "I remember how long it took me to adjust, but your mother patiently helped me get through it."

"Do you think that's why Joe didn't come home sooner?" Meg asked.

"Might be," Dad said. "Well, I'd better get to bed. See you in the morning."

As she brushed her hair that night Meg's thoughts turned to Joe. If he loved her as much as she loved him, he would have rushed home when he was released from the marines. Had he changed and now preferred loose women like Annie? Or intellectuals like Sylvia? Maybe Joe wasn't meant for her after all. But she had felt so sure that Joe would become a Christian and they would someday marry. It must have been only her plan and not God's. A tear slid down her cheek.

"Why do I love him so much, Lord?" she cried out in her heart.

CHAPTER XXXIII

Joe slept well Tuesday night and woke up feeling refreshed. After breakfast he got out his books to study but then the telephone rang. Sylvia was on the other end of the line.

"Joe, a couple of my aunts and uncles are coming to visit us. They usually do while I'm home. Would you like to come over for dinner and meet them?"

"No, I'd just be in the way. You're coming over here Saturday?"

"Wouldn't miss it. They'll be gone by then."

He spent the entire morning studying. After lunch, he walked to town and played pool. Annie wasn't there. When he got home he watered his garden and thought of the long evening ahead. There were leftovers in the refrigerator, but nothing appealed to him. Finally he decided to go to the Inn for supper. With that thought in mind, he bathed and shaved and drove out there.

It was six, and not many customers were there yet. Sally met him with a smile.

"I see you decided to try our food again," she said. "You must have been pleased the first time."

"Yes, it's very good food. Besides I'm bored at home with my own company," he said, returning her smile.

She started to seat him near the band, but he asked for a corner table.

"May I join you?" He looked up from the menu and to see Annie Graves standing at his table.

He stood up and pulled a chair out for her. "Sure. I'm glad for some company tonight," he said.

The waitress brought another menu.

"I think I'll have prime rib with a beer," Joe said. "What would you like, Annie?"

"I'll have the same," she said. "I shouldn't eat such heavy food before I sing, but, heck, I've got to do something different once in a while."

"I agree," he said. "The food is excellent here, also."

"I'm so tired of this town," she said. "Nothing exciting to do. This is as good as it gets, and I'm bored with it."

After the waitress took their order, Joe asked, "Why don't you try your luck somewhere else?"

"Because my boyfriend, Jack, wouldn't like it."

"Couldn't you leave him?"

"In case you haven't heard, he's very possessive of me. He thinks he owns me, and I guess he does."

"This is America. Everybody is free."

"The only way anyone ever leaves Jack is if Jack wants it."

The waitress served their dinner and they enjoyed a time of companionable silence for a while.

"Do you ever come here on Mondays?" Annie suddenly asked.

"The Inn's not open Mondays, is it?"

"No. I just wondered. Something put a scare into Jack. He thinks someone was here last Monday and overheard some of his business dealings."

"Why would he care if they were overheard?"

"I don't know," she said evasively. "He's funny that way."

While they ate Annie told him about her childhood in the slums of Chicago. "I began singing in the children's choir of an inner-city church," she said. "Everyone told me I was good so I thought that was my ticket out of there. At sixteen I left home and began singing in cabarets and nightclubs." She looked down and sighed. "I never reached the top. Then I met Jack. It's been downhill ever since."

"Leave him and try some other place," Joe advised her.

"I can't," she said and sighed again.

The band began tuning up.

"Do you have time for a dance before you go on?" Joe asked.

"Sure, if you don't mind Jack catching us."

"I'm not afraid of Jack."

"Good! A real man around here. Let's dance," she said as the band began playing "Begin the Beguine." She was a good dancer, and Joe enjoyed her grace and ease. On the way back to their table, he saw Sylvia and her relatives being seated. Sylvia waved at him, and he nodded in acknowledgment.

"Hope you don't mind being seen with me by your friends," Annie said.

"Of course not," he replied.

"You probably know most of the people in this town, since you grew up here," she added.

"Not too many. I left as soon as I graduated from high school. My uncle was the local bootlegger and, although a lot of men in this town supported him by buying his goods, they looked down on him. So I had two strikes against me, my uncle and the fact that I was part Indian."

"Well, you are the town hero now."

"Annie, it's time for you to get ready to sing."

Annie looked up, visibly shaken, to see Jack Phillips standing over her with a frown on his face.

"Annie can tell time, and she knows when she needs to leave," Joe said quietly.

"Who asked you to butt in? Mind your own business," Jack snarled.

"As owner of this place, I think it is my business," Joe said mildly.

"I don't like you, and I don't like my girl talking to you," he said and started to pull Annie up by one arm.

"Let go of her," Joe said, rising. His steel gray eyes pierced Jack's black ones as he towered over him.

"You'll be sorry for this," Jack threatened, and letting go of Annie's arm, he abruptly turned away.

"Uh-oh," Annie said. "You're in big trouble now."

"I can handle it."

"It's time for me to get ready to sing. Are you going to stay to hear me?"

"Wouldn't miss it," he replied.

Jack and Cal Blaine were seated at a table next to the bandstand when Annie came out to sing. Her green sequined dress sparkled and her auburn hair shone brightly. Before she took the microphone, she spoke to the band leader, and the band began playing "Temptation." Annie gazed at Joe with smoldering eyes while she sang the song in her husky contralto.

"She's using me to get back at Jack," Joe thought. "It means trouble for me, but I admire her spunk."

Jack sat with his eyes on the floor and a frown on his face. Cal fidgeted nervously.

Annie must have thought she had goaded him enough for her next song was "There I've Said It Again," and she looked at Jack. He kept his eyes on the floor, even when she moved around the audience and ended up on his lap.

As she made her way back to the stage, Joe decided it was time for him to leave. He passed the Ashleys' table and Sylvia grinned mischievously at him. Mr. Ashley nodded but went on talking to an elderly gentleman. The rest of the group seemed too deep in conversation to notice him, except Mrs. Hadley, sitting in her wheelchair. She put out a hand to detain him.

"Joe, isn't it?" she asked loudly.

"Yes," he said taking her hand and smiling into her eyes.

"Come see me and we'll play cards again," she said.

"I'll do that," Joe said.

Before he left, Joe went into the bar to have a beer. He looked around and saw it was empty except for a man sitting at a corner table nursing a drink.

"Hi, boss, what'll you have?" Mel asked cheerfully from behind the bar.

"A beer," Joe said and sat on a bar stool.

A burly man staggered in and sat on the stool next to Joe. "Whiskey," he said.

"Don't you think you've had enough?" Mel asked.

"Give me a drink or I'll bust your face in," he threatened.

"Why don't you go home and sleep it off?" Mel suggested.

The man stood up, grabbed Mel's shirt with his right hand, and drew back his left fist to hit him.

Joe jumped up and grabbed the man's raised arm and said, "You don't want to do that, buddy."

Suddenly the man released Mel's shirt. He swung around and his right fist connected with Joe's face. Joe reeled from the blow. His teeth cut into his lip. Blood spurted from his nose and lip and ran down his chin. The unexpected maneuver caused Joe to let go of the man. With his freed left arm he promptly punched Joe in the abdomen. Caught unaware, Joe doubled up with pain and hit the floor.

Mel leaped over the bar and pinned both of the drunk's arms behind him. "You're outta here," he said and pushed him toward the door.

The customer from the corner table came forward quickly and said, "I know him. I'll take him home."

Mel held him until he got him out of the front door, and then released him to his friend.

Joe looked up into a sea of concerned faces. A group of patrons about to leave had witnessed the fight. Someone helped him up, while another one gave him a paper napkin from the bar.

Joe pressed the napkin to his nose. "Thank you," he mumbled. "I'm okay."

Mel returned and told them he would take care of Joe, so they reluctantly left.

"How do you feel?" he asked.

"Like I was kicked in the stomach by a bull."

"Do you need someone to drive you home?"

"No, I can make it. I'll use your rest room here to clean up."

Joe dabbed gently at his bloody nose and cut lip with a wet towel. By the time he combed his hair he felt better.

"See you later, Mel," he said and left.

As he unlocked his car in the parking lot, a large man suddenly grabbed him from behind! Before he could turn around, both his arms were quickly pinned behind his back. The "drunk" from the bar, looking sober and mean, appeared out of the dark and stood in front of Joe while his "friend" held him.

"We'll teach you to make eyes at our boss's girl," the "drunk" said. Before he could use his fists, Joe kicked him in the shins, knocking his legs out from under him. He rolled on the ground clutching his legs and groaning in pain. This surprised the other one, and his grip loosened. Joe jerked around and swung at him. It was a glancing blow, which didn't throw the ruffian completely off balance. With doubled fists he came back at Joe.

Joe ducked and then feinted with his right and jabbed him in the abdomen with his left. When the man doubled over, Joe gave him a karate chop to the back of his head. He sprawled face down on the pavement. Joe grabbed him by the scruff of the neck, lifted his head up, and said, "Tell your boss that if he harms one hair on that girl's head, I'm coming after him!"

"What's going on here?" Joe looked up into Mr. Ashley's

shocked face. The rest of the family were staring at him. A small crowd began to gather.

"Just getting rid of a couple of drunks," he said. He helped the man up and told him to take his friend and go, which he did in a hurry.

"Joe, are you hurt?" Sylvia asked, concerned. "Your mouth is bleeding."

Joe took his handkerchief out of his pocket and dabbed at it. "It's nothing," he said. The crowd broke up and Joe got in his car and left.

At home he drew the bathtub full of warm water. Carefully he stepped in and lowered his aching body into the soothing depth.

"Ahh! That feels great!" he sighed as the warmth of the water covered him. His muscles gradually relaxed and the soreness eased.

He thought about the fight. Those men were sent by Jack to punish him! "How do I get into these predicaments?" he wondered. "All I want is peace and quiet."

When the water cooled, he gingerly stepped out and dried off. He looked at his face in the mirror. His lips were swollen, but he didn't think his nose was broken. "I look like something the cat dragged in," he said. "Tomorrow I'm staying home and resting. I don't want anyone to see me like this."

CHAPTER XXXIV

The next morning Joe ached all over but thought that in another day or two he would be okay. He ate a light breakfast and then went into his den to study football moves. When Mrs. Etheridge came, she looked at him strangely but didn't ask any questions. For lunch she prepared chicken noodle soup, stating it would be easier to eat with a sore mouth.

"She has noticed it," he thought, but was relieved that she didn't ask about it.

After lunch, he climbed up to his hilltop, his first visit since returning. Blueberry Hill, Maggie had called it. He surveyed the peaceful view for a time and then sat on the rock where Maggie had sat that day so long ago. The blueberry bushes were loaded with small green berries. "Some day I'm going to buy this property and build a house," he thought. "I'll build it here with the front facing west, and a garage attached on the north side." Mentally planning the house, he could think of sharing it with no one but Maggie. "A swing could hang on a branch of that oak tree for our children," he continued.

Joe spent several hours on the hill before returning home. Mrs. Etheridge had left a plate of cottage cheese and canned fruit in the refrigerator, along with a bowl of Jell-O. He ate with relish and was glad she was so thoughtful. When he finished the meal, he went out to water his garden. While he was there, Chief Bundy drove up.

"Nice looking garden," he said, coming around the house.

"It will be when it comes up," Joe said, smiling. "I'm finished here. Come in and I'll make a pot of coffee."

The chief sat at the table and watched Joe prepare the coffee.

"Some lip you got there," he said.

"Ran into a door," Joe replied.

"Not the way I heard it."

"Really? What did you hear?"

"Heard you got into a fight with a couple of Jack Phillip's thugs over that singer, Annie Graves."

"What?" Joe shouted.

"It's all over town."

"Did the Ashleys spread that rumor?"

"Nope. They're about the only ones not talking about it. Were they there?"

"Their car was parked next to mine in the lot when I had a run in with a couple of drunks."

"They weren't the only ones in the parking lot. Coffee ready yet?"

Joe got up and poured them each a cup.

"You've stirred up a lot of gossip since you came to town, Joe," the chief said. "I warned you to keep away from that bunch."

"I've done my best to stay out of trouble. What's all the noise about?"

"Mostly about you and Annie Graves."

"Annie Graves? What gossip could there be about her and me ?"

"Shall I enumerate?"

"Please do."

"Thursday evening you met her in the bar at the Inn and bought her a drink. Friday afternoon you played pool with her in Bailey's Saloon. Last night you bought her dinner and danced with her at the Inn. You got into an argument with her boyfriend, Jack Phillips. Her first number was a love song to you. Two of Jack's henchmen pretended to be drunk and attacked you in the bar. Mel ran them off, and then they jumped you in the parking lot. You came out the winner. How am I doing?"

Joe sat in stunned silence, his coffee forgotten. Finally he asked, "Who told you all of this?"

"Several people. It's all over town."

"Have the Mitchells heard these rumors?"

"They couldn't help but hear it. I brought this up to warn you about something else."

"I don't think I want to hear any more."

"You've got to hear this. Rumor has it that Jack beat up Annie. She isn't going to sing tonight or anytime soon."

Joe leaped to his feet. "I told them to tell that dirty cur what I'd do to him if he touched her. I'm going after him!"

The chief got up and took hold of his arm. "No, you aren't. Calm down. That's why I came to tell you this myself, before you heard it from someone else and went off half-cocked. We're so close to putting them all away, and I don't intend to let you spoil it. I'll lock you up first. Promise me that you'll let me handle this."

Joe's blood boiled, but he could see the chief's point of view. He would have to control himself for now, but the time would come when Jack would get his just desserts. If the chief couldn't do it, he would do it himself.

"Okay. I promise, but it better be soon or I'll do the handling, and it won't be gentle."

"I thought you'd see reason," the chief said, and shook his hand.

Friday morning, as Joe weeded his garden, his thoughts raced wildly about the rumors that Chief Bundy told him. No wonder Mrs. Etheridge hadn't mentioned his cuts and bruises. She must have heard the gossip. What must Maggie be thinking about him? He felt helpless, angry, and embarrassed that he couldn't do anything about Jack's treatment of Annie. "He must think I'm afraid of him," he thought, and that galled him so much that he chopped fiercely at the weeds.

"What have you got against those poor little weeds that you're attacking them so furiously?" asked a voice behind him. He hadn't heard Sylvia drive up.

"Because they dare raise their heads in my garden," he said. "How have you been, Sylvia?"

"I'm bored," she said. "Our visitors left this morning. Mother is helping in the store, Grandmother is playing cards with friends, Meg is working, and now I see you're working."

"I'm just killing time. I'll wash up, and we can sit out on the patio and drink lemonade."

Soon they were seated in the wrought iron chairs with a pitcher of lemonade and two glasses on the table between them. Joe poured a glass for Sylvia and then one for himself.

"This is delicious," Sylvia said. "Is that a cake I smell baking?"

"Mrs. Etheridge is baking it for the cookout tomorrow night. You're coming, aren't you?"

"Wouldn't miss it. I'm glad Amy is coming with Bob. I didn't get to see her the last time I was here. It's been a while since you've seen Bob, hasn't it?"

"Yes, several years."

“Joe, I want to thank you for making my visit here so pleasant. It’s good to come home and see the old town and my parents, but I get bored after a while. I’ve enjoyed your company, and you’ve certainly made it interesting this time,” she said with a twinkle in her eye.

“Thanks. You’ve been good company for me, too,” he said, deliberately ignoring her veiled meaning.

“Lunch is ready.” Mrs. Etheridge appeared with a laden tray. “Guess you want it out here. It’s such a beautiful day.”

Joe rose and took the tray from her and set it on the table. “You should have called me in to carry that,” he scolded.

“Oh, dear,” Sylvia looked at her watch. “I didn’t realize how late it was.”

“Stay and have lunch with me.”

“If it’s okay with Mrs. Etheridge.”

“When I saw you here, I fixed enough for both of you,” Mrs. Etheridge said. “Chicken salad with lettuce and tomatoes and fruit for desert.”

“Thank you. It looks delicious,” Sylvia said.

After they finished eating, Joe said, “I need to go shopping for the steaks and charcoal for tomorrow night. Wanna go?”

“Sure,” she said. “My parents’ car is in the drive. Let’s take it.”

When they returned from the store, Mrs. Etheridge had already gone, and Sylvia helped Joe put away the groceries.

“I’m leaving for Chicago on Monday,” she said.

“I’ll miss you.”

“Come to dinner tonight. My folks told me to invite you.”

“Can’t. Bob and Amy will be here. Why don’t you go to the Mitchells with me?”

“I’ll have to wait until tomorrow to see them. My folks expect me to spend the evening with them. Grandmother would be a grump if I didn’t. She asks about you all the time.”

“Maybe I could go by and see her before you leave.”

After Sylvia left, Joe cleaned and oiled his hunting rifle in case Bob wanted to hunt. He didn’t load it, but left the shells handy.

Shortly after he finished the phone rang. It was Bob. “Come over,” he said. “We just got here and are eager to see you. Meg says there’s plenty of food for supper.”

"Okay. I need to bathe and shave first."

Forty minutes later he knocked on the Mitchells' door. It was immediately opened by Bob.

"Come on in, you old Indian. I'm not in the habit of hugging men, but I'm going to make an exception." He crushed Joe in a bear hug, and then said, "Meet my future wife, Amy."

"I remember Amy," he said and shook her hand. "You don't look any older than you did in high school," he said.

Amy grinned, pleased, "Thanks," she said.

"What happened to your lip?" Bob asked. "Run into a door?"

"No, got attacked by a couple of drunks at the Candlelight Inn," he said and glanced quickly at Maggie. Although she tried to hide it, he could tell by the expression that passed briefly over her face that she had heard the rumors.

After supper Bob invited Joe for a walk.

"What have you been doing since the war, Joe, and why didn't you come home?" Bob asked bluntly.

"I spent the first two years in the hospital, and last year at Oklahoma A and M," he replied.

"I know how that is. I was in the hospital several months with my broken leg. It got infected and when that cleared up, I had to take therapy," Bob said. "Tell me how you got injured, or would you rather not talk about it?"

"It's hard for me to talk about it, but I'll try," Joe said. He paused and a sad faraway look appeared in his eyes. "We were on an island that we thought was uninhabited. A few of us went out on patrol to make sure, and we were ambushed. Everyone was killed except me, and I was unconscious when they found me. Said I was more dead than alive. After that I had terrible nightmares. The docs said it was battle fatigue. Physically it took a long time for me to recover, but it took even longer for me to recover mentally." He fell silent for a few minutes.

"The worst part was the war was nearly over and their deaths were so unnecessary. I was their leader and I felt like I had failed them. The guilt caused my breakdown, and the breakdown makes me feel like a coward. I should have been able to numb my mind to it. That's the main reason I didn't come home."

Bob looked at him earnestly and said, "Joe, you're not a coward! I'm living proof of your bravery. Man, I owe you my life. If those Japs had gotten hold of me, I can't bear to think what they would have done to me. I can't thank you enough for coming after me, buddy. No one can go through all you went through for over four years and not be affected. Never, never say or think that again."

"Thanks old pal. You make me feel better," Joe said as they continued walking.

"What are you studying at A and M?"

"History and coaching. I'm getting a teacher's degree. I want to teach in a small town like Oak Grove."

"I hear that Coach Brady is planning to retire in a year or two. Talk to him. Maybe he'll hang on until you get your degree. He teaches history also. Made to order for you."

"Maybe the school board wouldn't hire me."

"Are you kidding? Since you rescued me, you are the Golden Boy around here. A real home-grown hero."

"Other problems have come up, and I'm not sure that's still true. What are your plans after med school?"

Bob stopped walking and looked serious. "I keep thinking about those people who took care of me on that little island. Some had illnesses and deformities that I felt could have been prevented or healed with proper medical care. Amy and I both feel that God wants us to go to the mission field as medical missionaries. As a pilot I could cover several areas. We want to reach them for Christ, also."

"That's great, Bob. You have a lot to offer. Have you thought about the money you could make in private practice in a large city?"

"Of course I have. There are charity clinics that I could work in over here, too, but I feel God calling me to foreign missions. Amy and I are in agreement on that, and we want to be in His will." He turned to Joe and asked out right, "Have you thought about becoming a Christian?"

"Oh, no! Not you, too! Paul has already been on my case about becoming a Christian," he replied. "As long as this hatred for Dan consumes me, I don't think the Lord would accept me."

"Dan is dead. You aren't going to let him keep controlling your life, are you? If you let Him, Jesus will remove the hatred from your heart."

"Perhaps you're right. I'll think about it. We'd better get back before they send a search party after us."

When they approached the house they saw everyone sitting out on the porch.

"It's cooler out here," Sam said, fanning himself with a cardboard church fan.

"I need to go home and spend some time with my parents, Bob," Amy said. Turning to Joe she added, "Thanks for inviting me to the cookout tomorrow."

"Would you like to hike around in the woods in the morning, Joe?" Bob asked. "We could visit all of our old haunts."

"Sure, I'll be over after breakfast."

After Bob and Amy left, Sam said, "I think I'll go in and read the paper. Good night, Joe."

"Good night, Sam," Joe said.

Johnny also excused himself. "I'm going to my room and read," he said.

The chirping of crickets filled the air as Joe and Meg sat alone on the porch.

"I've been waiting for a chance to talk to you, Maggie. I suppose you've heard those rumors about me?"

"Yes, and I don't know what to think, Joe. I did see you with that woman."

"We're just friends. She's Jack Phillips's girlfriend."

"Ugh! That man gives me the creeps. I wish Johnny wouldn't work out there. Why did you fight over her?"

"I didn't fight over her. She's my employee, and I didn't like the way Jack treated her."

"I hope you're going to keep that gang of ruffians out of your club now."

"I plan to kick them out shortly."

"What about now?"

"I can't explain, but I can't get rid of them yet."

"Are you afraid of them? Or just afraid of losing your girlfriend?"

"Maggie, I know that you don't believe that!"

"How do you know what I believe? First you told me you loved me. Then you told me I was only a sister to you. You didn't come home until three years after the war ended. Now you tell me that you 'know' what I believe. You don't know me at all!"

She didn't give Joe a chance to answer but flounced into the house and slammed the door.

Joe spent a restless night. He finally had a chance to talk to Maggie alone and it had ended in an argument!

He loved her. How could he make her understand that when everything had gotten so complicated?

CHAPTER XXXV

The next morning Joe walked to the Mitchell house and found Bob alone.

"Everybody gone?" he asked.

"Dad and Meg are at the store, and Johnny is working at the auto shop," he said. "Buck and Duke are raring to go. They think we're going hunting."

"I cleaned and oiled my gun in case you wanted to hunt. Didn't bring it, though, since you didn't mention it."

"I just want to tramp around and remember the good old days. Let's go."

When they came to the river, Joe said, "Remember when we first met? It was here that those guys tossed me in, and you jumped in and rescued me. I was such a wimp. Hadn't been used to boys and rough play."

"You learned fast, though, both swimming and rough play. Sure glad you did."

"Yeah, it toughened me for the marines."

They hiked up the trail by the river and turned into the path that led to the treehouse. Joe remembered the last time he was here was with Maggie.

"Should we climb up, or do you think two grown men would look silly sitting in a tree house?" Bob said with a laugh.

"Now that you put it that way, I think it would."

Back at the Mitchells', Joe ate lunch with Bob and then went home to get ready for the cookout. Bob drove into town to see Amy.

After Joe put the charcoal in the barbecue pit, he looked around and decided he needed more chairs, so he drove to the hardware store. He saw Maggie talking to Alex, the mechanic from the auto shop next to the Inn. Her back was to him, and Alex was facing him. A stab of annoyance shot through Joe when he saw the look of admiration on Alex's face. The nerve of him looking at Maggie that way! Then he paused to think. What right did he have to get jealous? None. He had sacrificed that right when he had written that letter.

"Did you need anything else?" Maggie asked Alex, handing him a package.

"This is all for now," he said.

Joe had the feeling that Alex had mostly come in to see Maggie. "More competition," he thought.

As Alex walked away, Maggie turned and saw him standing there. "Hi, Joe. What can I help you with?"

"I need more chairs for tonight. Do you have folding chairs here?"

"You don't need to buy any. We have plenty of chairs. Lawn chairs and folding chairs. We'll bring them over."

"Maggie," Joe said, but she had already turned to another customer. "She's still upset with me," he thought.

At six o'clock Joe had just put on the steaks when Bob, Sam, and Johnny drove up in the pickup with the extra chairs and food Maggie had prepared.

"Meg and Alice are at the beauty shop," Sam said.

"Brock is bringing Amy and Sylvia," added Bob.

"Here's Paul," Sam said, as the preacher arrived. "Glad you could make it, Parson."

"Hi, everybody," Brock said as he and the girls came around the house. "I need some help carrying the chest of cokes. Don't want the girls to hurt themselves."

Bob got up and went with him. When they came back with the cokes, Brock looked around and said, "Where's Meg?"

"At the beauty shop. She'll be here soon," Sam said. "Let's unload these chairs."

As they finished unloading them, Maggie and Alice arrived. Joe had to look twice at Alice. Was this the dowdy-looking woman he first saw in the store? Her shoulder-length hair had been curled in back with the sides swept up into curls on top of her head. Golden glints highlighted the brown and gave her a more youthful look. Gone were the ugly black-rimmed glasses, replaced by pretty pink ones. Usually devoid of cosmetics, her face was expertly made up. A brightly flowered sundress showed off her slim figure, and white sandals replaced her walking shoes. She was younger and prettier than Joe had thought.

He turned to comment on her improved appearance, but paused when he saw the thunderstruck expression on Sam's face.

"Alice?" he asked in wonderment.

Maggie laughed and said, "Oh, Dad! Of course it is. She just had her hair styled and got new glasses. Isn't she a knockout?""

"She sure is. Sit over here by me, Alice," he invited.

"The steaks are done," Joe said and began putting them on a platter.

After Paul asked the blessing, they filled their plates and sat in the lawn chairs to eat.

"Great steak!" Johnny said.

"Am I as good a cook as Maggie?" Joe teased.

"Your steaks are better," he said.

When they finished eating, Joe went into the kitchen and brought out the cake Mrs. Etheridge had baked. Pink icing spelled out "Happy Birthday Maggie" on the white frosting.

Maggie's face flushed with happiness. "You remembered my birthday? I can't believe it."

Later they played badminton and everyone got hot and sweaty. Joe said, "I'm going to get some ice water. Want to help, Maggie?"

"Okay," she said.

They entered the kitchen and Joe noticed Maggie looking around curiously.

"Have you seen the house since Dan remodeled it?" he asked.

"No, but I'd like to," she answered.

"I'll give you a tour," he said with a smile and started into the dining room.

"What about the water?"

"They can wait."

Maggie admired the house as he led her through it. "I didn't know Dan had such good taste," she said.

"He didn't. He used an interior decorator. This study was once a downstairs bedroom," he said throwing open a door off the living room.

"I can see you've been taking advantage of it," she said looking at the books and papers stacked on the desk.

"Yes, I've been doing some extra reading and work on my courses for next semester. Now come see the upstairs."

"Hadn't we better make the ice water?"

"You aren't afraid to look at the bedroom with me, are you?" he asked with a grin.

"Of course not!" she said and started up the stairs.

"This is beautiful!" she said as they entered the master bedroom. "I love the drapes and the matching bedspread, and this furniture is grand. It looks unused. Don't you sleep here?"

"No. I sleep in my old room. It's the only room he left alone."

"He hoped that you would come home and live here, you know."

"He should have known better."

Maggie put her hand on his arm. "Joe, I'm sorry about the way I acted last night. Will you forgive me?"

Joe took both of her hands in his and looked into her eyes. She was so beautiful. He was tempted to take her in his arms and kiss her, but he didn't know how she would react.

"I want to explain everything to you, Maggie, but I can't yet. You'll just have to trust me."

"Hey, where's that ice water?" Brock called as he came into the kitchen.

When they carried the ice water out, Sylvia looked up and said, "What kept you?"

"Maggie had never seen the house since it was redone, so I showed it to her," Joe replied.

Sam and Alice were engrossed in conversation, as if they had just met. Sam hadn't really noticed her before, and Alice responded like a flower in the sunlight. Maggie sat down across from them with a pleased look on her face.

"I bet Maggie plotted this," Joe said to himself. "Alice has probably been attracted to Sam for a long time and he never noticed her. I bet he does from now on."

Paul took the seat next to Joe. "We'd like to see you in church tomorrow, Joe."

"I'll think about it."

"Meg is going to sing a solo," he said helpfully.

"Then I'll come. Haven't heard her sing since I've been home."

Bob leaned back in his chair on the other side of Joe. "After church come over for dinner," he said. "Amy and I plan to leave for the city in the afternoon."

"Thanks, I will," he responded.

Darkness descended on them, and the tree frogs croaked in full force. Suddenly a far away whippoorwill mating call sounded. Bob and Joe glanced at each other and grinned. Joe had used that signal on the Philippine island to let Bob know he was near. Since Joe didn't want the subject brought up, he shook his head imperceptibly, and Bob nodded that he understood. Turning his head, Joe saw Maggie looking at him with a grateful expression on her face. His heart turned over. She remembered. Maybe he did have a chance with her.

"It's nine o'clock," Paul said. "I need to go home and finish preparing for tomorrow. Thank you, Joe, for inviting me. It's been relaxing and fun."

Joe stood up and shook his hand. "I'm glad you came. Come back any time. You're always welcome."

The others left shortly after nine. Sam escorted Alice home in the car and left the pickup and chairs for Bob and Johnny. Amy sat between them in the cab and waved as they drove away.

Brock offered to take Meg home, but she declined. "You and Sylvia go on back to town. I need to walk off this meal," she said.

After they left, Joe said that he would go with her. "I need to walk too," he said.

The stars twinkled brightly and the moon shone down on them as they walked down the country road. Joe's heart overflowed with happiness to walk again with Maggie. He must tell her that he loved her.

She seemed to sense his mood because she said, "I have a lot of things to get straight in my mind, Joe. Let's just be friends for now."

"All right," he replied. "Just for now."

CHAPTER XXXVI

Joe sat in the church auditorium the next morning enthralled with Maggie's voice as she sang "The Old Rugged Cross." The blue of the choir robe brought out the blue of her eyes. Her brown hair curled softly around her face and framed her perfect features. He sighed. She was so lovely, not just outwardly but sweet and pure inside, too.

Paul preached an evangelistic sermon on the third chapter of the book of John. Joe felt like he spoke directly to him. The Bible said God loved him so much that He gave His only Son to die on the cross for him. Why couldn't he accept that and go to the altar and confess himself a sinner and receive salvation? There must be more to it than that. How could God love him after all the killing he had done and with all of the hate he had in his heart?

Following the service, Joe went home and changed into casual clothes. When he walked up to the Mitchells' house, he found Bob, Johnny, and Sam sitting on the porch. The aroma of roast beef wafted from inside.

"Have a seat," Sam invited. "Dinner will be ready soon. Meg has a lot of help today with Amy and Alice both here."

"Now why doesn't that surprise me that Alice is here?" Joe said with a smile.

"Dinner is ready," Maggie called through the screen door.

After the meal Maggie, Amy, and Alice cleared the table.

"I could help with the dishes," Joe volunteered.

"Okay," said Maggie. "I'll wash and you dry. Alice, you and Amy go sit out on the porch with Dad and Bob."

"I feel as if I should help," Alice said.

"No, you're guests and you've done your share. Dad and Bob will be lonesome out there by themselves."

Maggie ran hot water in the sink and put in a cap full of liquid soap, making lots of suds. She washed and rinsed the glasses first and put them in the rack for Joe to dry.

"I remember now. Glasses first, then silverware, then chinaware, and pots and pans last."

"Yes, I still do them the way Mom taught me."

"I miss your mother, Maggie. She was a wonderful person. She always treated me like a son."

Tears came to Maggie's eyes. "You were like a son to her. She was good to everyone. I wish I could be more like her."

"You are like her!" Joe exclaimed. "That little tomboy I used to know has grown into a beautiful, gracious woman."

Maggie blushed. "You don't know what a wretched person I really am," she said.

"I know that's impossible," Joe said solemnly. "Everywhere I go I hear reports that you are just like your mother. 'If you need any help, just ask Meg,' they say."

"I know me better than they do," she replied. "But God is so good to forgive and help me do better."

Embarrassed by the topic, Joe turned the conversation to other things. It was wonderful to be near Maggie. He wasn't sure afterwards what they had talked about. One subject they stayed away from, though, was love. Whenever he worked the conversation around to tell her his feelings, she skillfully turned the subject to something else. All too soon the dishes were dried and put away. Maggie made a pitcher of lemonade, and they carried it with glasses out to the porch.

When they finished the lemonade Bob said, "It's time for us to start for the city. We need to stop by the Whites' house on the way through town to say good-bye."

"I should be off, too," Joe said. "Sylvia is expecting me this afternoon. She leaves tomorrow on the bus."

"She could ride to the city with us and take the bus from there," Bob said.

"I mentioned it to her yesterday," Amy said, "but she said her parents want her to stay as long as possible."

Later at the Ashley's house, Joe and Sylvia sat in the porch swing.

"So you're going back to the Windy City tomorrow?" Joe commented.

"Yes, I'll be glad to get back. It's home to me now. Why don't you teach in Chicago after you graduate? You could earn more and there is so much more to do – theaters, pro sports, and all kinds of special events."

"I don't like large cities and crowds."

Sylvia turned abruptly to face him. "When are you and Meg going to let down your false fronts and admit you love each other?"

Joe looked at her in shocked disbelief. "Wha-what do you mean?" he demanded. "Maggie doesn't love me."

"Meg has carried the torch for you all of these years. I suspected it, and since you have been home, I see it in her eyes and in her actions. I've seen the way you look at her when you think nobody is noticing."

The appearance of her father in the doorway saved Joe from answering. "Come in and play cards with us before your grandmother has a fit," he said.

That night in bed, Joe tossed and turned, unable to sleep. Could it be possible that Maggie really did love him? When their eyes met, or when they touched, electricity seemed to flow between them. How could she love someone like him when she could have Brock, with his good looks and assured future at the bank. Or Paul, whom Joe suspected was halfway in love with her. She would be a perfect preacher's wife.

Finally sleep overcame him.

CHAPTER XXXVII

Sylvia's departure the next day drew quite a crowd at the bus stop. As Sylvia and her parents drove up, Joe was there to meet them. Meg and Brock also showed up to wish her a good trip back to Chicago.

Sylvia hugged and kissed everyone. When she hugged Joe she whispered in his ear, "Go for it, Joe."

Maggie looked at him curiously and he felt his face flush. He wanted to ask her to go for a cup of coffee, but he knew Brock would go too. "How does that guy get off work so much?" he thought. "He sticks like glue to Maggie."

The rest of the day passed slowly for Joe. He studied a while, napped some, and worked in his garden. In the evening he ate leftovers for supper. Going out didn't seem prudent. The guys at the pool hall would tease him about his "girlfriend" getting beaten up and wonder why he didn't do something about it. A long evening stretched before him. Since he had slept so much during the day he wasn't sleepy. Finding an old Reader's Digest, he read, engrossed in a story, until the telephone interrupted him. Startled by the lateness of the call, he glanced at the clock; the hands pointed to eleven o'clock.

"Joe, is Johnny there?" Maggie sounded frantic.

"No, he hasn't been here. What's the matter?"

"I don't know what could have happened to him. About nine o'clock he went to study for a test in driver's ed and discovered that he had left his workbooks and papers at the shop. I didn't want him to, but he insisted on going to get them. He rode his bike and isn't home yet. Dad took Alice to Wolfeton for dinner and a movie and is still gone. I don't know what to do."

Alarms went off in Joe's head. "I'll drive out to the shop and see if I can find him," he said.

"I want to go with you."

"No. You stay home in case he calls." He spoke a little sterner than he intended.

"I'd rather go. I can't sit here any longer. If you won't take me I'll go in the pickup."

"All right, Maggie, I'll be by for you."

Joe didn't want Maggie along in case of trouble, but he also didn't want her out by herself. He loaded his rifle, laid it on the back seat of his car, and put the rest of the shells in his pocket.

Maggie stood waiting for him on the porch and came swiftly to the car and climbed in.

They drove slowly through town. The streets loomed dark and desolate. Black storefront windows mirrored their headlights as they drove by. When they reached the garage, it too appeared dark. However, a light shone from the back window of the Inn.

Joe drove past the Inn and parked behind some bushes.

"Stay here, Maggie, while I look around," he said.

Taking his rifle out of the back seat, he crossed the yard and walked quietly up to the lighted window. A cement block turned up-end indicated someone had stood on it to peer in the window. Books and papers were scattered about on the ground. Standing on tiptoes he peered in. Four men surrounded the game table with papers and money stacked before them. No chips or cards were in sight.

Jack Phillips seemed worried. Cal Blaine and one of the men who had attacked him in the bar sat looking down. The other man, a large, well-dressed stranger had a frown on his face. There was no sign of Johnny.

"That kid has really thrown a monkey wrench into things," fumed the stranger.

"I think we overreacted," Jack said. "I doubt he heard anything. If that blockhead Larry hadn't drug him in at gun point, he'd have probably left us alone."

"Yeah, then why was he at that window spying on us," the stranger argued.

"What are we going to do about him?" Cal put in.

"That's your problem," the stranger said. "But whatever you do, it better happen far away from here."

Joe had heard enough. He moved around to the office door and placed his key in the lock. The newly-oiled door opened without a squeak. On tiptoes he crept down the hall to the game room and entered with rifle cocked. Johnny, bound and gagged, lay on the floor.

"Make one move and you've had it," he told the surprised men as he picked up the telephone and started to dial.

"I wouldn't do that if I were you." Joe whirled around and faced the other man from the bar. He held a gun to the forehead of Maggie! Joe looked into her terrified eyes and laid the rifle on the floor.

The man lowered his gun and Maggie's gaze fell on Johnny.

"What have you done to him?" she screamed and rushed to him. Jack jumped up and slapped her. With a howl of rage, Joe lunged at him and punched him in the face with his right fist, knocking him backward across the table to the floor.

"Stop him!" Cal cried in his high-pitched voice.

Before the others could reach him, Joe had scrambled over the table to get to Jack. He grasped him by the shirt front, pulled him up, and shook him like a rag doll. So full of fury was he that he didn't feel the blows hammering on him by the two ruffians. Finally he dropped Jack and turned his wrath on his antagonists.

He fought the two men with the strength of a man possessed! Punches, kicks, and karate chops instilled in him by marine training kept the men at bay. An occasional jab hit him, but, in his anger, it was like so many flea bites. One lucky punch squarely struck his face. Pain shot through his head. He could feel the blood from his nose spurting down to his chin. But this didn't stop him!

Abruptly, Maggie's terrified voice caught his attention. "Look out, Joe!" Too late he turned to see Cal with a raised pistol. The pistol crashed down on his head and blackness overtook him.

When Joe dropped to the floor, Meg scrambled to reach him, but the well-dressed stranger grabbed her.

Cursing and wiping their faces with their handkerchiefs, the two men struggled to their feet. One of them began kicking Joe as he lay unconscious.

Meg jerked free and dashed across the room. She jumped on the man's back and pounded him with her fists. "Leave him alone, you brute!" she shouted. "You couldn't whip him when he was conscious, so don't kick him when he's out!"

The well-dressed stranger said wryly, "She's right, Larry." He turned to the other fighter and said, "Earl, rescue Larry from the lady and tie her to a chair."

Meg struggled to free herself from Earl's grasp but he forced her to a chair and slammed her down into it. While he held her, Larry tied her to it with a rope. She was uncomfortable, but at least he had stopped kicking Joe!

All heads turned as the door burst open. Alex Davis stood in the doorway with blazing eyes. "What's going on here!" he said in a deadly calm voice. "Why are these people here?"

"Alex!" Meg exclaimed with hope rising in her chest. But all hope died at Jack's response.

"Calm down, Alex," he said. "They were caught nosing around."

"Well, that's just dandy!"

"We'll have to get rid of them before this whole thing blows up in our face," the stranger informed him.

"Alex! Don't let them hurt us," Meg pleaded.

Alex turned and stared coldly at her. Meg shrank back. His once twinkling blue eyes had turned to blue ice.

He slowly turned around and faced the others. Even they seemed to back off from his stare. "When I agreed to go in with you, I said 'no killings!' And that's exactly what I meant!"

"We can't jeopardize the whole operation," the stranger said.

"Then we'll have to open up some other place," Alex said with finality.

The stranger sat for several minutes in deep thought.

"Okay, we'll do it your way, Alex," he said. "How many cars are in the garage now?"

"Three," Alex replied.

"You, Larry, and Earl each take a car to our operation south of here. Jack, Cal, and I will pack all of our papers and close this place down tonight. We'll meet you there in the morning."

"What about them?" Alex asked.

"We'll leave them tied up here. They'll be found in the morning."

"You better be right," Alex said grimly.

Meg tried one more time, "Alex, please don't leave us here with these men." But Alex brushed by without looking at her.

After the three men left, Jack asked, "Are we really going to leave them alive to squeal on us?"

Terror filled Meg's heart as the stranger coldly replied, "Of course not. We'll leave them tied up alright, but a fire might just accidently happen. That will close this place down for good and keep their mouths shut."

"What about Alex?" Cal was nervous.

"That's what I told them we would do–leave them tied up," responded the stranger.

"Don't have any more rope to tie up that smart aleck Sullivan guy," Cal said. "I got all we had in the garage when we found the kid."

"He probably won't come to from that whack on his head in time," Jack said.

"You can't do that to us!" Meg screamed at them.

"Who says?" Jack snarled, "Shut up or I'll put a gag in your mouth!"

"Joe, Joe!"

It was Maggie's voice calling him. Had he had another one of his nightmares? He opened his eyes. Everything looked so hazy. Smoke! It filled his lungs and choked him. He raised his head groggily and coughed.

"Joe!" Maggie called him again and began coughing. He turned and focused his eyes on her. She was tied to a chair with ropes! Smoke filled the room and burned his eyes. He coughed again.

Joe forced himself to move. He wasn't tied but was so sore it hurt to move. Pulsing pain beat a rhythm in his head. His memory was returning. They must have set the Inn on fire and left them there to die. The smoke was getting to him. Had to hurry. Reaching in his pocket, he pulled out his pocket knife. Opening it, he crawled painfully over to Maggie and cut her hands free. The effort exerted him and he passed out again.

"Joe! Wake up." Maggie and Johnny tugged at him. He couldn't breathe. No air. Only smoke filling his lungs. The heat was becoming unbearable. His head felt as if hammers were pounding on it. He struggled to his knees and then fell back down coughing.

"Get out of here," he said between coughs. "Leave me."

"No! Get up!" Maggie yelled at him.

The urgency in her voice gave him renewed strength. He strained to get up again and, with their help, finally stood. They got on either side of him and put his arms over their shoulders. He laboriously put one foot in front of the other as they steered him out into the hall.

The heat and smoke made progress difficult and painful. All three were coughing. Flames licked closer and closer as they slowly went through the office to the outside door. Joe stumbled over the sill and nearly brought them all down. They regained their footing and staggered away from the burning Inn.

Joe took deep ragged gasps of fresh air. His lungs burned like fire. Just before he passed out again, he heard sirens.

CHAPTER XXXVIII

Darkness closed in on Joe as he crept through the jungle. He couldn't see his men, but he knew they were there. The overgrowth was so thick that they had to cut their way through. Suddenly lights flashed as machine guns rained bullets into them. Ambush! His men fell all around him. Screams of agony tore from the throats of the wounded and dying. Hordes of Japanese soldiers surrounded them. By the flashing lights he saw a raised hand with a grenade, and he opened his mouth and shouted, "No-o-o-o-o!" At the same time he raised his gun and fired. The soldier fell, and the grenade went off in his hand. Shrapnel pierced Joe's body. His chest burned like fire! They swarmed all over him, pinning him down. He fought them and cursed them. A sharp needle hit his hip, and he sank back down into the darkness.

When Joe had that dream, Meg was dozing in a comfortable lounge chair beside his bed. She had not left his room since he had been brought in unconscious in the early morning hours. They had escaped from the burning Candlelight Inn, and she and Johnny had not suffered any serious harm. His restless movements awakened her.

Walking over to wipe the perspiration off his face, she gasped when he suddenly shouted, "No-o-o-o!" She called for help as he pulled his oxygen mask off and jerked the intravenous needle out of his arm.

Nurses and orderlies rushed into the room in time to keep him from climbing over the bed rails. When they pushed him back into the bed, and held him down, he fought them furiously, called them "Japs," and cursed them. Meg fled crying.

A half an hour later the night nurse found her in the visitors lounge with a stuffed up nose and red eyes.

"He's quiet now," she said kindly touching her shoulder. "His temperature had risen, and he had a bad dream. We sedated him and bathed him with alcohol in cool water. His temperature is down some, but we are going to leave restraints on for awhile."

Meg gasped when she saw Joe. He lay asleep on his back with a sheet spread over him. His arms and legs were stretched apart and tied down with leather restraints. A leather belt around his waist was fastened on each side of the bed, and his oxygen mask and intravenous tubing were back in place.

"You can't leave him like that!" she cried.

"Dr. Newberry ordered it," the nurse said. "We'll remove the restraints in the morning. It's for his own protection." She raised the head of his bed a little higher. "We'll turn him every two hours."

Meg sat by the side of Joe's bed and took his hand in hers. She covered it with kisses and then laid her cheek on it. Tears coursed down her face and onto his hand.

Joe's face and body were badly bruised from the fight. His shirt had been ripped nearly off, and she had seen his chest pitted with scars from the war.

She heard again the terrible epithets that he had flung at the supposed Japanese soldiers. What had he endured during the war?

"I love you so much, Joe," she whispered. "I wish I could help you."

She spent the rest of the night at his bedside praying off and on, only moving when they came in to turn him. Toward morning she dozed off with her head on the bed near his hand. Suddenly she was awakened by his hand feeling her hair. She raised her head and looked into his face. His eyes were open and clear as he gazed at her.

"I love you, Maggie," he said. His eyes closed and he fell back to sleep.

In the afternoon Alex Davis came into Joe's hospital room. Meg welcomed him with a smile.

"You had me fooled, Alex," she said. "I thought you were one of them for sure. You looked and acted the part!"

"I had to, Meg," he said. "The hardest thing I did was to leave you there with those thugs. If I'd had my gun with me, I would have arrested them on the spot."

"Chief Bundy told us that you are an undercover cop. What happened after you left us?"

"Before we left, I told those bozos that we had better fill the cars with gas. We found a station open, and when I went inside to pay, I used the phone and called the chief and told him to get over to the Candlelight Inn. Back outside, I lurched against Larry and slipped his gun out of his holster. Then I arrested the two and hauled them off to jail. By the time the police got to the Inn, you were all outside and the Inn ablaze."

"We're grateful for all you did, Alex. What are your plans now?"

"I have to report back to Washington. It doesn't look as if there's any reason for me to come back here," he said, nodding toward Joe.

"No, unless you just want to visit," she said with a smile.

Joe awakened with a raging thirst. His mouth and throat felt stuffed with cotton. He had to get up and find some water. Sam sat by his bed and when he saw Joe arouse, he said, "What do you want, Joe? Don't try to get up."

"Water," he said hoarsely.

Sam poured water in a glass and held a straw for him to sip. When he had drunk his fill he asked, "Where am I?"

"You're in the hospital in Wolfeton."

"Why? What happened? What's this in my arm?"

"That's an intravenous. It's giving you fluid in the vein because you haven't been able to drink. You got pneumonia from all that smoke you inhaled and have been running a high temperature. Do you remember the fire at the Inn?"

Gradually it all came back to him and the scene played through his mind.

"Maggie and Johnny, how are they?" he asked.

"Fine, now. They had a little problem with smoke inhalation, but they recovered quickly. Dr. Newberry sent for your medical records and discovered that you had a lot of lung damage from shrapnel and that's why the smoke affected you so much."

"How long have I been here?"

"Three days. You've come in and out of consciousness."

"I don't remember a thing after I got out of the building."

The nurse came in and said, "You're awake! I want to take your temperature and other vital signs, and then I'll call Dr. Newberry and tell him the good news." When she finished she said, "Your temp is down and your blood pressure, pulse, and respiration are normal. The doctor will be glad to hear that."

Joe tried to stay awake to talk to Sam and find out more about the happenings at the Inn, but his eyes closed and he fell asleep. The next time he opened his eyes, it was evening, and Maggie was sitting by his bed.

"Hi, Maggie," he said. "I hear I've been on a three-day drunk."

She smiled at him and said, "If that's what you want to call it. How are you feeling now?"

"Maggie, I want to thank you and Johnny for pulling me out of that building. I was afraid I would hinder you so that you couldn't escape."

"We couldn't leave you, Joe. You know that."

"What happened after we left the Inn? All I can remember is hearing sirens before I passed out."

"You don't remember anything?"

"No, should I?" he asked puzzled.

"You've been very ill," she answered.

"Maggie–" He wanted to tell her that he loved her, but the evening nurse came in at that moment.

"Here's some orange juice," she said. "When you drink more fluids, we can take the IV out."

Maggie held his glass while he sipped through the straw. She left abruptly when he finished the juice.

Bright and early the next morning, Dr. Newberry came in. Joe was sitting up in bed eating a bowl of oatmeal.

"You're looking chipper this morning," the doctor said. "First time I've seen you with your eyes open. The nurses said you woke up, but every time I came you were asleep. I admit they're prettier than I am, but you could be a little more polite."

"Sorry about that," Joe said, "but I need my beauty sleep so I can compete with their boyfriends."

Joe pushed the over-bed table aside so the doctor could listen to his chest and heart.

"Br-r-r that's cold," Joe said as the stethoscope touched his chest.

"Are you coughing up much?"

"Quite a bit. When can I go home?"

"In a couple of days or so. You need to get stronger, and I would like for you to have at least two more days of penicillin."

"Why do you think I want to go home? My hips are killing me!" he complained.

He slept on-and-off most of the day. Sam and Maggie came by in the evening but didn't stay long. Joe went to sleep early and didn't cough as much.

The next morning Chief Bundy walked in to find Joe sitting up in a chair with a tray across his lap.

"Come in and have an egg with me," he said pointing to the poached egg sitting on top of a piece of toast.

The chief eyed it dubiously. "No, thanks," he said. "I've had breakfast."

"This is a wonderful meal. Sure beats that hot tea and colored water they call broth. Even have orange juice and oatmeal. Tell me about the other night. Where were you when I needed you? I thought you had a man on top of things."

"Alex had been watching things closely, but that afternoon he went to Wolfeton for spare parts. On the way back he had a flat tire, which delayed him longer."

"You mean Alex Davis, the chief mechanic, was your man?"

"Yeah. He's an undercover FBI agent. Alex thought it would be another week before the boss, Stan Melloti, arrived. So did Jack and Cal, but he surprised them all and came early. He's a gangster from Chicago and planned this operation. Stolen cars were brought in to the garage where they were repainted. They had dealers who sold them with false papers. We had the proof that we needed and were just waiting for Stan before we closed the net."

"Did you catch them, or did they get away?"

"We caught all of them. Alex arrested two of them and called us to go to the Inn. We picked the rest of them up at the garage. They figured all of you burned to a crisp, and there weren't any witnesses."

"I like the way you put that, Chief."

"Yeah, I have a way with words. They're in jail now. Since they crossed state lines, the FBI is going to prosecute. You, Johnny, and Meg will have to give witness about the arson."

"Is there anything left of the Inn?"

"Not much, but I'm sure you will have a good settlement from the insurance company. You wanted out of the business anyway, didn't you?"

"Yeah, but not like this. I have to think of my employees."

"Don't worry about the singer. She hates Jack and will 'sing' for the prosecution. We've offered her protection."

"Be easy with her. I have a feeling that she's had it tough all her life."

"By the way, I told Sam why you had kept the Inn open."

"Thanks. He's been really great about it, though."

In the afternoon the Bradfords came to see him. When Joe voiced his concern about their jobs going up in flames, they assured him that they would be all right.

"We already have new jobs in Wolfeton," Sally said. "I'm a waitress and Mel is the handyman at the Black Cat Café. He can do more than tend bar. In fact, he likes carpentry best."

"Which brings me to a question for you, Joe," Mel said. "Would you consider selling me the land where the building burned down? I want to start a lumberyard and we like the area. It already has that nice parking lot, too. Sally and I have been saving for a long time to go into business for ourselves."

"It's yours, buddy. I'll have my lawyer, Bill Hamilton, draw up the papers. He will also know what the land is worth."

"Don't worry about the cooks or waitresses. Jobs are plentiful. If they don't find one in Oak Grove, there are some in Wolfeton," Sally assured him.

The Bradfords hadn't been gone long when Joe had another visitor. Coach Jess Brady had been his coach when Joe was in high school.

"I heard about your accident. How are you feeling?" he asked.

"Good, except I'm tired of this room. What kind of a team are you going to have this year?"

"Hard to say. I'll have some good players coming back this fall. None as good as you and Bob, though."

"I love sports and intend to make coaching my life," Joe said.

"That's what I've heard," the coach said. "I met with the school board last night at their request. They knew that I planned to retire in two more years, but they offered me a bonus if I would stay an extra year so they could hire you after you graduate. Think you'd like to come back here?"

"Sounds good for you, but they haven't discussed it with me," Joe answered.

"What do you suppose your answer would be if they did?"

“I don’t know offhand. I’d have to think about it.”

“Hope you’ll take it. You’ll make a fine coach.”

After he left, Joe thought about living in Oak Grove. Only one reason he would stay here, which was also the same reason he would leave. Maggie. If she wouldn’t have him, he couldn’t stay in the same town. It would hurt too much to be near her and not have her as his own. She was the only girl he had ever loved or ever would love. He knew that now

CHAPTER XXXI

That evening the Mitchell family came to see him. Johnny looked downcast. "I'm sorry I got you into so much trouble, Joe. I was suspicious of them. That's why I was listening at the window. The cement block I was standing on turned over, and they heard the noise when I fell. Before I could get away, they were on me. I'm glad Alex wasn't one of the bad guys."

"The crooks might not have been caught if we hadn't drawn the cops attention to them at that time," Joe said. "I wish it had been less spectacular, though. Wonder why I wasn't tied?"

"They ran out of rope and thought you were out for the count," Maggie said.

"If anyone but Cal had hit me with the gun, I probably would have been. He is such a marshmallow," Joe said.

"After he knocked you out, one of those guys started kicking you," Johnny said. "Wish you could have seen Meg! She flew into him, hammering on him with her fists, and yelling at him to stop. They had to pull her off him and tie her to a chair. Told her they would gag her, too, if she didn't shut up."

Joe looked at Maggie in wonder. Her face flushed scarlet. "Thank you, Maggie," he said humbly.

"I-I couldn't stand to let anyone helpless get kicked."

"That explains why I'm so much sorer than I thought I should be," Joe said.

"Chief Bundy told us why you didn't sell the Candlelight Inn," Sam said.

"I hated not telling you, but he swore me to secrecy."

"That's one time the end justified the means," he said.

"You're looking so much better," Maggie said.

"I am better. Even had a regular meal this evening."

They visited until Nurse Jordan brought in his nine o'clock medication.

"See you tomorrow," Sam said.

On Sunday afternoon Joe had several visitors. Mr. and Mrs. Ashley came in but Mrs. Hadley was not with them.

"Mother wanted to come, but we were afraid the trip would be too hard on her. She sends her best wishes," Mrs. Ashley said. "I called Sylvia, and she was very concerned about you."

"You've really made a good impression on Mother Hadley. Never saw her take to anyone as she has to you," Mr. Ashley said shaking his head. "When you feel better, come play cards with us again."

After they left, Joe got up and walked to the lounge. He was there when Sam, Maggie, and Johnny found him.

"You look like you're improving every day," Sam said. "When are you getting out of here?"

"Maybe tomorrow," Joe replied. "I won't be able to do much though. I'm as weak as a kitten."

"Bob has been wanting to come down, but he's on call at the hospital this weekend and next weekend also."

"I'd like to see him, but I understand how it is."

"Hi, everybody," Paul said, coming into the room. "I'm glad to see you up and about, Joe. You didn't look this good last week when I was here."

"I was out of it. Didn't know who was here the first few days," Joe said.

"I would have come back sooner, but I have had a summer cold and didn't think it would be good to be around you."

"You're right. They tell me I've had pneumonia. Don't know how they would mix."

The Mitchells stayed a little longer and then took their leave.

"Would you mind if we went back to my room?" Joe asked. "I think I need to get back in bed for a little while."

"Let me help you," Paul said, taking his arm.

Joe was glad to have Paul to lean on. He wasn't as strong as he had thought. In the room, Paul sat quietly while Joe rested with closed eyes. Finally he opened them and said, "Thanks for helping me. I feel better now."

"You look better. Your face was white as a sheet," Paul said. "I brought you a Bible. Didn't know if you had one."

"I have one that the Mitchells gave me a long time ago when I was a boy. I hate to admit it, but I'm not sure where it is. The Christmas before I went into the marines, Mrs. Mitchell gave Bob and me each a small New Testament. They had metal covers. She told us to wear them in our shirt pockets to protect our hearts. I carried it there all through the war and still have it in my gear. There's a dent in it from shrapnel."

"Do you realize that it may have saved your life by keeping that piece of shrapnel from piercing your heart?"

"I hadn't thought of that, but it may have. My chest was full of fragments," Joe said in wonderment.

Paul looked at Joe seriously. "You nearly lost your life then and again last Monday night," he said. "God is keeping you alive for a purpose. He loves you and wants the best for you. Why don't you turn your life over to Him?"

"I've been thinking about it."

"Jesus died for your sins. Are you ready to make a commitment to Him?"

"I still have this hatred in my heart for my uncle."

"If you turn it over to the Lord he will help you rid yourself of this hatred. I know this to be true."

"I'll think about it."

"Pray about it. God hears the prayers of a person seeking Him."

They talked a few minutes longer, and then Paul said he would go and let Joe rest.

"May I pray with you?"

"Please do," Joe said and bowed his head.

Paul took his hand and said, "Father, we thank You for saving Joe's life twice, and now we ask for a total healing of his body, mind and spirit. Help him realize his need for You and turn to You for the forgiveness of sin and for eternal life. Thank You for answered prayers. In Jesus's Name. Amen."

"Thanks for your prayer," Joe said.

After Paul left, Joe lay in his bed thinking. Could he accept a faith so simple as Paul described? Shouldn't there be more for him to do than just repent and believe? "Lord, help me to believe," he whispered.

He got out of bed and walked in the hall until he tired. As he sat down in the chair in his room to rest, he noticed the Bible Paul had left. Picking it up, he turned to the book of John and read the first chapter.

"Time for bed," Nurse Jordan said as she came bustling into the room.

"Yes, Mother," Joe replied.

Her merry, dark eyes flashed at him. "You are a mess. I can tell you're better. We need to send you home and make room for a sick person."

After she had given him his medicine and turned out the light, his thoughts turned to all of his visitors over the last few days. He needed to make a few decisions. "Many of my problems have been solved," he mused, "but others remain." What about Maggie? Did she love him? What would he do about the tugging he felt inside when Paul talked with him about Jesus? When he read the Bible?

When Dr. Newberry examined him the next morning, he said, "You have improved so much, I'm letting you go home today. Is there anyone who can come after you?"

"I'll find someone," he said.

Joe went out into the hall to use the pay phone. An older man in a wheelchair, with a cast on his elevated left leg, sat in the doorway of the room directly across the hall from him.

"Howdy," the man said.

"How are you?" Joe asked politely.

"I'm fine, now that my leg is out of that traction and in a cast," he said. "Sure got tired of that bed."

"I imagine you did," Joe responded.

"Yeah, the only excitement I've had around here was the other night when you did all that hollering."

"What? I hollered?" he asked, astonished. "When was that?"

"Oh, Tuesday or Wednesday. Tuesday it was, the night after you came in, about eleven o'clock. I had just gone to sleep and you woke me up yelling 'No-o-o-o-o.' It was change-of-shift time, and all the nurses and orderlies came running. My door was open, and I could see it all. That pretty girl that was staying with you night and day ran out of your room crying like her heart was broken. You pulled your oxygen off and your IV out and were trying to get out of bed. They had to tie you down, and you cussed them out and called them names."

"I did that?" Joe was horrified.

"Oh, yes. I was in the army, but you used some choice words that I didn't even know."

"Did the–did the pretty girl hear me cussing?"

"She did unless she was deaf. You had everyone on the ward awake."

Joe was stunned. He went back into his room and lay on his bed. No one had mentioned this to him. What must everyone think of him? Especially Maggie! No wonder she was so distant!

It all came back to him now. He did have that nightmare one night. He thought the Japanese soldiers were swarming around him, but instead it was the hospital staff trying to control him. Maggie had stayed with him night and day, the man had said. She had fled crying. How disturbing it must have been for her!

CHAPTER XL

He didn't know how long he had lain in bed when a timid tap on the door aroused him. Mrs. Etheridge poked her head in and said, "I brought a pair of clean pajamas, and I'll take your others home to wash."

"You are just the person I want to see. Got your car here?"

"Yes."

"Would you take me home?"

"Gladly. I'm happy that you are well enough to come home. Your clean clothes are in that little closet. I'll wait outside while you dress."

Joe relaxed in his own home and enjoyed the good lunch Mrs. Etheridge cooked. "It's great to be home," he thought. Still needing to regain his strength, Joe napped most of the afternoon. When he awakened after three, Mrs. Etheridge was still there.

"The phone kept ringing," she explained, "and I didn't want it to wake you, so I stayed to answer it. Here's a list of people who called. Your supper is in the refrigerator. You can warm it in the oven when you're ready to eat."

"You are a jewel, Mrs. Etheridge," he said. "Thanks. See you in the morning."

Joe looked at the list of callers and groaned. He didn't want to talk to anyone at the moment. After he ate, he went out to water his garden. It didn't take much to tire him out. "I'm going to have to exercise daily to gain my strength back," he thought.

Several people called that evening, including Sam. He told them all that he didn't need anything, that Mrs. Etheridge was taking good care of him.

Sylvia called from Chicago. He reassured her that he was doing well.

"How is Meg taking all of this?" she asked. "Have you popped the question yet?"

"I think you're wrong about Maggie's feelings for me, Sylvia," he said.

"You'll never know until you ask her," she said.

After he hung up he thought about what she had said.

"Sylvia is wrong," he thought. "Maggie couldn't respect me after she witnessed the performance I put on in the hospital. She saw how rotten I am inside. I do love her, though. She is so good and pure."

Every day he worked out with weights, light ones at first, gradually increasing to heavier ones. One day he walked as far as the river. He worked in the garden some and read a lot. Two evenings Sam came over and played chess with him, and Paul did once. Johnny visited a few times, but Maggie never came.

"She witnessed that terrible scene I made in the hospital, and now she's too disgusted to want to be around me," he thought. "Would she even talk to me if I called her on the phone? I must apologize to her. Maybe it would be best to just let things lie and go back to school."

Every day he read the Bible that Paul had given him. Paul had recommended that he concentrate on the Gospel of John first. Then he read Romans, the next one he suggested, followed by the other gospels. It gradually began to make sense to him. "I want to believe," he thought, "but God can't accept someone like me."

The Friday night of the second week after he came home, Joe was restless and couldn't sleep. He looked through the drawer where he kept his clothes and found the small New Testament that Mrs. Mitchell gave him. He ran his finger over the dent in the metal cover and then opened it and began to read the Gospel of John. She had underlined John 3:16. "God does love me," he thought.

He got down on his knees by his bed and prayed. "Father God, I do believe You love me and sent Your Son to earth. Forgive my sins and help me to live the life You want me to live. Thank you for sending Jesus to die on the cross for me."

Peace and joy beyond anything he could understand filled him. He stayed on his knees a long time, sensing the presence of the Holy Spirit.

Before he got back in bed he had an urgent desire to go into the master bedroom. The wedding picture of Aunt Peg and Uncle Dan drew him in. His eyes fastened on Dan. Usually he ignored Dan's presence in the photograph, seeing only his aunt. They both looked so young. Aunt Peg had told him that they were both just eighteen when they married. Their inability to have children had disappointed them greatly.

When World War I broke out, Dan joined the army, even though he was in his late twenties. He came home wounded, and deeply disturbed by his war experiences. Joe could certainly identify with that. It was hard for him to find a good job. Then the depression came. Not able to make a living, he couldn't cope with the hardships that came with it. He began to drink and became abusive. Peg lost hope, too, and depended on alcohol to cover her disappointment, although she didn't mention that. Seeing a way out, Dan started the still and sold bootleg whiskey. When he had scraped together enough money, he bought the saloon.

While Joe gazed at the picture, pity overcame him. "What a waste," he thought. "Their lives together had been filled with so much unhappiness." Startled by his thoughts, he realized he no longer hated his uncle.

Fatigue swept over him. He put the picture down and went back to his own room and went to bed. Sleep claimed him immediately and he rested peacefully all night.

CHAPTER XLI

Joe awoke Saturday morning determined to talk to Maggie and apologize for his actions in the hospital. When he called the store, Sam told him that she had taken the day off. Upon getting no answer at her house, he thought about one place she might be. He put on his hiking clothes and headed for his hill, the one Maggie called Blueberry Hill.

Meg sat on a rock and watched a red-winged blackbird flitting from branch to branch. Memories of that day long ago when Joe had first brought her here and sat her on this same rock flooded her mind. Her pulse quickened when she heard someone approaching. The bird flew away as Joe wordlessly sat down on the ground beside her.

"Red-winged blackbirds are my favorites," she said softly. "They come here every spring, and I often come here to watch them. It's nice and peaceful up here on Blueberry Hill."

"Maggie, I want to apologize for what happened that night in the hospital," he said humbly.

"Who told you about that?" she demanded.

"The patient in the room across the hall. He was up in a wheelchair the morning I left, and he told me everything. I'm so ashamed."

"That nosy old man. He had no business telling you."

"He said that you left crying. It must have shocked you, seeing and hearing such things. I wish you hadn't been there."

"Oh, no, Joe," she said placing her hand on his arm. "It made me realize how terrible the war was for you. I saw a little bit of what you had gone through, and it broke my heart."

Her reaction encouraged him to go on. He took her hand in his and rubbed it gently. "Maggie, the last letter I wrote–I didn't mean it–about not loving you. I thought I was being noble not wanting you to sit home waiting for me. You were so young, and I realized there was a good chance I wouldn't come back."

"I know, Joe. It hurt me dreadfully at first. When I got older, I realized the truth. But if you loved me, why didn't you come home when the war was over?"

"I'd like to tell you," he said looking up at her with a question in his eyes.

"I'm listening," she answered calmly.

A sad and dejected expression crossed his face. He sat in deep silence for a few minutes before he spoke. "Just before the peace was signed, we were out on patrol and were ambushed by Japanese soldiers. I was the only one in my unit that lived, and I was nearly dead when they found me. A grenade had exploded a little way from me and riddled me with shrapnel." He paused thinking reflectively, then proceeded. "Since I was in charge of the patrol, I blamed myself. I guess it was more than I could stand, because I went berserk. It took a long time for me to heal. I had to undergo several surgeries and had part of a lung removed. All along I had these terrible nightmares, like the one you witnessed. For two years I was in hospitals and wasn't fit to be around anyone. The last few months I was in a psychiatric hospital."

"Oh, Joe, I'm so sorry. I can't imagine how terrible that must have been for you," Maggie said with tears in her eyes.

"I was ashamed and didn't want anyone to know, most of all you. When I was finally discharged as cured, I was afraid to come back here. Mainly I feared that you didn't love me or that you had married someone else. Then deciding that not knowing was worse than facing the facts, I had planned to come home even before I got the word that Dan was dead."

"I'm glad you came," she said softly.

His mood lightened and he spoke with excitement in his voice. "Maggie, I want you to be the first to know. Last night I made peace with God. I know He has forgiven me of my sins and has released me from the hatred I felt for Dan."

Meg glanced at his face. The despondent lines were gone. His facial expression made him seem younger. A light of happiness shone in his eyes and replaced the sad and haunted look he had worn since he came home.

"How wonderful!" she exclaimed. "We have all been praying for you. As I prayed last night, an unexplainable peace came over me. Somehow, I knew you were saved."

He turned her hand over and studied the palm.

"It's still here," he said solemnly.

"What's still here?" she asked brightly.

"The long lifeline with the happy marriage," He kept hold of her hand and a faraway look came into his eyes. "Sometimes in the hospital, I would dream of you, Maggie. I could see you so plainly, I thought I could reach out and touch you. Love for you would overwhelm me." He paused.

Meg said nothing.

"In my dreams you looked like I last saw you–a lovely dewy-eyed teenager. The other day in the hospital I had that dream again, but you were a beautiful woman. I told you that I loved you. Were you there, Maggie?"

"Yes," she whispered breathlessly.

He stood up and, still holding her hand, drew her up to face him. Gazing steadily into her eyes, he said, "Maggie, I love you. Will you marry me?"

"Yes, yes, yes," she replied, and he folded her in his arms and kissed her. The closeness of his body and the feel of his lips pressed on hers filled her with love for him. Joy swept over her. This is what she had waited for.

They stood locked in an embrace for a long time. Then Joe gently released her, set her on the rock, and sprawled down on the ground beside her.

"I didn't realize how much I loved you, Maggie, until I saw you again at the bus stop. You captured my heart completely, but I never had a chance to tell you. There were always others around–Brock, Paul, Alex, and I wasn't sure how you felt about me. Maybe I was a coward. I was afraid you didn't love me."

Meg looked down on his glossy black hair and brushed it back from his forehead with her hand. "I never stopped loving you," she said. "All other men fell short when I compared them to you. When I saw you at the bus stop, I wanted to throw caution to the wind and run into your arms. These past few weeks I've wanted to reach out and touch you, smooth your hair, run my hands over your face, kiss you. Watching you with Sylvia made me jealous. I wanted to sit beside you, laugh with you, be your partner."

Joe pulled her down beside him on the ground and kissed her again. "Oh, my love, we've wasted so much time. Marry me right away."

"Yes, that's what I want, too."

They sat on the ground leaning against their rock, planning the future. A short honeymoon to Galveston, Texas, where they could make up for lost time. Then go early to find an apartment in Stillwater where Joe would attend college.

"I can get a job while you go to school," Maggie said.

"No. I have enough money with my inheritance and the GI Bill. We can both go to school."

"I would like that," she said. "I'd like to work on a degree in music and then maybe teach school."

"The school board has asked me to coach here in Oak Grove when I graduate," Joe interjected.

"What did you tell them?"

"That I would think it over. I wanted to make sure you would marry me first."

"That's wonderful. We could buy this land and build our house here on Blueberry Hill like you planned."

Caught up in shared love and happiness, they didn't notice the passing of time until the shadows began to lengthen over the hills.

Maggie glanced down at her watch and exclaimed, "It's time for Dad and Johnny to be home! I need to be there to fix their supper."

Joe got up and helped her to her feet. Pulling her to himself once more, he kissed her before they walked hand in hand down the hill. When they entered the kitchen, they found Sam rummaging around in the refrigerator.

He straightened up, looked at their faces, and said, "Well, it's about time you two got together."

"You knew?" Joe asked in surprise.

"Anyone with eyes in their head can see that you're crazy about each other," he said.

Johnny came in and saw them and said, "Oh-ho, I think there's going to be a wedding."

"See what I mean?" Sam asked.

"Joe has more good news, Dad," Meg put in.

Joe smiled broadly and said, "I've accepted the Lord Jesus Christ as my Savior."

"Praise the Lord!" Sam exclaimed. "We've all been praying for you to make that decision."

Joe ate supper with them, and then stayed until bedtime while they discussed their plans.

"Will you and Johnny get along all right without me?" Maggie asked.

"I've given that some thought," Sam said. "You think Mrs. Etheridge would work for us until maybe October? I'm hoping there will be more wedding bells by then."

"Dad, that's wonderful!" Maggie exclaimed, running over to hug him.

"Actually, I haven't asked her yet. She might not have me."

"Yes she will. She's been in love with you for a long time. You were just too blind to see it."

CHAPTER XLII

After Joe left, Johnny went up to his room to read before going to bed. Meg and Dad sat in the living room in companionable silence. Finally Dad spoke. "Have you thought about how Brock is going to feel? He has been hanging around you for so long."

"I've told him all along that I didn't love him. When Joe was in the hospital and I stayed with him night and day the first three days, Brock saw that I cared a lot for Joe. I told him then that I loved Joe and intended to marry him. He will find someone else. His feelings aren't very deep."

"Would you have agreed to marry Joe if he had not become a Christian?" Dad asked quietly.

"No," Meg replied softly but firmly. "I don't see how I could, but I felt in my heart that he was under conviction. I've tried to stay away from Joe so he could accept the Lord on his own before he asked me to marry him. I would have had to tell him my reasons for refusing him, and then I wouldn't have been sure if he accepted Christ sincerely, or only for me."

"My little girl has really grown up," Dad said with a fond smile.

Meg smiled in return, and her eyes sparkled with a quiet excitement. "Last night I was reading the Gospel of John before I went to bed, and when my eyes fell on John 3:16, it sprang out at me. As I knelt by the side of my bed and prayed again for Joe's salvation, a great peace filled me. I knew then that he had accepted Christ as his Savior."

"Paul will be excited as well as the rest of the congregation," Dad said. "Joe has been on everyone's heart."

Meg slept well that night and awakened the next morning to a bright and sunny day. To her the flowers were more brilliant, the grass was greener, and the trees had more foliage. She sang as she cooked breakfast

"I wish I had invited Joe over to eat with us," she told Dad. "I should call him, but he's probably still asleep."

Later, at church, Meg came into the auditorium with the choir and was scanning the congregation when Joe walked in and sat by

Johnny. He smiled at her, and her heart sang. The service went by in a blur. Her thoughts were all on Joe. Why did she love him more than any other man? Was it his black hair, his piercing gray eyes, his firm mouth, his determined chin, or his athletic build? No. Brock was much more handsome, and Paul and Alex were just as attractive. Maybe it was his inner character. He had a good sense of humor, integrity, honesty, and a sense of justice. No, the others had these qualities, too, in varying degrees. She just knew she loved him, always had, and always would. It was as simple and as complicated as that.

Meg sat with her head bowed praying for Joe when Paul finished his sermon and offered an invitation. Paul recounted the Lord's desire for everyone to come to Him through belief in His Son Jesus Christ. He asked that anyone wishing to trust Jesus as Savior come forward and receive Him. He also extended the invitation to those wishing church membership by letter from another church.

"Let's stand and sing, 'Lord I'm Coming Home', as we invite you to come," he said.

As the choir and congregation began singing, Joe stepped out into the aisle on the first note and started forward. Paul saw him coming, met him with outstretched hand, and walked the rest of the way with him. Meg cried tears of joy. Shouts of "Praise the Lord," "Hallelujah," and "Amen" rang out all over the auditorium as praise filled each heart. The prayers of the church had been answered. Joe had come home at last.

EPILOGUE

On a bright September day in 1955, Joe drove the old Dodge station wagon up the winding road to his new house on Blueberry Hill. Football practice had run late, but he knew Maggie wouldn't mind. "Looks like we have a good team this year," he thought. "Maybe even win the division championship."

As he came around the last curve, his ranch-style house came into view. It was made of native stone and shingles, and he had built most of it himself. The sight of it gladdened his heart, and he was happy to be coming home.

He drove the car into the attached garage and entered the kitchen through the connecting door. Maggie turned from the stove and smiled at him. The children, four-year-old Mike and two-year-old Sarah, came running to him shouting, "Daddy!" Mike wrapped his arms around his legs, and Sarah held up her arms for him to lift her high into the air. When he did, she squealed with delight. He put her down, tousled Mike's hair, and took Maggie in his arms and kissed her.

"How is little Jimmy?" he asked as he walked over to the bassinet in the corner and touched the downy head of one-month-old James Lester Sullivan.

"Sleeping as usual," Maggie replied. "He's a good baby, and he even smiled at me today. It may have been gas, though."

While Maggie put the food on the table, Joe placed Sarah in her high chair, and Mike crawled up on his chair and sat on a big book, *The Care and Feeding of the Healthy Child.*

When they were all seated, they folded their hands and bowed their heads while Joe offered praise and thanks to the Lord.

The End